GLIMMER TRAIN STORIES

EDITORS
Susan Burmeister-Brown   Linda B. Swanson-Davies

CONSULTING EDITOR
Roz Wais

COPY EDITOR
Scott Stuart Allie

TYPESETTING & LAYOUT
Paul Morris

COVER ART
Herds, *by Jane Zwinger*

ESTABLISHED IN 1990.

PUBLISHED QUARTERLY
in spring, summer, fall, and winter by Glimmer Train Press, Inc.
1211 NW Glisan Street, Suite 207, Portland, Oregon 97209-3054
Telephone: 503/221-0836   Facsimile: 503/221-0837
www.glimmertrain.org

PRINTED IN U.S.A.
Indexed in *The American Humanities Index.*
Member of the Council of Literary Magazines and Presses

Glimmer Train (ISSN #1055-7520), registered in U.S. Patent and Trademark Office, is published quarterly, $36 per year in the U.S., by Glimmer Train Press, Inc., Suite 207, 1211 NW Glisan, Portland, OR 97209. Periodicals postage paid at Portland, OR, and additional mailing offices. POSTMASTER: Send address changes to Glimmer Train Press, P.O. Box 3000, Denville, NJ 07834-9929.

ISSN # 1055-7520, **ISBN # 1-59553-013-4**, CPDA BIPAD # 79021
DISTRIBUTION: Bookstores can purchase *Glimmer Train Stories* through these distributors:
  DEMCO, Inc., 4810 Forest Run Road, Madison, WI 53707 ph: 800/356-1200
  Ingram Periodicals, 1226 Heil Quaker Blvd., LaVergne, TN 37086
  Peribo PTY Ltd., 58 Beaumont Rd., Mt. Kuring-Gai, NSW 2080, AUSTRALIA
  Source Interlink, 27500 Riverview Center Blvd., Suite 400, Bonita Sprints, FL 36134
  Ubiquity, 607 Degraw St., Brooklyn, NY 11217
SUBSCRIPTION SVCS: EBSCO, Divine, Subscription Services of America, Blackwell's UK.

Subscription rates: Order online at www.glimmertrain.org.
or by mail—one year, $36 within the U.S. (Visa/MC/check).
Airmail to Canada, $46; outside North America, $59.
Payable by Visa/MC or check for U.S. dollars drawn on a U.S. bank.

Attention established and emerging short-story writers: We pay $700 for first publication and onetime anthology rights. We welcome your work via our **online submission procedure:** *www.glimmertrain.org.*

Glimmer Train Press *also offers* **Writers Ask**—*nuts, bolts, and informed perspectives—a quarterly non-newsletter for the committed writer. One year, four issues, $20 within the U.S. ($26 beyond the U.S.), Visa, MC, or check to Glimmer Train Press, Inc., or order online at www.glimmertrain.org.*

Now available in hardback from independent bookstores and online book sources:
The Glimmer Train Guide to Writing Fiction.

It is fall 2007.

In these last six years, there has been so
much devastation: the World Trade Center,
Afghanistan, Iraq, New Orleans and
Mississippi, the Indian Ocean tsunami, Darfur.

We dedicate this issue to those who have died,
to those who struggle to reshape their lives
around their losses, and to those with the will
to create a saner, more just and humane world.
The world is ripe for brightness.

PAST CONTRIBUTING AUTHORS AND ARTISTS

Many of issues 1 through 63 are available for thirteen dollars each.

Robert A. Abel • David Abrams • Linsey Abrams • Steve Adams • Diane King Akers • Daniel Alarcón • Susan Alenick • Will Allison • Rosemary Altea • Julia Alvarez • Brian Ames • A. Manette Ansay • Charles H. Antin • Margaret Atwood • Dalia Azim • Kevin Bacon • Michael Bahler • Doreen Baingana • Aida Baker • Kerry Neville Bakken • Russell Banks • Brad Barkley • Andrea Barrett • Kyle Ann Bates • Richard Bausch • Robert Bausch • Charles Baxter • Ann Beattie • Sean Beaudoin • Barbara Bechtold • Cathie Beck • Jeff Becker • Janet Belding • Sallie Bingham • Kristen Birchett • Melanie Bishop • James Carlos Blake • Corinne Demas Bliss • Valerie Block • Belle Boggs • Joan Bohorfoush • Matt Bondurant • David Borofka • Robin Bradford • Harold Brodkey • Oliver Broudy • Danit Brown • Kurt McGinnis Brown • Nic Brown • Paul Brownfield • Ayşe Papatya Bucak • Judy Budnitz • Susanna Bullock • Christopher Bundy • Jenny A. Burkholder • Evan Burton • Robert Olen Butler • Michael Byers • Christine Byl • Gerard Byrne • Jack Cady • Annie Callan • Kevin Canty • Peter Carey • Ioanna Carlsen • Ron Carlson • H. G. Carroll • David Cates • Brian Champeau • Vikram Chandra • Diane Chang • Mike Chasar • Xiaofei Chen • Yunny Chen • Robert Chibka • Chieh Chieng • Carolyn Chute • Christi Clancy • George Makana Clark • Dennis Clemmens • Aaron Cohen • Robert Cohen • Evan S. Connell • Joan Connor • Ellen Cooney • Rand Richards Cooper • Lydia E. Copeland • Michelle Coppedge • Rita D. Costello • Wendy Counsil • Doug Crandell • M. Allen Cunningham • Ronald F. Currie Jr. • William J. Cyr • Quinn Dalton • Bilal Dardai • Tristan Davies • C. V. Davis • Annie Dawid • Laurence de Looze • Toi Derricotte • Janet Desaulniers • Tiziana di Marina • Junot Díaz • Stephen Dixon • Matthew Doherty • Leslie Dormen • Michael Dorris • Siobhan Dowd • Greg Downs • Eugenie Doyle • Tiffany Drever • Alan Arthur Drew • Andre Dubus • Andre Dubus III • Stuart Dybek • Wayne Dyer • Melodie S. Edwards • Ron Egatz • Barbara Eiswerth • Mary Relindes Ellis • Sherry Ellis • Susan Engberg • Lin Enger • James English • Tony Eprile • Louise Erdrich • Zoë Evamy • Nomi Eve • George Fahey • Edward Falco • Anthony Farrington • Merrill Feitell • J. M. Ferguson Jr. • Lisa Fetchko • Joseph Flanagan • Charlotte Forbes • Patricia Foster • Susan Fox • Michael Frank • Pete Fromm • Abby Frucht • Daniel Gabriel • Avital Gad-Cykman • Ernest Gaines • Tess Gallagher • Louis Gallo • Elizabeth Gallu • Kent Gardien • Ellen Gilchrist • Myla Goldberg • Allyson Goldin • Mary Gordon • Peter Gordon • Jean Colgan Gould • Elizabeth Graver • Lisa Graley • Jo-Ann Graziano • Andrew Sean Greer • Gail Greiner • John Griesemer • Zoë Griffith-Jones • Paul Griner • Aaron Gwyn • L. B. Haas • Patricia Hampl • Christian Hansen • Ann Harleman • Elizabeth Logan Harris • Marina Harris • Erin Hart • Kent Haruf • Ethan Hauser • Jake Hawkes • Daniel Hayes • David Haynes • Daniel Hecht • Ursula Hegi • Amy Hempel • Joshua Henkin • Cristina Henríquez • David Hicks • Julie Hirsch • Andee Hochman • Alice Hoffman • Cary Holladay • Jack Holland • Noy Holland • Travis Holland • Lucy Honig • Ann Hood • Linda Hornbuckle • David Huddle • Sandra Hunter • Tim Hurd • Siri Hustvedt • Quang Huynh • Frances Hwang • Leo Hwang • Catherine Ryan Hyde • Stewart David Ikeda • Lawson Fusao Inada • Elizabeth Inness-Brown • Debra Innocenti • Bruce Jacobson • Andrea Jeyaveeran • Ha Jin • Charles Johnson • Leslie Johnson • Sarah Anne Johnson • Wayne Johnson • Allen Morris Jones • Nalini Jones • Thom Jones • Cyril Jones-Kellet • Elizabeth Judd • Tom Miller Juvik • Jiri Kajanë • Anita Shah Kapadia • Hester Kaplan • Wayne Karlin • Amy Karr • Ariana-Sophia Kartsonis • Andrew Kass • Kate Kasten • Ken Kaye • Tom Kealey • David Kear • Andrea King Kelly • Jenny Kennedy • Thomas E. Kennedy • Tim Keppel • Jamaica Kincaid • Lily King • Maina wa Kinyatti • Carolyn Kizer • Perri Klass • Rachel Klein • Carrie Knowles • Clark E. Knowles • N. S. Köenings • Jonathan Kooker • David Koon • Karen Kovacik • Justin Kramon • Jake Kreilkamp • Nita Krevans • Erika Krouse • Marilyn Krysl • Frances Kuffel • Evan Kuhlman • Mandy Dawn Kuntz • Anatoly Kurchatkin • W. Tsung-yan Kwong • Victoria Lancelotta • Rattawut Lapcharoensap • Jenni Lapidus • Doug Lawson • Don Lee • Frances Lefkowitz • Peter Lefcourt • Jon Leon • Doris Lessing • Jennifer Levasseur • Debra Levy • Janice Levy • Yiyun Li • Christine Liotta • Rosina Lippi-Green • David Long • Nathan Long • Salvatore Diego Lopez • Melissa Lowver • William Luvaas • Barry Lyga • David H. Lynn • Richard Lyons • Bruce Machart • Jeff MacNelly • R. Kevin Maler • Kelly Malone • Paul Mandelbaum • George Manner • Jana Martin • Lee Martin • Valerie Martin • Juan Martinez • Daniel Mason • Brendan Mathews • Alice Mattison • Bruce McAllister • Jane McCafferty • Sean Padraic McCarthy • Judith McClain • Cammie McGovern • Cate McGowan • Eileen McGuire • Susan McInnis • Gregory McNamee • Jenny Drake McPhee • Amalia Melis • Askold Melnyczuk • Susan Messer • Frank Michel • Paul Michel • Nancy Middleton • Alyce Miller • Greg Miller • Katherine Min • Mary McGarry Morris • Ted Morrissey • Mary Morrissy • Bernard Mulligan • Abdelrahman Munif • Manuel Muñoz • Karen Munro • Paula Nangle • Kent Nelson • Randy F. Nelson • Lucia Nevai • Thisbe Nissen • Katherin Nolte • Miriam Novogrodsky • Sigrid Nunez • N. Nye • Ron Nyren • Joyce Carol Oates • Tim O'Brien • Vana O'Brien • Mary O'Dell • Chris Offutt • Jennifer Oh • Laura Oliver • Felicia Olivera • Jimmy Olsen • Thomas O'Malley • Stewart O'Nan • Elizabeth Oness • Gina Oschner • Karen Outen • Mary Overton • Patricia Page • Ann Pancake • Peter Parsons • Roy Parvin • Karenmary Penn • Susan Perabo • Dawn Karima Pettigrew • Constance Pierce • William Pierce • Angela Pneuman • Steven Polansky • John Prendergast • Jessica Printz • Melissa Pritchard • Annie Proulx • Eric Puchner • Kevin Rabalais • Jonathan Raban • George Rabasa • Margo Rabb • Mark Rader • Paul Rawlins • Yosefa Raz • Karen Regen-Tuero • Frederick Reiken • Nancy Reisman • Yelizaveta P. Renfro • Linda Reynolds • Kurt Rheinheimer • Anne Rice • Michelle Richmond • Alberto Ríos • Roxana Robinson • Anya Robyak • Susan Jackson Rodgers • Andrew Roe • Paulette Roeske • Stan Rogal • Carol Roh-Spaulding • Frank Ronan • Julie Rose • Elizabeth Rosen • Janice Rosenberg • Jane Rosenzweig • Karen Sagstetter • Kiran Kaur Saini • Mark Salzman • Mark Sanders • Carl Schaffer • R. K. Scher • Robert Schirmer • Libby Schmais • Samantha Schoech • Natalie Schoen • Adam Schuitema • Jim Schumock • Lynn Sharon Schwartz • Barbara Scot • Peter Selgin • Amy Selwyn • Catherine Seto • Bob Shacochis • Evelyn Sharenov • Karen Shepard • Sally Shivnan • Evan Shopper • Daryl Siegel • Ami Silber • Al Sim • Mark Sindecuse • George Singleton • Floyd Skloot • Brian Slattery • Louise Farmer Smith • Roland Sodowsky • Scott Southwick • R. Clifton Spargo • Gregory Spatz • Brent Spencer • L. M. Spencer • Lara Stapleton • Lori Ann Stephens • Barbara Stevens • John Stinson • George Stolz • William Styron • Virgil Suárez • Karen Swenson • Liz Szabla • Shimon Tanaka • Mika Tanner • Lois Taylor • Paul Theroux • Abigail Thomas • Randolph Thomas • Joyce Thompson • Patrick Tierney • Aaron Tillman • Tamara B. Titus • Andrew Toos • Pauls Toutonghi • Vu Tran • Patricia Traxler • Jessica Treadway • Doug Trevor • William Trevor • Rob Trucks • Kathryn Trueblood • Jennifer Tseng • Carol Turner • Christine Turner • Kathleen Tyau • Michael Upchurch • Lee Upton • Gerard Varni • Katherine Vaz • A. J. Verdelle • Daniel Villasenor • Robert Vivian • Sergio Gabriel Waisman • Daniel Wallace • Ren Wanding • Eric Wasserman • Mary Yukari Waters • Jonathan Wei • Eric Weinberger • Jamie Weisman • Lance Weller • Ed Weyhing • J. Patrice Whetsell • Joan Wickersham • Vinnie Wilhelm • Lex Williford • Gary Wilson • Robin Winick • Mark Wisniewski • Terry Wolverton • Monica Wood • Christopher Woods • Leslie A. Wootten • wormser • Celia Wren • Callie Wright • Calvin Wright • Brennen Wysong • June Unjoo Yang • Paul Yoon • Nancy Zafris • Silas Zobal • Jane Zwinger

CONTENTS

The cast of the Baudette Community Children's Theater production of Tom Sawyer *around 1993. I was not in the cast but was one of the student directors. I'm standing at the right end of the last row next to the other student director, my best friend Kerry, although you can only see the top half of her face. We didn't have enough children for all of the parts, and had to beg our three friends Mike, Dave, and Greg (they are standing with us in the back row) to play the parts (right to left) of Muff Potter, Judge Thatcher, and Injun Joe.*

Cheri Johnson was raised in Lake of the Woods County in Minnesota. She has a BA in English from Augsburg College in Minneapolis, an MA in English and Creative Writing from Hollins University in Roanoke, Virginia, and an MFA in Creative Writing from the University of Minnesota. She has won the John Engman Literary Prize, the Andrew James Purdy Prize, the Gesell Award, a Loft Mentor Series Award, and a Bush Artist Fellowship. She has had work included in magazines such as *Clare, Pif, nidus, The Hollins Critic,* and the *Rio Grande Review.*

GURALNICK

Cheri Johnson

The sick child down the road, Letty, had a habit of waving with her toes instead of her fingers, perhaps because her legs were stronger than her arms. She did it every time I came into the yard. She also made a sweet, strange, gurgling noise in her throat when I came running at her. I pretended I was going to attack, then swung her up and turned her carefully upside-down in the air.

When I moved into the area it was Letty's family, the Tisdales, that I traded with first, on credit—mine—to clear the rotting cow carcass, the pile of dead dogs, and the pool of sewage out of my backyard. Their children helped to drive snakes out of the house. They beat from the raveling, braided rugs in the living room the damp smell of sheep or maybe pig.

This was in Minnesota, on a wooded northern part of it, two hundred miles east of the North Dakota plains. I had come to live on a place I had bought from a man in Wyoming, without having seen a picture of it. He said a strong young man would be able to farm there, but the most I ever raised on that land was a small herd of cattle and two crops of hay a summer, only one of which I kept. The other I traded for a winter's worth of wood. I would also trade cows, one by one, for planks, vegetables, fish, furniture, house painting, and truck repair, so that after I had bought the cattle and seed that first year, I hardly used any money at all—a good thing, because I almost never had it. I was thirty-five years old. Both of my parents

were dead of heart attacks, and I had two sisters in cities in California, where we had grown up. I wasn't sure if I had the right addresses
for them anymore.

When I first came to my new place, I pulled in in the middle of the
night. The property was out in the country, about halfway between—ten
or twelve miles on each side—two small towns, of three hundred
sixty-five people. The place was almost two miles north of a main road,
six miles south of a big lake. The land was flat and very green in the
summer, and even when you were in a field, deep timber—the tallest
of pine, poplar, and birch, with a thick tangle of undergrowth, black
willow, and wild raspberry—was never more than some acres away.
When upturned, the earth was very dark, sticky, and rich. There were
thousands of birds: pheasant, swallows, killdeer, grouse—even seagulls,
when you had just tilled. The land was always wet, and sometimes
soaked, especially in the spring, when feet upon feet of melting snow
made the steep, wide ditches run so fast and full and hard that water
lapped out over the gravel. In the spring the air smelled of wet grass
and leaves, and sometimes burning peat, and in the winter it smelled
of woodsmoke and cold.

That first night, there was a small car in my new driveway. A dog
began to bark in the house, and my border collie Mike answered beside me. There was not supposed to be anyone there. I got out of the
truck and looked around. I left Mike in the cab. It was late March, and
still winter there, very much so, the piles of snow from shoveling the
long dirt drive still over three feet high. The weather was warming
up, though; tonight it had to be in the fifties, and the snow would do
a lot of melting the next day. For now, the piles made a sort of tunnel
to walk through. I saw the house over one of these walls of packed
snow and ice: big, strangely shaped, colored white, green, and tan, with
multiple roofs. It looked like two houses that had been stuck together.
The garage leaned at about ten degrees. Farther back, by the yellow-
orange yardlight, I could see a tall, straight barn, a long, low building,
and two small ones, shed-sized. Pine trees over forty feet high edged
the yard, which was heavily drifted with snow. In the sideyard stood
a great ash tree, some of its branches so long and drooped that they

were partially buried in the ice crust of March; this I did not see until the morning.

No other animals called out. No lights went on in the house, but soon the door opened, and a short skinny man stepped out onto the porch and looked warily in my direction. "Hello," he called out. "What is it?"

"Hello," I said, and moved forward. Mike whined in the truck. "I've bought this place," I said.

There was quiet from the porch as he ducked his head back inside, then murmuring, and another voice. As I came closer a woman said, low, "Is it the oil? If it's the oil, tell him—" I looked at the long white tank along the side of the house.

"I'm not about the oil," I said, "but I've bought this place." I stopped about five feet short of the porch, but still I caught a whiff of someone unwashed. The man slid back into the house, the door slammed shut, and I was alone again. The dog inside had not stopped barking. I had been by myself for two or three minutes when finally I shouted in, "How about I'll leave for a while. I'll be back tomorrow morning about ten o'clock." There was no answer. I drove off with Mike, then, and went about a mile away. The man I had bought this place from had told me how to find the turn-off into the property, sixty acres of fields and forest. In my headlights, the wire fence sagged crookedly, and beyond it the tips of tall brown stalks poked out of the snow. I pulled in here, and slept, curled up with Mike. When I came back to the house late in the morning, the people were gone.

In the backyard, the body of the cow was partially covered by snow. It was mostly hide and bone. The animal had fallen on its side as it died. There was also the decaying carcass of a dog, and this body might have stayed hidden for a few more weeks of thawing if the just-stiffening body of another German shepherd, probably the dog that had been barking the night before, had not been dumped over the first one this morning, its warmth melting some of the snow. The second dog had been shot in the head, even though it looked as if it had been healthy and young. The dog that had been longer dead still had shreds of hide frozen across the skull, but its eyes were gone; the other dog's eyes, iced over, stared off into the fields. The Tisdales later helped me to clear the animals away, eased them with shovels onto a heavy wooden square that they hauled behind a decrepit tractor, and took them up into the woods where we buried them under rocks—because the ground was too frozen to dig in. But before they did, Mike, a few times, came up to lie beside the dogs and sleep. I thought it was too bad about the second dog especially, because Mike might have gotten on fine with her.

The Tisdales were a big family, and they lived in a sort of commune just down the road. They slept in all sorts of things around the place: an old trailer, a few vans, a delivery truck—and the best of them a cabin, or shack, depending on how forgiving you are. Gretchen, the woman who took care of them all, was the grown-up child of the oldest member, her father. She was crippled, and walked slowly with a cane.

To say that only one family lived on their place is not quite right, though, because one of Gretchen's daughters had a husband she lived with there in the trailer. This woman was Molly, and she was about thirty years old. She was hefty and slow-headed, her face faintly Mongoloid. She was Letty's mother. Letty, despite the obvious problems of her mother and grandmother—as well as the stranger, unidentifiable disorder cast over the whole place, on the sons, daughters, aunts, brothers, cousins, at least fifteen of them in all, the number sometimes changing—had, of the lot of them, been asked to bear the most. She had cerebral palsy and bad asthma, her eyes were severely hyperopic, and she could hardly hear a thing. What had to happen for a child to be born who would suffer like that? She could bear to walk only one or two steps, in a hunkered gait oppressively pigeon-toed. Usually they pushed her in a special stroller built for a growing child, or she was draped over her mother's pillowy front like a monkey, her eyes artificially gawking behind a bulk of dusty lens—the glasses Molly's husband had picked up at the bank in town, where they had been left in a cardboard box for the Lions Club—with her long white-blond hair. When you spoke to her she smiled brilliantly, even as she heard nothing of what you said.

Molly's husband was a Guralnick. I think one of his brothers may have lived on the place, too, from time to time. I never knew the husband's first name, and it did not seem important, because he called almost all of his neighbors and relations by nicknames or curses, as they came to him. He was black-haired like his wife, but thin like all of the men there, including the eldest, the patriarch of them all, who had lost all of his teeth; from this old man I hardly ever heard a word, except for a few times in town, when he was hobbling behind his daughter, the lame Gretchen, as they all did—even Guralnick—in a strange slow line, and the old man would reach forward to pull his daughter's sleeve, and mutter, "Hung-y. *Hung-y!*" Gretchen would look back at him, and tap his hand like a piano key: "Okay, Pa…"

Guralnick, like the others, did not bother much with bathing, but he was the first to smell what was wrong with my bathoom, and he was also a great help to me with the well. I had an artesian well. The people who had been squatting there had not known to keep a fire going in the wellhouse, so when I first went out there, the run-off had built in front of the tank a three-foot wall of ice. Guralnick helped me to set up a little wood stove in there. Water began flowing to the house again.

The squatting couple had had only one tiny oil stove to heat the whole house; it was a miserable, dangerous, leaking thing, and I hauled it away. They had managed to trick the oil company into thinking they had a right to be here, and the oil man had kept coming to fill the white tank until they'd stopped paying. This I heard from the Tisdales. I had been living in the house for a week or so, and had installed two other stoves in the living room and kitchen, so I wouldn't freeze to death, when the extra heat began to thaw the house out. Guralnick came in one afternoon and said, "Goddamn, you son of a bitch, it smells like shit in here, don't it?" In the bathroom we moved the bathtub and discovered underneath a thick layer of sewage. I had to pull out that tub and get a new one, so I could not afford to put new carpet into the living room, and lived for a long time with the stink of the squatters' goats.

Beyond the backyard, but in front of the fields, marked off by a fence, was a middle ground of bluestem and cheatgrass, where there were the remains of old cars, combines, tractors, and a corral. When the snow melted, I even found three little school desks there, with wooden seats and black iron legs.

One night in that first November I sat down and wrote a long letter to my younger sister, who had at least one baby now, and told her about my place: the water pipes that had been buried too shallow and always froze; the beautiful boggy fields of alfalfa and foxtail, and the deep stands of timber; the bear and gray wolf and the moose that sometimes blocked the narrow wild road; and my wicked red bull, with his heavy horns. The letter came back, with the rubber stamp outline of a hand, its finger pointing to my name. I was going to take the letter out, cross out Sally's name, and address it to my older sister; but winter came then, with a whole new set of challenges, and I did not ever get to it.

A year after I came, Letty turned five. That April the Tisdales began to talk of whether or not she would go to school in the fall. Molly wanted her to go. She had not been able to stay in school herself, because the district had said they did not have the resources to teach such a child (if you could believe Molly; I suspected the family might have taken her out, to spare her from the teasing). Letty, though, was as bright as any child her age. Someone on that place—I marveled over it—had even taught her how to read, and she would do it silently, slumped in Molly's lap in the yard, out of a picture book. I tested her one day, to see if it was really true. I brought a new book over that I had gotten out of the children's section in the library in Boucher. I sat her in my lap, to read aloud to her, on the metal steps of her mother's trailer. She could hear you if you read loudly, and directly into her ear.

The other children shrieked in the back, playing Police. For guns they had small tubes of cheap handcream, which they shot onto the grass. A pack of barn cats wandered between the Tisdales' place and mine, between the Ludtkes' to the north, and the Schües' to the south, and these animals trailed behind the children and ate the ribbons of white lotion. Some of the men and women were hanging out laundry, on a rope strung between the red-and-white delivery truck and a tall birch in the middle of the yard. Gretchen was in the cabin, which was on the edge of the yard, closest to the woods. She sang loudly in there. The air smelled wet, both growing and dead, messy and clean. Letty's blond hair blew oily against the skin of my arms. She felt like an unwieldy sack of sticks in my lap. On the second page of the book, I began to ignore the real words and make up my own…Letty howled and honked and slammed her head as much as she could into my chest. I squeezed her and laughed. "I'm sorry, honey," I said. "I'll do it right this time, how's that?" But she was mad, and wouldn't giggle over the silly parts, even when I tickled her. When I left that day, she frowned her goodbye. Guralnick pinched her toe gently and said, "What's up your butt?" But I was afraid I had really made her angry; and when I came back the next afternoon, bringing her a roll of mints, I was re-lieved when she beamed as dazzlingly as ever, and wrapped her scrawny arms around my neck.

Gretchen and Molly took Letty to the school in Boucher to see what they would be able to do with her. The school said they could teach Letty, although her mobility would be a problem. An aide could carry or push her around all day, but Molly could not bear the idea of it being done by a stranger (I had known the Tisdales for three months before Molly would even let me pick Letty up). Then the kindergarten teacher got squeamish and balked when Molly suggested that she or some other member of the family could do it. So Letty would have to have a wheelchair, Molly decided, and a motorized one, because she was not strong enough to push the wheels. A school nurse said that with hearing aids, it might be possible for Letty to hear almost as much as a normal child. So, Molly said, the family would have to get their hands on some of those, too.

Between the school's restrictions and Molly's, it was going to be hard to get anything done. Despite all of the problems, though, Molly was ecstatic at the prospect of school for Letty within her reach. I was there when she told Guralnick. I was helping him, and Molly's three pale-haired brothers, to put up a flimsy lean-to of greasy particle board onto the house where Gretchen lived with her father. I could see through the window of the cabin a bed and a mattress, a black woodstove, and a crock pot with no plug for its cracking brown cord. The old man slept on the bed under a quilt, despite our hammering. The trailer, which was also what Gretchen hooked to a pickup and used to haul her pile of scrap iron to craft fairs and flea markets, was the only dwelling with a cook stove. "Hey, hon," Molly said, and came to stand in front of Guralnick. Her hands were on her hips.

Gretchen stood back with the stroller, and with Letty in it, asleep. Gretchen wore dark pink sweat pants and a plain sweatshirt of the same color. She was hefty like her daughter and wore her hair in a dark, frizzy bun. When she stayed in one position too long, her cane began to sink into the soggy ground, and she had to pull it out again like a root. Molly had on an old blue-and-white checked dress with a large brown stain like rust near the hem. They had Letty in a little dress, too, yellow, and it fit on her thin, disjointed body like a too-heavy coat slung unevenly over a flimsy hanger. One of the other women, a cousin of Molly's, I think, came and lifted Letty out and took her into the trailer, which Gretchen had parked in its usual place on the lawn, across the yard from the cabin, and on the other side of the drive. Letty made a small sighing noise in her sleep and her glasses slid down her nose.

Molly's three brothers stepped back from the lean-to, and I went with them, toward the west wooded edge of the place. We were in the shadows of the trees now, and it was chilly there. One of the brothers, the middle one, a few years older than Molly and shorter than all the other men, watched after Letty as she was carried across the yard. To the east was my alfalfa field. I could look out over it and see my house and cows from here. Guralnick turned to face Molly, who squinted in the sun. "What is it," he said.

She told him what the school had said and what she had decided about it, in her halting, loud way. As she talked she sliced her plump hands in the air like a politician. Her mother spoke up when she got things wrong. When Molly came to the part about a wheelchair costing nearly four thousand dollars, and her hands went higher, above her head, and she began to stomp her foot, too, to emphasize, Gretchen broke in to say, "Two thousand, Molly," and Guralnick swore.

"Fucking-A, Molly," he said. "What are you even thinking about? We don't have no fucking two thousand dollars." Molly stared at him for a moment with her mouth open, then narrowed her eyes. Guralnick turned back to the lean-to and looked at the three blond brothers, who watched Gretchen and waited for her signal; she did not give it, and Guralnick slumped back around to face the women. "Your mama don't have no two thousand dollars," he muttered.

"That's why—*you* gotta get a *job*." Molly's narrow plump mouth hung open.

The cousin who had attended to Letty came out of the trailer, shut the door quietly, and sat on the ridged steps. A few of the other women and children sat around it in patches of sun and washed laundry in black plastic tubs. There were still dirty piles of snow on the sopped flat brown grass. Across the yard to the north, two of the other men worked on a car, and one little girl, wearing only a white sweatband and blue jeans, stood on a wood block and looked into the engine. Every few minutes one of them would drop a tool with a thunk on the grass. One of the men whistled "The Yellow Rose of Texas." Beside me, Molly's youngest brother crouched down to rest his legs, his fingertips pressed into the shaded wet ground, and began to snicker. There was the small quick scramble of a squirrel or rabbit in the brush. Guralnick stood quiet and still, his eyes on Gretchen's feet, for so long that finally Gretchen tapped Molly's shoulder and led her away.

Guralnick frowned as we nailed the rest of the rotting boards into place and said almost nothing. Usually it was hard to get him to be quiet. Only one time did he say something about what had happened, and he directed it to me, ignoring Molly's brothers: "Hey, dickhead, it's not like—right?—that I could make that much even if I worked at Linnet's for a goddamn year." Linnet's was the wood treatment plant in Auchagah, about thirty miles away.

I straightened up and stared at him and grinned. "That's just—of course it would—goddamnit, Guralnick, a *year*?"

Guralnick only laughed with his mouth wide open, closed his eyes, and plugged in a nail that way.

But Molly did not let it alone. A week later she was sewing a blue school dress for Letty, out on the lawn, and she came up to Guralnick where he and I were crouched in the driveway, drawing out a plan in the dirt for my vegetable garden. She stuck him in the arm with her needle. "Mom says she won't be needing the pickup for anything today, so you should take it to see about going to Linnet's," she said.

Guralnick said, "For fuck's sakes, Molly!" and held his arm, in a green-and-black flannel shirt, where she had pricked it. But he was not talking back to her much. I was surprised, because I had seen him give it to her before. Guralnick liked to call Molly fat and dumb, and a few times when I'd run into them in town I'd seen him trying to humiliate her in stores, by attempting to engage the high-school girls who worked there. It was hard to shame Molly—but usually he tried, and picked at her whenever he could. When Molly left us this time I tried to talk more to Guralnick about rows versus hills, onions and pumpkins, marigolds to keep the bugs away, but after a while he threw down the stick he had been sketching with and stalked off into the woods.

One of the older children had Letty out in the driveway, and he was trying to see if she could walk any better yet. He walked behind her, holding her arms like a toddler's, then let her go. One of the Schüe boys rode by on a four-wheeler on the road and kicked up mud and water, but Letty did not even turn her white-blond head. She fell onto the drive and slumped there until this cousin, or half-brother, or uncle, came and gathered her up. I said goodbye to Gretchen, who was sitting at the little metal table in the trailer with her chin in her plump hands, staring off into space.

She smiled when I came in. I stood with one foot on the steps and the other on the main floor of the trailer. The air smelled of cigarette smoke and soap and cologne. I shut the door behind me but not all the way, so that a line of sunlight shone from the ceiling to the floor. "Gretchen," I said, "please don't—but I wonder, what do you all live on out here? I mean—how do you buy peanut butter and things?" As soon as I had asked it, I felt miserable. It was a rude question, and none of my business at all. But how strange, it seemed to me, that I had known these people for a year now, and had never figured it out—nor even wondered, really. Gretchen did not seem offended, or surprised. She tipped her head and closed her eyes for a moment, with an odd solemn smile.

"Well," she said, "well, one thing—we've got Pa's pension. He was in the army. Didn't you—it surprises me that no one's ever told you. The boys are all awfully proud of it." I didn't know if I thought they really were or not. But that was a peculiar moment—to realize that that decrepit, seemingly worthless old man had been, all this time, supporting them all, on a sum probably meant for only one person, but doled out, I was also beginning to understand, to all his descendants—and to whomever they brought into the family—by Gretchen. I wondered if the old man was even aware of it: eating whenever they brought him something to eat, sleeping all day in his bed.

I left them to see about the cows, and dinner, but I came back later to spend the evening. It was nine or ten o'clock and the sky over the pines and the scrubland was a strange dark blue, a deep beautiful color. As I walked over, the brush wolves started their delicate howling. Whenever one of those little wolves came in on the same pitch as another, the first wolf lifted or dropped its voice to make it sound as if the pack were growing all the time. At the house Mike joined in with them. I was eating a piece of red licorice and I stopped chewing, and walking, to listen, and laughed. He did pretty well. I might have thought he was a little coyote, himself, if I hadn't known different. But then the timber wolves came in, and in their cries there was something so low and wild and grave that the adult coyotes dropped out immediately, and only their pups continued, undaunted, in their fervent yipping; and poor Mike, too; it was as if he couldn't help himself. But he could not even hope to catch that fullness, the chilling, wavering notes—he barked and gulped like a seal. I had just been laughing, but now it made me want to cry to hear him. I jogged back home and brought him over to the Tisdales with me.

That night Molly had gotten wild about the whole thing with Letty. She may have even had something to drink. The children had built a fire for marshmallows. Near it Molly's black hair was wild, and her broad resolute face flushed and sweaty, as she railed on Guralnick. When I came up the drive with Mike, she was saying, "I would do it—I would do it, in a minute I would do it, but I need to be here to watch her." She was stalking a circle around the fire. No one said—they did not need to—that no one at Linnet's would trust Molly with a saw, or a machine, or even a can of varnish. Guralnick sat on the ground with his legs out, pointed toward the fire, his back against a blackened stump. When Molly came by him, she would step over his feet but kick back at them with her heels before going on. Her three brothers, and two of the other men, were also at the fire, back a little from it to avoid Molly's path, and all of the six children—minus Letty—were so close to it I was afraid they would burst into flame. Their whittled green poplar sticks were turning black. I gave them each a piece of licorice. Two of the children dropped their pointed sticks when they saw Mike, and ran off to chase him in the dark. The flaming marshmallows smoldered, then went out. When I picked one of them up it burned my fingers and charred sugar flaked off. It was too hot to eat and I dropped it again on the lawn. Two bats swooped, but stayed high above our heads. Over the spit and pop of the fire, I could hear the first of the peepers, thin and young and high in the marshy land across the road. In a few weeks they would fill the night.

Guralnick was looking at his hands, and did not notice I had sat down until about five minutes after. When he finally looked up and saw me sitting a few feet away, I moved closer to him. "What do you think about that crazy bitch?" he said. He only glanced at me, before studying again the flames, which sent out tiny sparks that I ground into the grass with my boot. Molly heard him, and grunted like a bear on the other side of the fire, clenching her fists.

"Well," I said, in a low voice, only to him, "well, it's just that she wants—"

Guralnick straightened up and stared at me. For a fraction of a moment his mouth fell open a bit in surprise; then he tightened his lips again and glared. "Dickhead," he said, and clapped his hands on his thighs as if he were really going to rail into me. I cringed. I wished I hadn't said anything, and I looked in another direction, across the fire. I was happy when he only grunted a few times but did not go on. Molly went off on a rant again, as if she guessed what we had been muttering about.

This went on almost all summer. Molly did not give up, and Guralnick was finally pressured into starting at Linnet's. He worked for about three days late in July. Then he showed up at my house in the middle of the day, to help me weed peas and till the corn. I didn't ask why he wasn't at work because I needed the help. I had planted a huge garden and I couldn't keep ahead of all the weeds. I would not be able to eat it all, either, even what I would freeze now, then thaw over the course of the winter. In this same week, we cut the first crop of the summer's hay, and left it in the sun for a few days to dry.

Guralnick worked the gas tiller while I weeded on my knees, lifting the delicate pea stems with their little white flowers. If you didn't lift the whole plant, it was hard to see where the main stalk was; you might yank it out when you got a piece of lovegrass or thistle. My knees and palms got gray. I kept taking my gloves off because my hands got so hot. I had forgotten to put a hat on, and my hair was burning up when I touched it. I moved down the row, and the hard lumps of dirt hurt my knees through my jeans. Every few plants or so, I plucked a medium-plump pod, swept the peas out with my thumb, and tipped them into my mouth, spitting out the dirt that had gotten on them. The best peas were somewhat flat, oblong, and juicy-sweet.

Behind me, through the beans with their flat, velvety leaves, and the taller pepper and tomato plants, and a row of growing corn, I could see Guralnick's wiry body shake along with the jolting tiller, as he forced the big blades of it through the black-clay earth. He wore a dark brown cowboy hat. I began to think of him working at Linnet's, of Letty—when he had shown up today, I had been relieved, grateful; I had wanted to throw my arms around him. I poured him a huge glass of red Kool-Aid instead and filled the glass with ice, and we sat down at my kitchen table and organized a plan for attacking the exuberant garden. At the same time, I felt awful about Letty. I couldn't help but think of the wheelchair, of Guralnick's choice, and how it was not one he would be able to sustain. How could a person work as he wanted to? What wouldn't stand resolutely against him? How could he dare? Not that Molly was wrong. If Guralnick had been a different sort of man, he would have just left.

When he saw me watching him through the leaves, Guralnick grinned and flicked me off.

I didn't want to see what it would be like over at the Tisdales now, so for the next day or two, I didn't go over there, but just stayed at home. The whole house creaked and settled all the time, especially at night, but I had grown to love its doing so. There were too many rooms for me, but I wandered through them all every day, and thought of what furniture I would put where, when I could get it. I had put up insulation by now, and filled in some of the other cracks, but I still saw daddy longlegs and crickets on the floors. In the bathroom the new tub still shone. The steps going upstairs were splintery, and the ceilings there slanted down too low for my head. Mike liked to go up there, though, and stare out the small window overlooking the driveway and bark at anyone when they came in.

Guralnick came over a few more times, once with a few of the other men, so we could cut the hay. We did not talk about Letty. Another time he brought the other children with him, and I paid them a dollar each to weed one whole half of the enormous garden. It looked beautiful when they were done: black with carved green trimming.

Then one morning later that week I woke up to a noise. I lay for a while in my small bedroom off the kitchen before I thought, Well—that's somebody yelling. I went onto the porch in my bare feet to listen. One of the Tisdale children had come over to play with Mike a few weeks earlier, and his foot had gone right through the porch floor. I would have to tear the whole thing down soon.

I listened to the screaming. I knew, immediately, that it was coming from the Tisdales', and even though I had heard shouting over there plenty of times before, this time there was a frantic note in it. So it had happened; it had all come down with Molly and Guralnick. I dreaded finding out what this was going to look like. But after I had decided to do it, I put on shoes and pants in a hurry, and went over there right away.

From their yard came a thick wailing, piercing at its highest pitch, and at its lowest as resonant and keening as a big drum. It swelled between these two points like a wave, or the wheezing of a bellows. It made me want to crumple over. Except for this howling the yard was terribly quiet. I knew that scream had to be Molly's. Gretchen had her sitting in a green and white upright lawn chair when I came, and her wide short legs filled it. She cried as though she were vomiting, not with her hands over her face, but gripping the arms of the chair, with her head down and her tangles of brown hair falling over it. Gretchen leaned on her cane, her other hand pressed to Molly's head. The children sat close together with some of the other women and men, by the trailer. Letty was not with them. Molly's three brothers and Guralnick stood by one of the cars, an old blue LTD parked crookedly in the drive. There was a lump of something behind the car, with an old brown towel thrown over it.

I stood at the end of the drive for a minute. No one looked over at me. I looked at Guralnick, but there was something about the way he stood, with his hands in his pockets, and leaning against the car door, but more rigid than you would imagine a person to be in this posture—and the way the brothers looked straight out over the lawn, almost defiantly, at Gretchen and Molly—that made me nervous to approach them. After a moment, I jogged back around the men and the car, giving them a wide berth. I came up to the trailer, and finally one of the women looked up at me. She frowned, then quickly, consciously, blanked her face. I stopped a few steps from her and dropped my arms. "Someone hit something?" I said.

She turned from me again before she spoke, and looked where everyone was looking, at the crying woman. "They accidentally—they backed into her," she said, and one of the other women, an older one—she might have been Molly's older sister—looked at me sharply and said, "Don't call the police yet, because we're going to."

"What?" I said. "What—Letty?" The first woman who had spoken nodded. I jerked my head around at all of them. This woman had crossed her arms tightly under her breasts. She was thin and bony faced. The children looked at the ground and fiercely braided grass. No one would look at me; finally I broke away, and ran to Guralnick. When he heard my steps on the gravel, he looked up, squinting, and then gave the line of brothers, leaning against the car, a hard sweeping look. They straightened, and looked back at him, before nodding to me. "Guralnick," I said, and reached out a hand to him, even though the gesture felt strange, and not just because of Guralnick, of who he was, and what our relationship was like, but because of this whole situation, how odd it felt—"I'm sorry." He nodded and clasped my hand once, quickly, before dropping it and looking at the ground. The brothers stared coolly at me. Usually they all looked at least somewhat different from one another, but at that moment I could not sort them out, tell which one was which by name or age.

I said, low, leaning in to Guralnick, "What happened?" He shook his head, and I shook mine slowly back at him. "It wasn't you," I said.

"No."

I was nearly whispering when I said, "Which one?" Guralnick shook his head again, harder this time, and he stood up straight and crossed his hands behind his back, then turned completely away from the brothers to look at only me, and it may have been the last time that he did so—looked me fully in the face.

"It was an accident, now," he said. "I don't think there's any fucking need for that. I think you'll want to stop that." His face was calm, as if he were talking to a child: his leathery, tan skin, flat, oily black moustache, and small chin. As I stared back at him, I could hardly think of what needed to be said. I wanted to repeat what I had asked before, but it was not a question one could ask again. And I knew even then—didn't I?—that no one was ever going to tell me, because it didn't matter, it didn't make any difference at all, which one.

Still I went on, recklessly: "But how did she get into the driveway? What was she doing there? Who was watching her?" My hands had begun to tremble. Guralnick swore at me again, and told me to shut up; and then Gretchen was coming. One of the other women had taken over with Molly, who had not quieted yet.

"She couldn't hear the car," said Guralnick.

Gretchen walked as slowly as ever, but as Guralnick and I had nothing more to say to one another, we turned to watch her come. When she had, she looked at Guralnick, and then at her three sons, who stared ahead impassively, their arms all crossed. The early sun glinted orange on their pale heads. "Which one of you was it that done it," Gretchen said in a low voice, tentatively. I nodded and looked at the four men, but no one looked at me. The brothers had remained silent for a few seconds when she sighed and looked at the ground, then over at the covered bundle on the drive. When I looked at it with her, I felt my mouth fall open, then come cracking back together as my teeth began to chatter. "I do want to know," she said, trailing off. They stayed silent. Finally, she flicked a glance over at me, then at Guralnick. "All right," she said. "All right." Her voice had grown quieter with each speech. She shrugged, and as she turned away I clutched her shoulder.

"Gretchen!" I said. "What?"

Guralnick reached out and pushed my arm away, and I yanked it to myself and glared at him. He moved toward me as if he were going to punch; and then suddenly his body relaxed. His face sharpened out of its frenzy, and a new look came over him, like sunlight passing over the ground. "Hey, shithead," he said, grinning viciously, "hey, shithead, is it going to rain on that hay of yours today?" The sky had clouded; it had been getting grayer all morning. Guralnick pointed to blacker clouds in the east. If it did rain hard, the whole crop might mold and be ruined. I stared at him for a long time, but his face did not change. Finally I turned away and started to walk back around the car, so I could leave without having to see the small pile of cloth that was Letty. Behind me, Guralnick made a hissing noise with his lips. "We'll be over in the afternoon with the baler, shithead," he said—and he did not fail me. But after the haying was done, we did not go to see each other anymore.

Later on that morning, I heard an ambulance and then a police car come. I heard much later from the Schües that responsibility was pinned on the youngest brother, who, because he was only sixteen and the death was declared accidental—and Guralnick, the only competent parent, did not press charges—got off with a light punishment. I did not stay close with anyone in the family.

I did go to Letty's funeral. When it was Molly's turn to go up and look into the casket, was let to do so, irresponsibily, alone; she began to fiddle with and fix Letty's dress. Then she reached in, and talked to the dead child. I realized that she was trying to sit Letty up, but the stiff body would not bend. It was the minister who came to stop her, because Gretchen could not get up fast enough, and none of the others came forward to do it. The only way there had been a funeral at all was that the church had raised the money for it. I had not given any money to the fund, because I could not spare it, and I did not go up to look into the casket myself.

After the service I bolted out, but Guralnick was there on the steps. He must have left in the middle of the service, because I had seen him come in and sit down, looking hard at his hands. I was not going to ever talk to him again, but I was so sick over the image of Letty's rigid pointy shoulders and her pale rabbit face without glasses, rising like a puppet out of the casket in Molly's clumsy grip, that I came and stood close to him on the cement steps, and said, "You put them up to it. You put one of them up to it." Guralnick was jumpy, and he moved back, looked nervously around him, and said, excitedly, his eyes sad and wild, "They had to do it," slapping his thighs in old jeans. He had on a faded Pepsi sweatshirt. "And they should have done it without me having to tell them to—those boys knew that *somebody* had to—and it wasn't *me* who—why should *I* have to—who knows which one of them it was. But she had that kid coming before I ever—" He stopped, and I did not want to hear what he had to say, anyway, and left. What difference did it make, if what he was saying about the little girl was true? It didn't matter how it had all started, only how it had ended up.

I drove home. I took a longer way now, so I wouldn't have to go past the Tisdale place. I couldn't tell, though, which hurt more: the times I didn't think, and accidentally found myself on the same old road and drawn to look into the yard, and saw them all out there, working on something; or the times I did it right, and went the long way around

24

on County 5, which included a stretch of blacktop and went past the Schües. The Schües were nice people, a couple in their fifties with grown children somewhere. I stopped on the afternoon of the funeral to say hello, but they weren't home. At least they didn't seem to be; it seemed there had been someone in the living room when I drove up. I thought I had seen someone. But no one came out into the yard, even when I had been standing there for five minutes or so. You didn't go up to a house and knock unless it was winter or raining. So I got in my truck and left.

I wrote to my sister.

Sally—The ground is so good here. Anything will grow if it doesn't freeze first! You can only get hay twice. I have had some trouble with some people (I am not in trouble)...

I had finished the letter before I remembered I had nowhere to send it. I stayed in that house for another year, and finally I sold it. I drove all the way to Santa Cruz, and showed up at the building my oldest sister had used to live in. She was gone. The two boys living there now had no idea where she was. They were nice enough to pretend that they had seen her while they were moving in, and that she had seemed to them like a really nice lady. Yes, there might have been a couple of children, too, now that they thought about it. But I don't think they ever even saw her. I thanked them because they were kind, and it wasn't their fault. She had moved, like people do, and there were a lot of things I could have done before she went away so that now I would know better what to do with myself.

I drove to the coast, and Mike had a great time on the beach.

In the months after the funeral, before I left Minnesota, I had sometimes seen Molly in town, with Gretchen and a few of the other women. Molly would look at the toys and clothes and pink plastic brushes for little girls. She would pick them up and croon. Finally one of the women would come to lead her away: "Come on, Molly..." They would show her something else, a picture she would like. She looked, and seemed to enjoy it, but her sadness was slow to leave, and the pleasure even slower to come. What I saw most sharply in her was the place she came to, in between—I can only compare it to the vacant way that children fill up their days, between meals, and chores, and excitements, and surprises.

I would not know anything else, if someone could tell me the worth of this.

FICTION OPEN AWARD WINNERS

1ST PLACE

Cheri Johnson receives $2000 for "Guralnick."

Johnson's bio is on page 6, preceding her story.

2ND PLACE

Sari Rose receives $1000 for "As in Life."

The former mayor was jailed, re-elected, then died. The rubber factory moved away and the Naugatuck rubber workers took office jobs in Waterbury or line jobs on the other side of town, where they made lipstick tubes and safety pins.

Sari Rose has received the Katherine Anne Porter and New Millennium Writings awards for her short stories. In 2003 she was a PEN New England New Discovery recipient. Her stories have appeared in the *Iowa Review*, *Nimrod*, and *New Millennium Writings*. She is a graduate of the Iowa Writers' Workshop, and, at a slow and steady pace, is working on both a novel and a story collection.

3RD PLACE

Dana Cann receives $600 for "Forty Days."

And suppose at night you dreamed about suicide bombers, about hiding indoors, with your family, your extended family, cousins and in-laws you've never met before. Your dream is like a family reunion, except that you're hiding indoors, because suspicious strangers in flowing robes roam the streets and sidewalks.

Dana Cann lives in Bethesda, Maryland. His stories have appeared in *The Sun*, the *Florida Review*, and *Blackbird*, among other journals. Honors and awards include two residencies at The Virginia Center for the Creative Arts and a Creative Fellowship from the Mid-Atlantic Arts Foundation.

---

*We invite you to visit **www.glimmertrain.org** to see a list of the top twenty-five winners and finalists. We thank all entrants for sending in their work.*

Me, age four, with my beloved Cotton. I had wanted to name
her John, but my parents and sister wouldn't go for it. In a bright
move, however, they agreed to give her John as a middle name,
and so she was known (at least to me) as Cotton John Perabo.

Susan Perabo is Writer in Residence and Associate Professor of English at Dickinson
College in Carlisle, Pennsylvania. Her story collection, *Who Was I Supposed to Be*, was
published in 1999 by Simon & Schuster and named a Book of the Year by the *Los
Angeles Times*, the *Miami Herald*, and the *St. Louis Post Dispatch*. Her novel, *The Broken
Places*, was published in 2001. Her fiction has recently appeared in the *Missouri Review*
and *The Sun*. She holds an MFA from the University of Arkansas, Fayetteville.

WHY THEY RUN THE WAY THEY DO

Susan Perabo

Ginny, the cleaning woman, knows what I've been up to. How could she not? For almost two years I've been bumping into her after midnight, at least twice a week; she looks up from her vacuuming or polishing, smiles congenially but not warmly, then returns to her work. Sometimes she's on the elevator when I get on, and we ride down eighteen floors in silence to the gaping, vacant lobby. Sometimes she's got a bag of trash that's bigger than she is, and I wonder how she's possibly going to get it to the dumpster. But my purse is heavy and I have wadded underwear in my pocket and I have to be back in this building in six or seven hours, so I don't offer to help. When I feel guilty about this, I remind myself that cleaning is her *job*, that she wouldn't walk past the reception desk at Wrona, Blake, Mulcahey, and Kramer Law Assoc. and see me juggling six impatient clients and offer to lend a hand.

"Do you really think she knows?" Donald (he's the Mulcahey) asks me. We are on the foldout in his office and he's shuffling his feet around under the covers trying to locate his socks.

"I don't know," I say, though of course I know, of course she knows, of course everybody in the office knows, and probably half the people in the damn building, not that they care. But Donald lives under the delusion that we are being discreet, that if we don't leave the premises together at two a.m. or make extended eye contact during working hours that no one will be the wiser, and I allow him to enjoy this delusion because if he knew all the people who know, it would make him sweat. And he's a big man, and he doesn't need to sweat any more than he does already.

"One of these days he's just going to keel over," Tommy says, clutching his chest and tipping over onto the couch. "And then what're you gonna do? You'll have to get him off that foldout bed, prop him up at his desk with a pen—"

"Okay," I say. "Enough."

"You'll have to *dress* him." He howls with laughter. "You're going to have to ask that housekeeper to help you. The two of you are going to have to—"

"Okay," I say. "I get it. You can stop now."

"Just don't call me," he says, grabbing a fistful of Cheetos. "I don't want any part of it."

On nights I do not stay late at the office, Tommy and I sit in my apartment in sweats and slippers and watch television for hours and hours. It is hard to find a friend who loves TV as much as you do, who is not ashamed to admit that he watches television for six to eight hours every single day, that he watches truly indiscriminately, moves seamlessly from *Gilligan* to The History Channel, from *Seinfeld* (the seventh or eighth viewing of most episodes) to *Nightline*, talk shows, game shows, re-runs of *old* game shows, decorating shows, C-Span, soaps, even the occasional sporting event. We watch without excuses, without pretexts or apologies, without fear of judgment. We just watch. Christ, do we watch.

(Devoted Gay Friend + Adulterous Affair = Simplicity and Contentment.)

Tommy's partner of four years, Gil, is a doctor. He's one of these appalling high-energy people, works in the ER, almost exclusively the graveyard shift. This plays out well for all of us. When I am at work Tommy is downstairs with Gil. When Gil is at work Tommy is here with me. When both Gil and I are at work, Tommy rides his bike. To see him splayed across my couch in the evenings, his hand buried in a bag of Cool Ranch Doritos, you would never know he logs forty miles every morning. He is a competitive racer. He was in the Olympic trials when he was eighteen. Now he competes in local races where he wins trophies and gift certificates to Applebee's. He doesn't have a job. He defines himself not as independently wealthy, but as independently comfortable. And except for his racing gear, he and Gil can live off what Gil makes at the hospital.

The fourth letter from Mariela arrives on a Monday. Donald flashes me a glimpse of the flimsy gray air-mail envelope when he passes me after lunch; he is bursting with excitement, but it is a rule that we cannot open the letter until the office is closed and we can do it alone, without fear of interruption. At five o'clock Donald sends me the official signal that he can stay late—he opens his door halfway. This means I should go kill a few hours, until much of the office has cleared out, and then return. Sometimes I go to the movies, the rush-hour special, though because I am still in my work clothes—fitted blouse, gabardine pencil skirt, heels—the movie feels like another part of my job, and I find myself sitting unnaturally straight and smiling pleasantly regardless of what is on the screen.

Mariela was Donald's anniversary gift to me. When we had been together one year he presented me with her picture and her paperwork. She is ten years old and lives in an orphanage in Paraguay. Every month we send her twenty-eight dollars (less than a cup of coffee a day!) to help pay for her food and clothes and school books.

"This is our little girl," he'd said that night, touching the photo with tender fingertips. "Look at her, Lauren. She's ours, yours and mine."

Donald and his wife have three children, two in high school and one in college. They pose on his desk in matching silver frames.

"Isn't she beautiful?" he'd said, squeezing my hand until the blood stopped at my knuckles. "She's all ours. She's nobody else's. She's yours and mine."

That was a little over a year ago. And the truth is, it had totally creeped me out in the moment. I didn't tell him this, because he was so obviously moved by it, so blown away by his own gesture, but the whole idea of it made me queasy. Weren't we using her, this innocent little brown orphan? Wasn't she an accomplice to something torrid and dirty? But then, almost overnight, it seemed perfectly acceptable, just as most everything in my life that had ever made me inconveniently queasy (i.e.: my parents' grisly divorce, my absurd broken engagement in college, my temp-job career) had swiftly morphed into *perfectly acceptable*. After all, I told myself, it wasn't as if we had taken Mariela from someone else, someone more deserving. Before us she had nothing, and now she had twenty-eight bucks a month and she meant something to someone. So I have grown used to the idea that she is out there—out there and ours—and Donald and I devour the letters with equal pleasure. She is, I am quite certain, the only child I will ever have. She has never barfed on me and she will never break my heart. And yet when we hold her picture surely what we are feeling is all the joy and pride of real parents.

She sends us actual letters. When I first heard about it, I imagined the letters would be something like the sweepstakes notices you get, the ones with your personalized information spliced in:

Dear *Lauren and Donald*,
Thank you for your generous gift of *$28*. I used it to buy a *new goat*. Now there is *milk* for my *classmates*. I hope the weather in *Chicago* is pleasant.
Sincerely,
Mariela

But I was wrong. The words are her own—translated, of course, and typed on a piece of flowery stationery:

Dear Family *(this new letter begins)*,
Today at school we talked about rivers and why they run the way they do. After school we played football even though it was raining. I was on the red team and I scored one goal and then a boy named Jorge who

was on the green team rubbed mud in my hair. Last week I was sick but I am getting better. Thank you for writing me and helping me to have books and clothes for school.

Love, Mariela

"Jorge better watch his back," Donald says. "I'm gonna kick his ass."

The agency has included an updated photo and we sit there on the foldout couch squinting at it, as if even in the photo the distance between us and Mariela is immense. She is standing on a gravel road in front of a squat building that I assume is the school, because she is holding two thick books pressed against her chest, in the same way I and many girls had held books at the age of ten, a shield that hid our bodies, the only thing we could hold so tightly at that age.

"She looks so old," I say. "She's not a little girl anymore."

"Soon she'll be casting spells on all the boys," he says. "Just like her mother." He pokes me in the ribs, a gesture I despise. I suspect he is one of those men who tickled his children until they begged for mercy, that he was so pleased with their laughter that he was able to overlook the dismay behind it.

"I'm not her mother," I say. "And Donald, your socks have holes in them, okay? You make a hundred and eighty—"

"You're as much her mother as anyone," he says, setting the letter aside.

"That's nice," I say. "I'm sure that would be a great comfort to her. You can't buy a week's worth of decent socks?"

"What's wrong, honey?" he asks. He puts his big palm on my cheek, a gesture I love, and I forget about his socks and Mariela. Sometimes I feel like I could sleep curled in his hand, like a hamster.

"Nothing," I say.

"No, really," he says. "What is it? Is it me?"

This is his favorite question: is it me? is it me?

"Don't freak out," Tommy says. He is standing in my doorway with a supersize bag of Barbeque Fritos. "Whatever you do, just don't freak out."

"What?" I say, closing the door. "What happened?"

"Just don't freak out."

"Okay, whatever, I won't freak out."

He sits down on the couch, picks up the remote, and turns off the television.

"I'm freaking out," I say.

"Me, too," he said. He pauses, then inhales and exhales deliberately like he is on an infomercial for yoga tapes. "We're moving."

"What do you mean *moving*."

The word itself feels strange in my mouth. Moving. Moo-ving. A cow plus *ving*. You might say *I'm moving this couch to the other wall* or even *they're moving my office at work*, but people themselves do not move. Things move. Tommy and I have lived in this apartment complex for seven years, since literally the day after we graduated from college. When Tommy and Gil became a couple three years after that, Gil moved in; Tommy did not move out. Because Tommy did not move.

"Gil got this amazing offer to run the ER at this hospital in—"

"Gil?" I explode. "Since when is this about Gil? Since when is every goddamn thing about Gil?" The irony that Gil's name comes up approximately once a month, usually in passing, is popping around in the back of my brain like a Mexican jumping bean, impossible to grab.

"Sweetie," Tommy says miserably. And right then it becomes apparent that one of us is going to start crying. I'm not sure which of us, but either way it's something to be thwarted at all costs.

"Go home," I say. "I have stuff to do, all right? Just get out of here. I have like a million things to do."

He doesn't move from the couch. "Can I just turn on the TV instead?"

"Okay," I say. "Want a Coke or something?"

"Okay," he says.

We drink our Cokes. We eat the Fritos down to the crumbs. We watch a special on The History Channel about a British soldier in WWII who was dropped from an airplane, already dead, with bogus top-secret documents in his pockets, sent to confuse the Nazis. It's always good, when you're feeling really lousy, to watch something about Nazis.

Usually I skip the company picnic. Usually, as soon as the date is announced, I remember something very important that it conflicts with. This was true even before Donald and I were together. Didn't I see these people enough during the week? What did I need, exactly, with a bunch of tipsy lawyers and legal secretaries smeared with sunscreen and bug repellent, a bunch of kids running around screaming their heads off, their faces stained with watermelon? But this year an unfortunate turn of events has made it necessary for me to attend. I have won an award. In our annual client survey, the email marked Urgent informs me, I have received an "unprecedentedly unanimous vote of ten (excellent) for friendly customer service…both in person and on the telephone!"

"It's a big deal," Donald calls to me. He is standing in his private bathroom, in front of the mirror, poking a small red bump that has appeared below his left eye. "If you don't show up…well, it'll look really, really bad."

"You're telling me I might get fired for not coming to the company picnic?"

"I didn't say that." He pokes his head out the door. "Just…it'll be weird if you don't come. People might think it's because, you know, whatever."

"I might be sick," I said. "I might get the flu."

He's back at the mirror. Bug bite? Acne? Cancer? "Okay, it's dumb to you. Okay. Fine. But some people have been here for twenty years and never won something like this. It means something."

"Something besides I'm screwing the boss."

He abandons his prodding and comes out of the bathroom. "Are you kidding me? Really, Lauren, you think I had something to do with this? Is it that hard to believe that people think you do your job well?"

"I'm so proud," I say, twisting my heels into my shoes. "My college education has finally paid off. I think I'll call my mother. And imagine how proud Mariela will be when she hears."

"Babe, what is it?" he asks. "Is it me?"

"My friend Tommy is moving," I say. "In three weeks. He and Gil are moving to New Mexico."

"Wow," Donald said. He sits on the foot of the foldout beside me, puts his hand over mine. "But he's your best friend."

"I told him that. It didn't seem to make the difference."

"I'm really sorry," he says. And he is. He's not a bad guy. You hear about a guy like this, a guy—a *lawyer,* for crying out loud—banging his receptionist at the office two nights a week while his wife keeps his dinner warm, and you think you've got this guy all figured out. But you don't know that, when he sees a spider crawling across his office wall, he'll catch it in a plastic cup and when he has a minute to spare he'll run the spider downstairs and shake it into one of the plants that line the front of our building.

"I'm sorry, too," I say.

"You have to be my date," I tell Tommy the next night, during *Animal ER.* "You owe me big and I'm not going alone."

"Sure," he says. "I'll be your date. I'd love to be your date. Is Fatty going to be there?"

"He's not fat," I say. "Just because you weigh seventy pounds doesn't mean everyone else is fat."

"Ouch," Tommy says, because on TV a golden retriever is having a fishhook removed from his floppy ear. He changes the channel: *$100,000 Pyramid,* the real one, with Dick Clark.

"Yes!" we say, in unison.

"Is the wife coming?" he asks.

"Probably," I say. "I don't see why she wouldn't."

"What's her name again?"

"I don't know," I say, which is a lie. Her name is Carol. But I prefer to refer to her in my deliberate, detached way as "the wife," "the missus," or "the old ball and chain."

"I've never been to a company picnic before," Tommy says.

"Are you packing?"

"For the picnic? Too soon, I think."

"You're funny."

"I'm packing a little," he says. "You could come help, you know. We could hang out at my place."

We rarely hang out at his apartment. It smells a little, I think, like aftershave.

"I have more channels."

"This is true," he says. "I only have a hundred and five. We'd never be able to find anything to watch."

"New Mexico," I say. "Have you ever even been to New Mexico? Have you ever even been *through* New Mexico?"

"I've been to Arizona," he says.

"I can't believe he's making you go," I say. "Of all the selfish—"

"He's not making me go," Tommy says. "It's exciting, okay? Going someplace new, starting over. I might even get a job myself. I'm ready for a change."

"Since when? Since last week? Since he *told* you you were ready for a change?"

"Lauren—," he says harshly. He starts to say something, then thinks better of it.

"What?"

"Nothing," he says.

We leave it at that. And I realize, as I turn back toward the TV, that I am all about *leaving it at that*. If I could *leave it at that* forever, if I could get away with never having another conversation of substance, with anybody, I might just take it and run.

Dear Family,

Today a dentist came to look at our teeth. He said mine were second best and all he did was give me a toothbrush. Some other kids had to have some teeth pulled and Jorge was one of them and his cheek swole up and everyone laughed at him. But I didn't. The dentist was a tall American man with a beard and one of the girls asked if he was Santa Claus. Then later somebody said that the dentist might adopt one of us so we all tried to guess who it would be. I think it will be the girl who asked if he was Santa Claus.

Thank you,
Mariela

"Poor Jorge," Donald says. It's the night before the company picnic and we are sitting on the middle of the foldout eating Chinese food from stained boxes. "Nobody's ever going to pick poor Jorge."

"I don't think anyone's going to pick any of them. After they're babies, nobody wants them."

"You never know," he says. "They might get lucky."

"Maybe I'll go get her."

"Who?"

"Mariela."

"Oh," he chuckles. "Right."

Of course I'm not even remotely serious, but as soon as he says *right* the whole thing racks into focus and makes more sense than any thought I've had in years.

"So what would you do?" I ask. "What would you do if I just showed up one day with her? Just one morning I come in to work and she's tagging along behind with my briefcase."

"Lauren," he says. "Come on. Cut it out."

"You started it," I say. "You're the one writing the checks. So what do you say? Let's go get her. We'll bring her back. She can live here in the office and we'll raise her. Two nights a week we'll order in pizza, rent some movies. The rest of the time she can just hang out around the building waiting for us to show up."

He looks weary. I know what he is thinking. Someone probably told him this would happen—one of the other lawyers, or his psychiatrist—that at some point the receptionist would get needy, go a little crazy even, that at some point his joy ride was going to end and the stakes were going to get higher and he was going to have to get rid of her somehow.

"I love you," he says. "Do you understand that? This isn't just like…a thing. I'm not like other people who do this. You know that, don't you?"

"I know," I say. "You're like…like you who does this."

"Tell me what to do," he says. "I need someone to tell me what to do."

"That's the most pathetic thing I've heard in my entire life," Tommy says. "Jesus Christ, what a big baby."

We are on our way to the picnic. The sun is blazing in the sky. My feet are up on the dashboard and I realize I shaved only my left leg this morning. The end is near, I think. But what the hell? First you stop shaving your right calf, soon your fingernails grow ragged, eventually you stop brushing your teeth. Even the simplest matters of personal hygiene fall by the way. Next thing you know the health department is knocking on your door, and there you are on your couch, all alone, covered in bags of Doritos. And you, not even quite thirty. What happened to you?

"You're a little pathetic, too," I tell Tommy. "Don't forget that. We're all a little pathetic."

"Exactly," he says. "Everybody gets to be a *little* pathetic. But you can't have more than your share, or there's not enough to go around. You can't be a hog about it."

The wife is adorable, cute as a shiny little button in that pushing-fifty kind of way; her brown hair is bobbed, her makeup tastefully applied, her blouse bright and sleeveless, her walking shorts khaki and slimming. I can't think of a single bad thing to say about her, watching the two of them standing by the barbeque pits, standing close enough that their matching shorts brush against each other. Owning not a single outfit that falls between what I wear to work and what I wear in front of the television, I am grossly overdressed, despite my one stubbly leg.

"I should have worn my sweat pants," I say, trying to not allow my eyes to linger on the wife.

"You're making a statement," Tommy says. "You're telling the world that no occasion is too casual for heels. Soon women all over America will be playing softball in two-inch pumps."

I look at the schedule of events posted by the picnic tables, hoping that the awards ceremony is early on the agenda, that we can eat a quick burger and I can collect my prize (framed certificate, coffee mug) and be headed home inside of an hour. To my dismay I see that the ceremony comes last, after food, volleyball, and—

"Races!" Tommy says. "I didn't know there were *races!*"

I refuse the potato sack and egg-on-a-spoon, but after considerable badgering I agree to be Tommy's partner in the three-legged race, despite the fact that even with the heels kicked off my skirt promises to slow us down. Just before the starting gun—a teenager popping a baggie—Donald and the Missus hustle up to the starting line, all giggles and flushed faces. We are on one end of the line of competitors; they are on the other. Between us are three other couples who tumble into heaps barely out of the gate. Tommy drags me along; I feel like dead weight, and see Donald out of the corner of my eye, grimacing, trying to catch me. I believe in this moment he has forgotten who I am, so intent he looks upon winning the race. Tommy hurls himself through the blue-streamer finish line and drags me with him. We high five and bounce off each other. We make complete fools of ourselves, long after it is appropriate. The wife comes over to congratulate us, and Donald comes panting along behind her, a slightly panicked look on his face.

"Congratulations," the wife says. "You're quite a pair."

"This is Lauren," Tommy says.

"Oh, the famous Lauren!" she says. "Congratulations on your award."

"Yes, congratulations!" Donald exclaims. He shouts it so loud his wife winces and gives him a look. "We're all very proud," he says at a normal level.

"Is this your husband?" the wife—Carol—asks.

"No," I say. "This is just Tommy."

In the car I completely dissolve. One moment we're sitting calmly at a red light and the next moment I'm blubbering.

"I can't believe you're actually going to leave me. I can't believe you're actually—"

"I'm not leaving you. For God's—"

"You stupid shit...mother...damn...freaking—"

"Good one," he says.

"Shut up," I say. "Don't you dare make me laugh, you—"

A horn blares behind us. The light has turned green. Tommy guns the engine and the car jolts into the intersection, shudders, chokes, and dies.

"Shit!" Tommy says, slamming the gearshift into park.

"What's wrong with it?"

"Stupid piece of—"

The horn blares again. "I know!" Tommy yells. "I know! Thank you very much!"

The guy whizzes around us and offers the predictable gesture. The car starts. Tommy puts it in drive and we move forward again, in silence. Tears eke out of my eyes and roll to the corners of my mouth. I am furious that I cannot stop them. We are only a mile from home when Tommy says, "It does that sometimes when you give it too much gas. Dies at intersections."

"You should get that checked out," I say.

"I guess." He clears his throat, stares at the car in front of us. "Come to New Mexico," he says.

I sniffle gracelessly, lick the salt from my lips. "What?"

He glances at me briefly, then turns back to the road. "Come to New Mexico. Just do it. What do you have here?"

"You," I say.

"Yeah," he says. "And I'm going. So we could go together."

My tears have dried up. "All three of us? You, me, and Gil."

"Sure," he says. He pulls up in front of our building and turns off the car. "I mean, me and Gil. And…and me and you."

I take off my seatbelt. I feel that Tommy and I are at the tail end of a very long date. I blow my nose before I turn to him.

"I think that's a little more than my share of pathetic," I say.

On Monday I start packing my things at 4:45. I want to be standing in the elevator at 5:00, out of the building before Donald can signal me with his door. But then someone calls and I have to put them on hold forever, and then a delivery man comes by with something stupid and important, and then it's 5:05 and the office is almost empty and it's just me and a couple other girls and Donald's door is open halfway. I look at it, weigh my options. I think: So my best friend has moved away. So what? It's not as if there's a dire shortage of fags who like TV and junk food. It's not as if anything *has* to change.

"Come out for a drink?" one of the girls says.

Her voice so startles me that I literally flinch.

"Sorry," she says. "You wanna come out with us?"

"Me?" I say.

"Your boyfriend can come, too."

"Who?"

"From the picnic. He's cute."

"Yeah," I say. "Well, we have plans tonight."

And then they are gone and it's just me and Donald's door. And I hear the girls' laughter down the hall and then I hear Ginny's vacuum cleaner start up in the office next door and I hear—don't I?—Donald on the phone with Carol telling her he's going to be late and I hear Tommy taping up his boxes and I hear the din of the television in my own apartment and my bag is packed and I'm out the door in the hallway and Ginny is there with her vacuum and the thick black cord is blocking my path.

"I'm not who you think I am," I shout.

She turns off her vacuum. "Excuse me?"

"I'm not who you think I am," I say.

She smiles vaguely. "I'm sorry," she says. "Do I know you?"

I will go to Paraguay, I decide, as the elevator begins its descent. I will go to Paraguay, and I will never return. In the morning I will leave a note for Tommy, telling him what I have done, wishing him smooth pavement and two hundred channels in New Mexico. Then I will go to the airport and board a plane. By noon I will have cleared the airspace of my country, and by dinnertime I will be on a bus on a gravelly road. The seats will be torn and the windows will rattle loose in their frames. The bus will smell. Maybe I will smell, too. Maybe I will be happy to smell. And at nightfall I will get off the bus and there she will be, running toward me with bare feet and windblown hair.

"Mama, Mama," she will shout. "Mama, is it you?"

"It's me, baby," I will say.

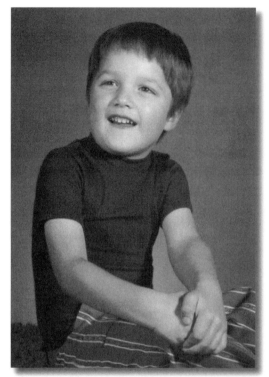

With my modeling career on the rocks, I soon turned to writing. (Pants courtesy of Tony Randall.)

James Sepsey is completing his BA in English. After that he'll teach. This is his first published story.

NOT WHEN A DAY
CAN BE THIS GOOD

James Sepsey

Today our VCR exploded. Mom and I were watching *The Bank Dick*, with W. C. Fields, and right as the plot thickened, smoke shot up the back of the machine, and it died. I told Mom a long time ago I thought we should get a new VCR. "You just watch," I said. "One of these days it's gonna blow up before our very eyes." It did, but all Mom said was for me to get it fixed.

So here I am lugging this enormous VCR down the street. People of today have DVD players, computers, gadgets. We have a 1983 Pioneer Century. Mom's real sentimental about it. She paid three hundred and seventy-five dollars for it in 1982. I was thirteen, and I remember the day she brought it home. There it was, like a crate of food that had washed to shore on our deserted island. We hovered around it, plugged it in, hooked it up to the TV, stood back. Then Mom said, "Be nice if we had a movie to watch."

So we went to the video shop and rented *Duck Soup*. It was all we watched for a week. We returned it late, and our late fees were so staggering we didn't rent another movie for two weeks. We just monkeyed with the VCR—opened the hatch, set the clock, read the manual, stuff like that. Wished.

This morning I go to the Video Mote to see if they can fix our VCR. They can, but it'll cost over a hundred dollars. Apparently some belts have melted, and a capacitor is fried, and something else is wrong with a gear. The guy at the Video Mote, Ian, says why not buy a DVD player? He's right. I saw one the other day for ninety-nine dollars. But since I only have ten, I tell Ian to start work on the VCR and I'll bring him the rest of the money next week. He says sure.

I tell Mom how much it's all going to cost.

"Why so much?" she says.

"You really don't understand VCRs, do you?" I say. "Some belts have melted. A capacitor is fried. There's something wrong with a gear. Perfectly common problems, yet not cheap repairs."

"When will we have it back?"

"Just as soon as we raise ninety dollars to pay it off."

"I hope you have a plan."

I say I do. Mom asks what it is. I tell her I can't tell her.

"Is this plan of yours legal?" she says.

I tell her it is. "But," I say, "it involves a little magic."

"Not that again, Virgil," she says.

I became a magician probably twenty years ago. One night I was watching TV, sitting with our cat Lefty. Lefty was a fat Siamese, and one of his paws was larger than the other, hence the name. Although in reality, it was his right paw that was larger, so how he became Lefty I'll never really know. Dad named him. Dad was kind of a comic genius. Since his death, from cancer, the comedy around the house has petered out. I do what I can. But I'm filling some pretty big shoes.

Lefty and I were watching a variety show, and Doug Henning was the variety. Chances are you don't know who Doug Henning is. In his day, he was the best magician around. He had long, feathered hair, a moustache, buckteeth. He wore a jumpsuit, white boots, stuff like that. I don't even remember what trick he did, but I was so taken by his mystique—and by his blond, leggy assistant—that I said to myself, *Now there's a life worth living.*

I went out the next day and bought a magic kit. It had foam multiplying bunnies, multiplying balls of yarn (with cups), some colored rags, and a wand. I practiced all day, then later that night I made a sign and put on a magic show. I wore a bathrobe, and tried to make a magician's hat out of black crepe paper. I did the multiplying bunny trick for Mom, but all the bunnies shot out of my hand at the wrong time. Then I did the multiplying balls of yarn for Dad, but I got them out of order and revealed the secret of the trick.

"The thing to remember with magic," Dad said as I bawled, "is you don't wanna show how it's done. Remember that, okay?"

I have this old magic book called *Magic Revealed*. On the cover is a guy in a cape holding a rabbit up for some spellbound kids. In the background there's a collage of magical acts—a woman floating in the air through hoops; gloved hands holding cards—all aces!; a puff of smoke that has the phrase "How Is It Done???" spelled over it. The book was written in 1938, a pretty good year for magical achievements, I imagine.

I read the table of contents. I'm looking for tricks involving money. There's one where you make a coin go from one pocket to the other. And one where you fold a dollar bill and turn it into an IOU. But neither of these seem legal, or really magical, so I put the book away and think things over. I have a headache so I lie down.

About 4:30 the phone rings and wakes me up. Mom's taking a crap, so I get up to answer it. It's Ian. He says he has something he wants me to see. "The weirdest thing," he says. "Come right down. I mean, I close at 5:00, but that's subject to change when something like this happens."

I tell Ian I'll be right down. Mom says to get some tin foil while I'm out. So there's seventy-five cents down the drain.

I get to the Video Mote about 4:53. I have a digital watch, so my timing is always precise. Ian's inside smoking a cigarette, and in the background he's playing a laser disc of *Duel*. *Duel*, Ian says, prefigures *Jaws* in a number of ways: You have the menacing antagonist—the diesel, the shark—and you have the guy who has to do away with said menacing antagonist. Another good film, according to Ian, is *Two-Lane Blacktop*. It has nothing to do with either *Duel* or *Jaws*, but it's supposed to be pretty good, and Ian is always recommending I watch it.

"Good evening," Ian says, in a Vincent Price kind of way.

"Hey, Ian," I say.

"Virgil?" Ian says. "Where'd you buy this VCR?"

"I don't know. I think it was Merrill's Electronics."

"Out of the box? Untouched by human hands?"

"As far as I know."

"You've got something here. Something incredibly unusual and rare."

"I do? What?"

"I think it's better if we talk about it tomorrow. Over beers. Can you spring for a six-pack, meet me here around noon?"

"Well," I say, "I do have to buy tin foil first."

"I see," Ian says. "I just thought you'd be interested to know what you have here, that's all."

"You can't just tell me now? The machine's right in front of you."

"I need the night to ponder this. It's so unusual, so rare, I don't know what to make of it. *I'm coming out of my skin, Judah.* Know what movie that's from?"

I say I don't.

"Tell you tomorrow," Ian says. "Are we on?"

I say we are. Where I'll find money for a six-pack, though, I have no idea. Mom's on disability, and her check doesn't come for another two weeks. At the moment, we're flat broke. But I'll think of something. I always think of something.

But I can't. Not with Mom on my back all night about getting a job. "You're thirty-seven. I need you to be a man. Like your father, your grandfather, your great-grandfather. All men. God, you'd think it'd run in the family at some point. Did you remember tin foil?"

I tell her I didn't. Then I say I'll work on being a man. After dinner she falls asleep on the sofa. I watch TV and think about my problem.

I guess I could sell something. This guy, Ace, he said once he wanted to buy my *The French Connection* poster. I take one last look at Gene Hackman, his plaid hat, then go call Ace. I ask does he still want the poster. He says am I kidding? Of course. But for half what I was originally asking.

"What was I originally asking?" I say.

"Ten bucks," Ace says.

"So I'm to sell it for five bucks?"

"Yeah, but I only got four right now. Let me owe you a dollar."

"All right," I say. "Come on over."

For four bucks I can get a six-pack of Lucky Lager. Ian and I can do the puzzles on the bottlecaps. Those are always pretty challenging.

The next day I go to buy a six-pack of Lucky Lager, but as it turns out they only come in twelve-packs. The guy at Liquor Land says how about Hamm's? "It's only four dollars and ninety-nine cents," he says. I tell him I only have four bucks. He thinks it over. "Okay," he says. "I'll sell you five cans for four bucks." I buy them. Then I go to see Ian with five cans of Hamm's. But he's not at the shop.

It's about 12:47, and I'm standing outside the Video Mote with five cans of Hamm's, and it's getting warm. The beer is. People keep walking by and staring at me. They're probably thinking, *There's that somewhat-retarded guy that lives with his mom still.* That's the general consensus around Branch Peak, the town where I live. I can't say I blame people for thinking like that. I am a little old to be living with my mom. But people probably don't know that guys like Herman Melville, author of *Moby-Dick*, lived with his in-laws even after he was a famous genius.

But where the hell is Ian? My guess? He skipped town with my VCR. I mean, what he found so unusual and rare about it, I have no idea. We once watched this Michelangelo Antonioni movie about a pretty girl who did nothing, and I remember Ian commenting on how mysterious it all seemed. The way nothing happened. The way empty spaces suggested loss. The way the woman and her lover stared ahead at what appeared to be nothing. "But you take something from it, don't you?" Ian said after we watched the movie. I was drunk, so I don't remember if I had a snappy comeback or not. I probably didn't. I probably just agreed with him.

Well, nothing is certainly happening at the moment. Ian owns the Video Mote, so he pretty much decides if it'll open for business from one day to the next. Things have been tough on him lately with the DVD boom. He's an old-fashioned merchant who still firmly believes that laser discs are superior to all forms of video entertainment. He is also quick to point out that Woody Allen steals everything from Ingmar Bergman.

At about 12:57 I tear a piece of the paper sack, take the pen from my pocket, and write a note to Ian. Simply:

> *Ian. What gives? I was here when you said to be here. I brought beer and all that. But you were not here. I'll be at home if you need me. Virgil.*

I tape the note to Ian's door and leave. My other guess? Ian probably got high this morning and forgot what he told me yesterday. Ian does that. Gets high. But to each his own. If he did get high and forget, he'll eventually remember. I won't hold it against him.

When I get home Mom says Ian called. "I told him you went out for tin foil," she says. "Because you did, didn't you?"

"No," I say. "I was supposed to meet Ian about our VCR."

"Is it fixed?"

"No, even better: something mysterious has happened to it."

Mom shakes her head, shuts her eyes. She asks me to get her pills from the dresser. I ask which ones and she says all of them.

"You're not going to commit suicide, are you?"

"Not really," she says. "It's just another migraine."

In addition to being a manic depressive with a heart murmur, Mom gets migraines about twice a month. Movies, especially old comedies, cheer her up. The remedy to her woes. So it's vital that I get the VCR back so she can finish watching *The Bank Dick*. "I want our VCR back by tomorrow—no matter what you have to do."

I tell Mom I'll do whatever it takes.

"Did Ian mention if he was at home?" I say.

"No," Mom says. "But he did mention he was in jail."

Mom sits on the sofa and waits for me to get her pills. I walk down the hall, a little shaky, wondering if this is all true. Jail? For what?

I call the jail, the Branch Peak Police Department, and ask to speak with Ian. The lady on the phone says I can't, but if I'd like to visit I can do that tomorrow afternoon. I tell her thanks and she says to have a nice day.

• • •

Today I go to see Ian, but I can't visit him until 4:30. Right now it's about 4:17. I have to sit in a little waiting room for thirteen minutes. Next to me is a tall, nervous woman wearing a green felt hat. She has the Holy Bible on her lap. Across from me is a Mexican family—a woman, three boys, two little girls. Next to them is an elderly couple, probably in their seventies. A cop is standing in front of a door, one of those doors with a window where they put chicken wire between the glass. I guess that's in case if the convicts bust out, glass won't shatter all over the place. On the wall behind the cop a sign reads:

No Smoking. No Items Past This Point. All Conversations Are Recorded. Thank You. Branch Peak Police Department.

At 4:32 the cop tells us to follow him. We do. I let everyone go first. The elderly couple takes a while to get to the door. I help the woman through, her husband not even noticing I have taken her by the elbow. We go to little windows, as directed by the cop. I sit at the end. After a minute, Ian comes to the window, crying, in an orange jumpsuit, his hands shackled in handcuffs.

"Are you okay?" I say.

"Okay?" he says. "What kind of goddamn question is that?"

I shrug. "What happened?"

"I can't go into it right now. I'm in court tomorrow. This sucks so bad."

Ian buries his face into his forearms.

"Well," I say, "I hope it all works out, Ian. Anything I can do for you?"

"Yeah, spring my bail. Can you do that?"

"Well, probably not. No. With what? I can't even afford to pay for my VCR."

"I need to talk to you about that," he says. "But not here. Not now. As soon as I'm out, we gotta have a long chat about that VCR."

"I was hoping to do that today," I say. "Remember you said to bring beer?"

"Is that all you can think about at a time like this? Jesus, Virgil. I've had it with you."

Ian gets up and walks toward the guard behind the glass. The guard lets Ian into a little room, and he is escorted away by two cops. The other visitors keep visiting. I scoot my chair back, stand up, leave. I'll have a hard time telling Mom about the VCR. I hope Ian doesn't get killed in jail. They say it's a no-man's-land in there. I wish I had a shiv or something to give him.

Back at home I return to my book of magic. Surely there's a way to resolve the ninety-dollar issue while simultaneously freeing Ian from jail. I know it sounds strange, but magic is more than just sawing attractive women in half, or making milk disappear into a newspaper. If you really put your mind to it, you can do just about anything. I just need to find a chapter in my book of magic that tells me how to do that. Just about anything, I mean.

But tonight will be difficult. Mom's depressed. She shows me the *TV Guide* crossword puzzle she's been working on, and in every square she's written something depressing: *Misery. Tears. Grief. Drowned. Will Someone Please Let Me Die In Peace!* I hold her hand. I sit beside her. I tell her it'll all work out. She disagrees.

"Look at us," she says. "The whole town thinks we're incestuous freaks."

"Why?" I say. "Because we happen to still live together? Because I don't work? Because I'm nearly forty and still living here? Because people can't mind their own business?"

"You're goddamn right that's why," Mom bawls. "People have a right to think it's sick."

"People stink," I say. "Let 'em think what they want."

"No," Mom says, shaking me by the shoulders. "It is sick. You are too old to live here. You've never worked a day in your life. Get out of here!"

Mom stands up, points to the door. I guess she wants me to leave. So I do. I stand in the front yard for a while. Then I sit on the steps. It's pretty cold, but Mom says I can't come back in. I wonder what Ian wants to tell me? I wonder if I'll have to move to a house for idiots. Uncle Rex did. Maybe that's the problem. Maybe that's what runs in the family. Idiot's blood.

Around 9:36 Mom opens the door. She's put on a clean dress, shoes, a hat. She asks would I like to go to the Burger Odyssey for a double-pastrami French burger. A double-pastrami French burger is the greatest hamburger on earth, and I would love to go have one with Mom. We walk to the Burger Odyssey, four and half blocks, talking along the way.

"I don't think it's sick the way we live," she says. "I was joking."

"Me, either," I say.

"But maybe you can find a job. Anything. I used to throw papers when I was a girl. I can show you the ropes of that industry."

I tell Mom that would be terrific. I'd love to have a paper route.

"How's the magic coming?" she says. "I know how much it means to you."

"Fine," I say. "Magic is a mysterious thing, you know."

"I bet you sometimes wish you could make me disappear, don't you?"

"Never."

"I know. I'm kidding. I know you'd never do that."

I tell her not in a million years. She hugs me. I take her hand as we cross the street. She looks beautiful. We arrive at the Burger Odyssey. And we do so in style. I open the door for Mom, ask for a table for two. The girl in the red visor laughs, but she obliges. She seats us, and I ask for a menu. She points over her shoulder, at the wall. I tell her thanks. Dinner is wonderful.

When we get home there's a message on the answering machine from Ian. "Hey," it says. "I'm okay. I mean, I'm out. Look, come on down tomorrow about that VCR. I won't screw you this time. Shit, I didn't mean to say *screw* in front of your mom. Is she there? Hey, but come down tomorrow. Nine's fine. No beer. I'll make some coffee. Bye. Oh, it's me, Ian. Bye."

Mom laughs. I laugh. We listen to the message again and laugh some more.

"Does that mean he's fixed it?" Mom says.

"You never know with Ian," I say. "Lord knows."

Mom turns on the TV and we watch the last half of *Stagecoach*. Good movie, if not entirely a riot in the comedy department. Mom falls asleep on the sofa. Later on, so do I.

The next morning I tell Mom I'm going to see Ian. She wants to come, so I tell her to put on some tennis shoes. We stop for coffee at Perky's, then go on our way. It's a little cold for September, but it feels all right. The leaves are a nice yellow, and they almost glow when they fall to the bright sidewalk. Mom hums "The Way We Were" as we walk. I can't sing, so I just listen.

We go inside the Video Mote, and Ian is cleaning his *Lawrence of Arabia* laser disc. When we approach the counter he says, "The guns face the sea in Aqaba."

"*Lawrence of Arabia*," I say, only because I saw Ian cleaning the laser disc.

"Good, good," he says. "What about the last quote?"

"Oh, yeah," I say. "What was the last quote again?"

"I'm coming out of my skin, Judah," Ian says.

"Hmm," I say. "I have no idea."

"*Crimes and Misdemeanors*," Mom says. "Woody Allen."

"Nice work, Mrs. Capsian," Ian says. "All right!"

I look at Mom. She smiles and shakes my hand. "Thought I was an idiot, didn't you?"

I tell her absolutely not. Ian calls us over to the counter, points at our VCR. "Well," he says. "Are you ready? Can your heart stand the excitement?"

"Probably," I say. "What is it? What's the big mystery, Ian?"

Ian points to the front of our VCR, running his fingers over the Pioneer logo. "Outside, this is a Pioneer," he says. "Good brand, everything's just fine. But inside. Do you have any idea what you have inside this machine?"

"Other than dirt?" Mom says. "God only knows."

"Your circuit board was smuggled in from Sweden," Ian says. "Someone put a Pioneer cover over the chassis. To save money. It's a Locke inside."

"So our VCR is Swedish?" Mom says. "You mean our troubles are over?"

"That's hysterical, Mrs. Capsian," Ian says, a little irked. "What you have here is cheap, cheap electronics, yet it somehow has lasted all these years."

"Because it always thought it was something else?" I say.

"Yes," Ian says. "Along those lines."

"So," Mom says, "can you fix it?"

"Sure," Ian says. "You think it's neat, right? You guys don't seem too impressed."

"We're very impressed, Ian," Mom says. "It's just, we miss our VCR."

"I know how it is," Ian says. "I'll have it ready by tomorrow. You can make payments. It's an easy fix."

"How long will it last?" I say.

"As long as love will let it," Ian says, sort of striking a thinking man's pose, losing sight of life's greater simplicities.

Before we leave I ask Ian what happened the other day.

"You mean jail?" he says. "Yeah, I was drunk and decided to cross a street. I passed out halfway along the journey. Next thing you know, I'm sleeping next to a bologna sandwich and an orange. A tall black guy is pacing the cell in his underwear. Can't tell you how much it sucked."

"You should avoid doing that," I say.

"I know," Ian says. "Probably should."

Mom and I leave Ian and head out. On the way home I hide behind a tree. Mom can't find me. She calls for me. Panics. I finally jump in front of her, laughing.

"I was worried you'd disappeared," she says, her hand over her heart.

Mom puts her hand on my cheek. Her palm is cool and soft. The sky is wide and bright and blue. Two clouds crash together. I tell Mom not to worry. I tell her I'll never disappear. Not from the life we have together. Not when a day can be this good.

INTERVIEW WITH
D.B.C. PIERRE

by Jennifer Levasseur and Kevin Rabalais

When dark horse D.B.C. Pierre won the 2003 Man Booker Prize for his first novel, the farcical **Vernon God Little,** *headlines across the world screamed his criminal past. "Reformed cocaine addict is £50,000 Booker winner," the* **Daily** Telegraph *wrote. Pundits questioned whether his win spoke more to the public's fascination with his until-then-hidden drug- and theft-filled past than to his skill. Some even questioned his right to the prize, since Pierre has spent much of his life in North America and Europe, and* **Vernon God Little** *is set in Texas, featuring a high-school massacre and the American media's response to it.*

Born Peter Finlay in Reynella, South Australia, in 1961, Pierre (whose initials stand for Dirty But Clean) moved with his family to Mexico when he was seven years old and remained there until early adulthood, where the poverty of his surroundings exaggerated the wealth of his ex-pat American community. At a young age, he fell into drugs and scams,

D.B.C. Pierre

Glimmer Train Stories, Issue 64, Fall 2007
©2007 Jennifer Levasseur and Kevin Rabalais

which continued through his subsequent travels, culminating in his most publicized theft: writing a bogus contract in order to sell a friend's house and take the profits, leaving the elderly man homeless.

In his repentant Booker Prize acceptance speech, Pierre pledged his winnings to the people he conned. He now claims to have repaid everyone he owes, barring two people he says he can't locate.

Pierre's follow-up novel, Ludmilla's Broken English, *contains the same kind of wild, over-the-top language and impossible scenarios that fans expect from him and critics love to hate. In the novel, recently separated conjoined twins find themselves entangled with a mail-order bride service operating out of the Caucasus.*

D. B. C. Pierre now lives in County Leitrim, Ireland. Jennifer Levasseur and Kevin Rabalais interviewed him in Melbourne, Australia.

You've been quoted as saying that part of the impetus for writing Vernon God Little *was the desire to pay your debts. Yet many first novels aren't published, are published to small advances, or aren't commercially successful. Did you realize this when you started?*

Twenty years earlier, out of a sense of unreality, I might have attempted to do something like that, but I knew that I might as well buy a lottery ticket as write a novel in order to provide financial headway. It was much more of a creative statement. I had tried for years to be an artist and never got anywhere. I had just gone through a very frustrating decade, one thing following another. Deciding to write a novel was a way to prove myself to myself. I couldn't find a regular job, especially in London, let alone get a novel published. I actually knew going into it that the odds in London for publishing unsolicited manuscripts was something like five thousand to one. As I wrote *Vernon,* I couldn't think of anyone I knew who would like it. There was no one I could send it to.

Was that freeing?

Being in a position of having nothing to lose is fantastic. When I sat down to write *Vernon God Little*—and this is probably like most writers—I automatically imagined an average reader. I had started to write something that I thought was what a book should be. But I quickly discovered that I might end up with something that I didn't necessarily like and readers mightn't like either. Learning from scratch, though, I had no one to please but myself.

What kept you going during the process?

Vernon took eighteen months to write. I finished the first draft in five months. Finishing the first draft got me through the rest of it. It was crap, but the voice was there. I had no experience. I had the essence of it but none of the craft. I had to go back and build a plot. Along the way, I had to learn how to put the carpentry together.

What did you learn during this "carpentry" stage?

It was an odyssey. That's the only way I can describe it. I felt like I was swimming the Atlantic at night. I was completely blind. In hard times, I got superstitious and started believing in kismet. Information and details about the plot and characters started to come my way just when I needed them. I learned about the nature of tension and how to put obstacles in front of characters. I didn't want *Vernon* to be a traditional novel because it was a bit of a two-way piss-take on how the media tell stories or how a TV movie might be put together. I wanted it to feel a bit that way. In the end, I was watching television news and movies in order to see the way they maintain tension, and I forged the characters' desires along the way.

Aside from that, was there a model you had in mind, something that helped you so that you didn't feel as though you were inventing a new form?

I often use a lot of limes in cooking and in mixing drinks. One day at the beginning of writing *Vernon*, I was in South London, where there are good West Indian markets, and I brought a lime home and cut into it. This was the most extraordinary lime. It was so far from all the other limes I had ever had. Underneath its bitterness, it was sharp and bright. You could almost smell it in the color. That's the only way I can describe it. Around that was an incredible perfume, this extraordinary fragrance that, even from a distance, engulfed me. It drew me in. I knew that's how I had to write the novel. It was just a feeling, but I knew that if I could capture that as the dynamic of a work, then it would be exciting. I wanted it to be perfumed and mysterious and have not just a sting but a bright sting, one that wasn't muddy or grungy, because darkness comes in many shades. I wanted a really crisp darkness in *Vernon*. That lime showed me how I wanted the reader to *feel* the novel. But in terms of the practical craft of writing, I was really bashing my head against a brick wall. I wrote three drafts.

Were you beginning again each time?

Vernon's voice from the first page was fine. I had to do a lot of editing. I also liposuctioned him because he was incredibly verbose. He spoke like he would have on the street, and I learned to sharpen that voice. All of his reflections were there in the first draft. What I didn't have was a storyline. The gunman was already there. The main characters were set, but nothing really happened. It was just Vernon talking on and on. He also died in the first draft, which I thought was correct, but it wasn't true to the big movie the thing had to be. I knew that he would have to live and improbably triumph in the end. I made a reference document with an index that had all the writing in it. I put a couple of hundred pages of material that I liked in it and kept that as a master file. If I had a new draft with a new skeleton, I just transferred it. But I had to learn the craft, which was a whole other thing.

You've said that you weren't someone who dreamed of becoming a writer. Was there a stage during Vernon God Little *when you knew that you could do this, or that writing is what you want to do?*

Every day. And then in the same day I would believe that I was just wasting time. Half of the exercise of writing seems to be to manage that incredible roller coaster. The truth must be somewhere in the middle, I figure. I suspect writers and artists have this feeling all the time, this oscillation between euphoria and despair, a real sense that you're on to something and then a real certainty that you aren't and that you're only deluding yourself. All of that happens, often in the same day. It's like a love affair. The smallest things can suddenly turn your world upside down. I was going through all of that. You get used to it. A few months in, I decided, for the sake of sanity, that the truth was somewhere between those extremes and I just needed to write and press on. That was a hard thing, knowing that I was going to sit down and write shit and go to bed knowing that I had written shit and just hope that down the track the thing would come together. It's still all very mysterious.

Was it difficult to get rid of Vernon's voice once you completed the novel?

Vernon was originally going to be a trilogy. I drafted three books. There was the "black" book, which now exists. Then there would be the opposite viewpoint, in which society was supportive. The third book would draw a line down the middle. Everyone is always arguing in black and white. I'm fascinated not so much with the way something happens but with the way it's argued. My publisher said that I shouldn't push my luck, though, so I said, "Fair enough." My third novel will be a much more proper book. With the experience of *Vernon* and *Ludmilla's Broken English*, I've picked up some craft.

What did writing the first novel teach you about writing the second?

Writing the first novel taught me only how to write that novel. For the second one, I made a decision to come out of my comfort zone. The thing I found easy with *Vernon* was to get into the skin and talk through the mouth of that character. After I won the Booker Prize, I had major internal tussles. I seriously, seriously want to become as good as I can. I define good as being able to write and cry or laugh spontaneously at the page as I write. I'm enchanted with the idea that I'm sitting in the dark and almost charging a battery with energy. I hope to share that energy with the reader as we sit together in the dark. If I can make that journey rich, then I'll be happy. After the Booker, it obviously wasn't useful for me to think I had made it or reached anything spectacular. It was much more useful to think I had been given permission to proceed. It did put a duty on me not to capitalize on that success and take things easy. I couldn't say, "You can do this now. Just churn out another, similar novel." I've made the decision to be as good as I can, and I'm not going to be able to do that if I'm safe and comfortable. I've put a lot of pressure on myself to get cracking and do all of the work I can now because I wasted too many years doing nothing.

Do you think Ludmilla's Broken English *is as far as you could have gone from* Vernon God Little?

For the purpose of growth, I knew that it had to go against what's natural for me. Maybe that's the kind of book you should write in an extracurricular sense and not publish, but I haven't got the time for that. I thought I best come into the third person and not put any autobiographical energy into the second novel. Vernon and I agree about a lot of things. That's a fantastic, powerful fuel for writing. But I decided to take that personal connection away and detach myself from the narrator's voice.

Are you more at home in the first person?

For some time, I've felt it was certainly my corner. Having said that, I'm going back to it now for the third novel, armed with some new knowledge.

Was Ludmilla's Broken English *your first idea after* Vernon God Little*?*

After *Vernon*, I wrote a list of twenty-one ideas and showed them to my agent. I knew nothing about the market. She pointed to *Ludmilla* and said, "Try that one." She thought it was important that I have a British setting for the second novel because people were so confused with the setting of the first one. They thought it was an American novel. I got cracking on it sometime before *Vernon* was published. Then my life was massively interrupted for about twelve months after the Booker announcement.

When you went to your agent with those ideas, were you already thinking of a long-term body of work?

I'm conscious of the trajectory of one work to another and see the connectedness. The third novel will probably bring the first two into context. I haven't got an idea of the shape of that novel yet, but I can feel it. Now I just have to tack into the breeze. But I won't be able to write those twenty-one ideas, not in my lifetime.

How long did you work on Ludmilla*?*

I spent a couple of years on it. I went through more drafts than I did with *Vernon*. I must have written fifteen hundred pages and ten drafts before I boiled it down. This is the problem. Since I'm learning from scratch, I seem to be always chasing a feeling. It's like the feeling I had with the lime. If I could explain it, then that lime is *Vernon God Little*. That's what I was after. But how, in practical terms of writing a novel, are you going to get that feeling onto the page? It was a lot of hit and miss.

There is a taste I want to leave in the reader's mouth. *Ludmilla* started out as what you would expect: a man having a dialogue with himself. Two halves of himself, that is, were having an argument. He was a believable character in a believable place. I also had the idea for a very plausible story involving a mail-order bride. But another set of arguments quickly developed, and symbolism began to control the story. I knew that I had to make the characters rise above the symbols. I had to rework the material because the novel couldn't survive if the characters were merely standing in for the symbols. So I struck on the idea of two people stuck together, adult Siamese twins who suddenly found themselves pulled apart. It wasn't a political agenda.

But to what extent do you think politics informs the book?

I would have to go to some length not to let my writing be infected by the world around me. *Ludmilla* is infected with politics because I couldn't escape this constant set of liberal and conservative arguments when I was writing. So I let those political arguments enter the narrative. During all that time of working out the novel, I was observing the way reality is made reasonable by the media. Look at the question of Iraq. The statement of action that moved this event forward seemed transparent to a lot of people, blatantly transparent. But very quickly academics and commentators, an entire industry of people who chat on television, broke the argument into little pieces. Over time, they made the argument reasonable by diffusing that first moment when you said, "This can't be right." Suddenly, the issue over weapons of mass destruction shattered into a hundred other issues. They built it into a rational thing. I thought if I spent a lot of trouble making the work subtle and doing all of those traditional things, I would be no different from them.

How did the novel grow?

The plot and characters grew together. I had the symbols. It was like a mechanical framework, and the charcters had to flesh out. There was a lot of going through the whole thing and then starting over. I don't know if I found it hard. When I finally read it through, it had the pace

I was after. I disagree with most of the characters in *Ludmilla*, but I didn't want the novel to support one argument or another. I wanted the argument to appear like a Kandinsky double painting. While you think the whole thing tends to have a liberal agenda, it becomes quite conservative. I took out the one character who was an active promoter of change because I wanted there to be a balance.

What kind of research did you conduct for the book? Is it true that you visited the region with Doctors without Borders?

They took me for about a fortnight to the borders in the Caucasus where the refugees were. It was amazing. I had already drafted the scenes in the novel dealing with this and wanted to go to see how close I was. I immediately had to downgrade Ludmilla's lifestyle. I had given her a hard life, but the reality is far too brutal to describe in fiction, even too vulgar for me. There are a couple of emblems in the novel of how brutal it is, but nothing near the real thing. It would have been too ugly for any kind of comedy. That's for nonfiction. So I downgraded her character, put her back in coach. The setting, the pace, and the smell of it is from that trip. The Caucasus is an amazing part of the world. At the time I was there, about five people were kidnapped. There are so many disparate activist groups there that they trade hostages among themselves. You can set up these incredibly complex rescue deals and find out that at the eleventh hour they've traded the hostage to another group and you have to start from scratch. A lot of Western volunteers are kidnapped, so we couldn't visit some of the places I wanted to see. Some of the scenes in the book were rendered from that experience. There were people living with unexploded RPG missiles that had landed in their house some years earlier, and they didn't know what to do so they moved into the garden shed in case the missiles went off.

Many critics want to read Ludmilla's Broken English *as a traditional novel. Does this surprise you?*

I don't know what they're expecting because I haven't come out of a literary culture. This is another area where I'm swimming blindly. I'm not particularly widely read. I don't know my position or the position of contemporary British or any other English-language literature. Many people do, though. They can see the curve, where it's come from and where it is at present. I have absolutely no idea about these things. It's taken me a long time to be educated up to the level of where we are in contemporary literature. I'm completely disconnected from this, and I don't know if that's good or bad. One danger is that I might write something that's already been done. And so my work is humbly submitted as a taste of something I had personally.

What is your reading background?

I've always been a reader, and I love language, especially the music of it. Because I grew up in Mexico, I've been influenced quite a lot by American culture. My challenge is that I'm slow. If I'm reading and I see a beautiful passage or turn of a phrase, I'll go over and over it. I sometimes get stuck on a page in an almost autistic way. I can spend months and months reading a book. It's not for lack of reading that I find myself at a disadvantage, but there are fashions and trends that I'm unaware of for not having grown up in any single place for a particular length of time. It's the same thing with music. I like symphonic music, but I only discover it by hearing it and then trying to find out what it is. That doesn't suggest that if I love the second symphony I will like the third one.

You said you have the idea for your third novel. Have you begun writing it?

I've got a hundred pages of notes that I've winged along the way. It's the first novel that's been fully formed in my mind, and I don't think that I'll have to explore because this is a nicely structured clock full of explosives.

Was it on that original list of ideas?

Yes. It's grown since then. I know exactly what I want to do now. It will be nice and almost mathematically crafted with a constant tension. You'll quickly see that it's going to be hardcore and that it's not going to relent. It's just going to climb and climb, and at the end you'll wonder if you've fallen. That's the feeling I want, anyway.

You mentioned that you're going back to the first person for this one.

I think I found a way to narrate an incredibly decadent novel about sexual excess and desire from a point of view that will keep me as a writer and readers on the correct side of the moral equation.

Which side is that?

It means that we can be voyeurs without being complicit in some of the issues in the book. We live in decadent times, and this interests me. With the internet, sexual desire has suddenly found enormous outlets. I want to write something in which really lurid things are played out, but without doing it like the Marquis de Sade.

Lurid behavior seems to run throughout your books.

This behavior fascinates me. That's why this one needs to be polished. I don't have to have arguments about what kind of book it should be. It needs to be a beautiful container for volatile subject matter. The Marquis de Sade often wrote like the deviance was all great fun. That won't last a minute today. I'll have a crack at it. Now I have to do research and then hope that I can write it in a way that it cannot be banned.

Are you writing with a set of specific ideas, or are you moved by a feeling, as you were with Vernon God Little*?*

There's a performance in writing, a kind of energy, that I love. I can sit for ten days and hack away in an intellectual fashion and only come up with a single set of reasonings, but if I sit down with passion and let that passion be carried along the wave of an idea, the work seems to have energy as well. There's the emotional component. The more emotional I am when writing, the more emotion the reader will notice in the work. Then I don't need to make too many decisions, either, because I know instinctively what has to go in instead of the usual thing of thinking about the mechanics of it. I described this as an odyssey earlier because I'm often making these discoveries from scratch.

Does anyone read your work in progress?

I don't even print it out until I'm finished. There's a little sweetness in the printed page. I reckon that you get ten to fifteen percent more resonance off the page than you do off the screen. So I save that experience as a little sweetness for myself. If I can be happy with it on the screen, then I figure it will be really nice on the page. This is my reward.

What happens once it's printed?

From there, I play with it some more. It also goes to my editor. Many things in the book will become obvious to me because I've seen them so much. I tend to make clues too subtle and I often rely on my editor to tell me what he didn't see something coming because I had shaved some of it off. I'll get a better sense of how to do this over time. My editor doesn't interfere. If the errors don't distract from the reading experience, he'll let them stand. But he may say, "I had to read that three times to understand what was going on."

Do you read fiction while you're writing?

I don't have a rigid discipline, so I don't have the time. I never quite believe writers who say they're up at seven a.m. to write a thousand words. They have a cup of tea, and then write two thousand words after lunch. I can't see that happening to me. I tend to work throughout the day and then move ahead in the night. So I'm normally working at night, which is the space I would like to read, but when I'm finished writing I just fall straight into bed.

This sounds like an intense period for you.

It's not healthy. Apart from anything, I don't sleep. I get too excited. For *Vernon*, I was with a doctor every fortnight. I'm a hypochondriac, and writing that book gave me all kinds of anxiety. There was a period when I wouldn't even leave the house. I finally went to my doctor and said, "I think I have temporal-lobe epilepsy," which I had diagnosed myself with after a search on the internet. I was like a first-year med student, discovering illnesses, and he would sit back and listen, occasionally shaking his head and saying, "No. I don't think so." Finally, after three or four visits, he said, "What do you do for a job?" I said, "I'm trying to write a book." He said, "Then go somewhere to write and then go home." I still have problems, though. The analogy of drag racing comes to mind. They pour gasoline on those big, rubber wheels, and then do a burn-out to make the tires stick as an adhesive to the track. The first drafts of the novel and the final run-through should have that heat to them. I think the first draft needs to be written in a fever without regard for structure. Do it as quickly as possible. Then develop a routine and pull back to work it through in the middle. The end should be a frenzy.

Is there any pleasure in this?

It's in the odd thing. There is a general, slightly destructive pleasure that comes a bit from suffering. I'm chuffed generally, and feel a bit honored to be writing. At times, I feel in the presence of something greater than myself. I don't think writing originates from us, given that our stories are often just the usual things rearranged. I feel like an arranger of something, and that's great. I get specific pleasure when something comes out exactly as I wanted it. You collect a sentence that works. If you sit there long enough, you collect enough sentences to make a book. It's just chipping and chipping away.

Kevin Rabalais and Jennifer Levasseur, editors of *Novel Voices: 17 Award-Winning Novelists on How to Write, Edit, and Get Published*, have appeared in numerous international publications, including *Brick, Glimmer Train Stories*, the *Kenyon Review, Tin House, Missouri Review, World Literature Today*, and *Five Points*. Louisiana natives, they live in Melbourne, Australia.

Me and Bobby, my grandma's cat, circa 1965.
I'm the one with the cheeks.

Antonya Nelson has published eight books of fiction, most recently *Some Fun* (stories; Scribner 2006). She teaches in the creative-writing program at the University of Houston, and lives there, in Las Cruces, New Mexico, and in Telluride, Colorado with her husband, writer Robert Boswell, and their two children, Jade and Noah.

FALSETTO

Antonya Nelson

"All your friends are weird," Michelle's little brother Ellton had said to her that morning. It was a statement with staying power. She would be thinking of it for years to come. She thought of it now, not twelve hours later, as her boyfriend gave her brother a playful sock on the shoulder. The resigned look he turned on his sister said, "See?" He seemed then like the most mature person in the room, although he was only eleven; she was eighteen years older, old enough to be his mother, and her boyfriend was in between, twenty-two.

Plus, Michelle was accustomed to thinking the opposite: that her *family* was weird.

Ellton realigned his video camera, a sleek little unit cupped in his palm, replete with secret abilities. Far too complicated for their elderly parents, the device—a gift from their sister—had been handed over like a bomb to the boy for defusing. It made him seem sneaky, unpopular, destined to someday be accused of a crime he hadn't committed.

Her brother was the opposite of Teacher's Pet, Michelle thought: Teacher's Bane. The clever kid who never failed to name the emperor naked. With him you got away with exactly nothing, although he took no smug pleasure in correcting people—he just liked to have the facts straight. Things could be got right.

"Yo, Elton John," said Michelle's boyfriend Max, still in sparring position. He looked to Michelle for affirmation of his "whimsical tendency." It was the dinner hour, for which Michelle had prepared by drinking a lot of beer during the cocktail hour. Now Max tied an apron over his Polo shirt and stuffed his feet into his sheepskin scuffs. He enjoyed cooking even though his repertoire included just the one dish, a green-flecked, chunky, orange-colored vegetarian sauce: part chili, part marinara, part sloppy joe, you could pour it over pasta, or rice, or beans, or a bun, depending.

"Why is that funny?" Ellton responded, aiming the camera away from his tabletop drama and into Max's face, capturing the gape-mouthed, faux-innocent prankster's expression that Max put on when he thought he was being endearing. He wasn't used to not being liked. Everybody liked him, with his lazy Georgia accent and his bundle of homey bromides handed down from some grandmother. At Ellton's fingertip a red light blinked, accompanied by the electronic whirring. "Ellton is a family name," the boy explained for the tenth time in as many days, his voice tolerant yet fatigued. Max couldn't know that Ellton was showing admirable restraint, not mentioning that Max was a name his and Michelle's family had once chosen for their rooster.

They'd eaten Max for dinner one day, fed up with his early-morning antics.

Ellton did say, "And why must you keep hitting me?"

"'*Hitting*' you?" Max looked to Michelle as to a kind of referee. What sort of sissy was her brother, anyway? The camera followed. In its lens, Michelle corrected her posture. She told Ellton that Max was just playing.

"Playing what?" the boy asked. And Michelle wondered too why Max thought that making fun of a person's name and cuffing him on the shoulder was somehow evidence of good sportsmanship. "It's like he thinks I'm Leroy," Ellton said. Leroy was the dog. He was a dog who invited getting kicked, stubborn, stinky, self-absorbed. *All your friends are weird.* Her brother's thin arms and unmuscled body afflicted Michelle; he was so fearless, yet so unprotected. He'd hung around in his mother's womb for ten months and still only weighed six pounds when he finally came out. He had no defense except the one he'd just employed: weary inquiry. He'd been raised by adults as if he were an adult himself. It was her parents' nature, as a caretaking pair, not to apply much pressure, to more often sit back and observe. Their tolerant philosophy, this entropy in action, yielded mixed results, Michelle thought. Her brother was extraordinary, in her opinion, but the dog she could envision euthanizing.

Her boyfriend, if he hadn't been a Southern gentleman, would have expressed the opposite opinion. "Lighten up," he told the boy now, his mush-mouth accent softening the command.

In the greasy glass of the tall kitchen window Michelle saw the three of them—herself, Max, Ellton; woman, man, child—reflected against a dark mass of approaching clouds. The sky was bigger in Montana; she never remembered this until she had left and then returned. Trails of steam wandered like tears down the glass, while outside the storm front rushed over the Bitterroot Valley and Rock Creek toward them. Their home sat on a hill, and weather could be anticipated for hours before arriving. She felt poor and pitiful, watching the clouds, like an orphan, undeniably bereft. Just that quick, she quit loving her boyfriend. He did not belong in the window reflection: the oncoming storm, two sad siblings. The sensation came as a relief, as if she'd taken the advice Max had offered Ellton, and had lightened up herself, opened a hatch in her heart, at last relinquishing its contents, the confusing and crowded affections like caged birds, set free in a burst of wind.

"Hey Ellton," Max had said days earlier, "you ever seen anything as weird as a fennel bulb?" He held the object up by its hairy stem. Yes, Ellton had said, yes, he had seen many things as weird as, if not weirder than, a fennel bulb. Undaunted, Max asked how Ellton felt about a wedge of parmesan sitting in the sauce. The reply to this was that the cheese smelled like feet. Tough audience, Michelle thought, forcing Max into Trying Too Hard: kids could sense it a mile away, especially this kid.

And now Michelle no longer had to love Max. She thought he had been kind to come with her, but maybe he was guilty of trying too hard with her, too. They'd only been dating for a couple of months. He hadn't met her parents, so it did not naturally follow that he should join her. That his eyes should have filled with tears when she told him what had happened. She'd been touched, back in Houston, but now she was skeptical. He was adopting her family, glomming onto their grief. It had real substance, grief, unlike the ethereal contents of their college classes. "Us," he said, often; the word made her avert her eyes as from a disfigurement. "We." From Houston to Missoula, with a gloppy layover in Salt Lake, he had thrown himself into the role of "support system" in her "time of need."

It was Ellton who had phoned to tell Michelle about the car accident. "They aren't dead," he'd said, right off. He'd always had a masculine voice, husky, unsentimental. "Mom and Dad were in a crash," he said with this voice; in the background, the shadowy, concerned conversation of the neighbors whose house he'd gone to after school that afternoon. His mother and father were driving home from Missoula, where they'd been purchasing sprinkler pipes and mulch, seeds, and saplings: the hopefulness of spring that would lead to a summer garden. They didn't often leave Portersburg; they preferred pleasures that cost nothing and did not require going anywhere. This had been their annual pilgrimage to the garden center, where Michelle could imagine the quiet coupled contentedness they shared, something she both envied and resented. They didn't mean to exclude. They didn't realize how insular their marriage seemed, how it had not really required children in order for it to feel like a family.

Only later did she admire her little brother's sequencing of information: "They aren't dead," he'd known to tell her first.

His videotape was a re-creation of the accident. Max, who was studying elementary education, found the project disturbing. His reaction was to chide the child, nudge and tease him into some other, acceptable sort of person. Didn't he want to help cook, grate some odoriferous cheese? But Ellton was a detail freak. For him, facts offered consolation. He was using toys and rocks and twigs to simulate the pileup in Antelope Canyon; the cop who'd attended at the scene had drawn up a quick diagram on a yellow pad that Ellton consulted like an instruction manual. He'd never been an ordinary boy. He was so thin that people grew angry when he wouldn't eat. When tickled, he didn't laugh so much as suffer a sort of spasm. His solemnity frightened most adults; it was as if they understood he could not be embarrassed himself, but he could embarrass them. Constantly, aggressively, people were insisting that he *smile*.

He made Michelle's heart hurt.

Finished with Max, Ellton swung his camera back to the tabletop. "This guy swerved to miss an animal. Or something."

"A U.F.O.," Max suggested. "Sasquatch."

"Whatever," Ellton said. The Matchbox red convertible that represented the first driver dodged the Scooby Doo figurine and left the lines of the braided placemat that was the road. "The log truck was coming downhill and couldn't stop." Lincoln Logs made for the spill of lumber that had forced their parents' car, a little Matchbox Wonder Bread van, off the kitchen table. Their car had hung suspended upside-down in a ridgepole pine before falling finally to the ground.

Every day, on the drive to Missoula, they passed that broken tree. It looked as if it had been struck not once but twice by lightning.

"The police told me Mom wasn't wearing her seatbelt." He reiterated this daily, as if it might eventually make sense to him, spoken enough.

Michelle responded with her lines: "She was napping." Late every afternoon her mother napped. A creature of habit. A creature, Michelle thought, subject to her instincts, respectful of those of others. "She doesn't like how the shoulder part cuts into her face." Her mother's sleeping form came to mind—on her chenille bedspread at dusk, hands palm-to-palm beneath her cheek as if in prayer—supplanting, briefly, the stiff, comatose form face-up in the hospital bed.

"They say," said Max, gesturing with a wooden spoon, "that sometimes a seatbelt can kill you. Sometimes, they say, wearing a seatbelt is the worst thing you can do." He had taken it upon himself to be their cook, their captain, their bossy cow, and plunged the spoon back into the onions spitting in oil at the stove while Michelle and Ellton studied the tableau on the table. It was a large, round, wooden table, sticky with many meals, the table that had always sat there collecting the most important of the family matter. Max had tried to remove that stickiness, spraying greasecutter, rubbing with sandpaper. For ten days the siblings waited while Max, shirtsleeves metaphorically, literally rolled, busied himself at the stove, at the sink, at the washer and clothesline. His teeth were straight and white, his hair thick, his clothing fresh: shipshape. At each station he remarked on the improvements he foresaw: brighter lighting, handy shelves, Lysol, fumigation, flat-out gutting. He'd spent a long time rattling the kitchen drawers searching out a knife only to discover its rusty dullness. Then he began the rattling quest for a sharpener. In lieu of that, he used the rough bottom of a ceramic plate, swiping the blade back and forth till it gleamed, till it could nick an arm hair from his arm, a piece of legitimate ingenuity Michelle was impressed by, despite herself. Tidy, handy, gallant, comely: what more did she want? Or maybe it was *less*?

"Splatter cover?" Max asked. "Colander?" These had long ago become rhetorical inquiries; theirs was the most poorly stocked household Max had ever encountered. And he couldn't have found a worse town for fresh produce, nor a more lackluster audience for tonight's vegetarian lasagna. Ellton loved meat, and Michelle seemed to have lost the capacity to taste anything besides grief and fear. The flavor was wretched; it occasionally choked her.

She put her fourth beer to her lips and closed her eyes, letting the warm, sweet fluid fizz in her mouth, all texture, no taste. This was her father's brand, dark and thick. He drank it at room temperature. Neither she nor her brother bothered to interrupt Max as he nattered on, adding garlic, herbs, a couple of cans of tomatoes. Their mother stocked a lot of tomato products because the dog was always getting skunked. Leroy was a profoundly self-indulgent dog, Michelle thought; the habits her parents allowed him to acquire and keep were dreadful. Unlike the children, Leroy had had no peers or teachers or friends to instruct him how to fill the gaps, behave in a civilized manner. For the last week and a half, he'd been holed up behind their father's easy chair, growling if anyone dared come close. If he needed some basic necessity—water, kibble, a trip outside—he climbed stiffly out of his cave, grizzled and blinking, and approached the door with his gray head sternly lowered, as if he would butt right through it, given provocation.

Just before the phone rang, Michelle could feel its jangle coming

toward her; you always could, in this house. Ellton said, without looking up from his cinematography, "That'll be Roxanne."

And of course it was.

"Hi Roxanne!" chimed out Max, who'd never met her.

"Who was that?" Roxanne asked.

"Max," Michelle answered.

"Doo Wop?"

"The one and only." Michelle had broken Max of his annoying
habit of saying "Do *wha'*?" It was a tic, something he'd picked up in
Georgia and brought to Rice University. "Do *wha'*?" he responded,
no matter what you had just said to him. At first she thought he had
a hearing problem.

"I can't wait to meet Doo Wop."

"Yes you can." *All your friends are weird.*

Roxanne and Michelle were identical twins. Enough work for any
two parents, especially parents who didn't seem to particularly want
or need children, merely to accept them, the occasional byproducts
of sex. Twins: surprise, surprise. Michelle could imagine her mother's
pregnancy, the rising bulk of her girls beneath her dress, the way she
and their father must have looked down alarmed at what was happening. Her parents loved all growing things—animals, flowers, weeds. Yet
overseeing their own offspring had not come naturally to them. They
were unconfident parents, daunted. Michelle and Roxanne were wild
children, left quite often to their own devices, driven home by neighbors,
looked after by shopkeepers and teachers. Portersburg itself had raised
them. Then, the year the girls graduated high school, their mother had
another baby, a bigger surprise. Why had she waited so long, the sisters
complained? Why, now that they were leaving home for college, had
their parents finally gotten around to delivering their brother? There
was no answer but a pair of sincerely perplexed shrugs.

It was Ellton's arrival that had most likely accounted for Michelle's
dropping out at semester break and moving back home. No doubt her
baby brother was responsible for her remaining in her old bedroom
for another five years, thereby permanently separating her life's path

from her twin's. It was probably Ellton whom Michelle could thank for what her current professors named "life experience," that commodity that was serving her so well as a "non-traditional" undergraduate right now. Junior year, at age twenty-nine and a half.

Her sister Roxanne had been a sparky, daring girl, but was a busy, irritated woman. She seemed to believe that their parents had perpetrated a terrible injustice on their children, raising them the way they had. Away from Portersburg, when she'd discovered how freaky she was, she'd made big changes. Mother of a five year old and pregnant again, she cut immediately to the chase. "What's going on with them?"

"Mom's still unconscious. Dad's stable." In traction, in a full body cast, he couldn't be any more stable, Michelle thought.

"Mom's eyelids were twitching," Ellton reminded her. He had run upstairs to ransack his room for a more suitably sized animal figure, returning with a lifelike, big-shouldered bison to take the place of Scooby Doo.

"What'd he say?"

"He said her eyelids were twitching," Michelle repeated. Her sister's daughter was shouting in the background, hundreds of miles away in Seattle. She was spoiled in the most pedestrian and uninteresting ways. Roxanne's household operated with the child as the centerpiece, like the sun; Michelle wondered if every home had its most radiant member. If so, theirs was their mother. Their slumbering mother, a mild, cool star, undemanding, a little inobtrusive as far as heavenly bodies went, yet the nucleus, nonetheless.

"I can't fly out there because of the fucking baby," Roxanne said. "And Bobby won't let me drive by myself." Her husband grumbled, reasonable arguments being laid out like bullet points, Michelle could tell by the intonation. Roxanne's husband Bobby was a manager at Boeing and wore a suit over his pear-shaped body; his closet resembled a rack at a dull department store, dozens of white shirts hanging ironed in a line, gray pants creased beneath, red and blue neckties hanging above the row of black dress shoes. Their house, which Michelle had visited just once, was part of a subdivision named after the trees it had obliterated, a house brightly lit like a catalog display, everything new and smelling of recent manufacture, the floors golden oak, the rooms painted creamy ivory, the appliances silent and tucked into the walls. There were shelves and baskets and drawers designated for all of their belongings, a peculiar and alien tricky neatness to it all. The girls had not grown up this way. Their home was dark, filled with, oh, birds' nests and shucked antlers, dated magazines and obsolete kitchen tools, broken mantel clocks that their father collected, dried flowers their mother pressed between the pages of all of the heavy encyclopedias, rust rings and shed hair everywhere, piles and piles of books like pieces of furniture, a cloud of enveloping dust when you sat down in a stuffed chair. Serious, sedimented strata on every surface—history, mystery. "So we'll all come on Friday," Roxanne was saying, "just as soon as Bobby gets off work." A door closed in Seattle and there was sudden silence, Roxanne's breathing. "I have to go to the damn potty to get any privacy around here. I'm gonna tinkle, sorry."

"That's okay." Michelle would have liked to find some privacy, too, but there was only one phone in the house, and it was attached to the wall, receiver tethered.

Roxanne and Michelle had frequently confused their mother over the phone, when they were young, but Roxanne's adult voice was flat, imperious, loud with assurance—*potty? tinkle?!*—while Michelle's remained tentative. Their mother never mistook them when they called home nowadays.

What if, Michelle panicked, her mother could never answer a phone again? A sudden strange heat fell upon her, like a flood of molten wax flowing from her skull to her knees. This heat wave ambushed her several times a day, leaving her afterwards in a film of sweat, dizzy and disoriented. Meanwhile her sister was lauding a Seattle neurologist, recounting the phone calls and fact-finding activities she'd been engaged in since last they spoke. In these anecdotes, Roxanne always played the bully who would not take no for an answer. As soon as it was possible, her mother would be airlifted to the university hospital in Washington. Then Roxanne would be the one who visited daily. She would bring flowers and a bedjacket and fragrance. She would know what to ask the doctors, nurses, therapists, and orderlies. And even though they all dressed exactly alike in their scrubs, she would know how to tell them apart.

Maybe if Ellton hadn't been born, Michelle would have finished college when Roxanne did, and met and married a man in graduate school, as Roxanne had, and become a young, presumptuous matron with a mortgage and a minivan and a cigarette-smoker's mature, knowing voice, even though she didn't smoke. The acquisition of these things seemed to insure the compliance of officials and professionals. You could sense Roxanne's belligerent expertise even over the phone, even big as a house with a baby.

"I didn't want to alarm Chelsea," Roxanne said. "I haven't told her Ma'am and Pop-pop are in the hospital. She's going to spaz." The toilet flushed, in Seattle.

"You know what?" Michelle said, under the sedating influence of her father's beer, looking at the back of her little brother's head as he bent over the table. "Ellton is closer to Chelsea's age than to ours." Her sister's silence let her know that this was no brainstorm. Roxanne frequently allowed a deep pause to convey her disappointment in Michelle. Michelle, the undergraduate. "I mean, I know he's closer to her age, but, like, these are his *parents*. Not his grandparents," she added, in case Roxanne wasn't following. Max, she noticed, was shaking his head in sorrow at the sink as he sluiced water off another thick, wet noodle.

"I know that," Roxanne said. "I am well aware of that. What are you, stoned?"

Ellton said, "Can I talk to her?" holding out his hand for the phone. Michelle passed it over after saying, "No, I am not stoned."

"Roxanne?" Ellton said, "Will you bring back that Lego guy Chelsea took at Christmas? I said she could *borrow* it, not *have* it." He described the missing figure in detail, down to the expression on its tiny plastic face. By now Chelsea would have lost it—she would have lost it in the car, swallowed it or flung it out the window, the first five minutes of their drive back to Seattle in December—and Roxanne wouldn't have known to return it even if she'd been aware that the girl had taken it. Ellton had two personality traits that would now battle inside him: one was that he loved particular things, studied them carefully, remembered them, used them, needed them. The other was that he was generous, unconsciously so, giving his beloved things to other people, sharing.

He handed the phone back to Michelle. "You have a million Legos," Roxanne was saying. "You've got crates—"

"That's not the point," Michelle said.

"Oh, it's exactly the point, it's just heartbreaking how he's fixated on that thing and I wish I knew where the hell it was, but I don't, and really, the point is that Mom and Dad are in the hospital and I feel so frustrated I can't just get there right now. I feel like a turtle on its back, just waving my legs waiting for somebody to put me right. Tell him I'm sorry, I'll buy him a dozen of his goddamn little Lego men. Is he bathing?"

"As we speak?" But Michelle hunched uncomfortably, as if Roxanne could see her and their ripe little brother. In fact, Ellton had not, to her knowledge, bathed recently. She hoped Roxanne wasn't going to ask if he had returned to school yet. "And did you see her eyes twitch, or did you just hear about it?"

Again she flashed on her mother sleeping here at home, on the butter-colored chenille spread in a block of autumn light from the window upstairs. Outside the window tall aspens quaked, and their leaves cast a flickering shadow like water, shimmering over her in the late afternoon. It took an effort to superimpose the true sleeping form of their mother. The no-season gray light of the hospital, the inky bruise where an I.V. needle had been inserted, the dark hairs on her chin. It almost seemed that you should be able to make her eyes open by sitting her up, like a doll. The nurse—doctor? candy striper?—had stood behind Ellton when they visited, ready to catch him if he fainted, though it was Michelle who'd felt woozy. Max had decided that his role was Rock, and he kept kissing Michelle's cheek and squeezing her shoulders, as if he had the power to bolster her. Michelle was sorely tempted to throw an elbow into his torso. The nurse had mistaken the three of them, thinking Max was Michelle's husband, Michelle Ellton's mother, Ellton the grandson of the injured woman. You couldn't blame people for jumping to the obvious conclusions, could you?

"I guess there was a kind of flinch, if you can call that movement." Seventy-five miles away, their parents slept in two different parts of Saint Pat's. Their father, who'd broken a great many bones, was expected to live. Their mother's damage was of the internal and hidden sort, shrouded by coma. This was considered a mercy, a gift her body had given itself, a cocoon inside of which no one knew what transpired.

"This is going to sound awful," Roxanne said, "but I wish it was Dad who was in the coma. I mean, we love him, of course, and maybe it's different for a boy, you know, to grow up without his dad, but I can't help thinking that Ellton needs Mom." Now her strong capable sister was crying. "I get contractions when I cry," Roxanne complained. "I can't cry, or I get contractions." But she didn't stop. "Think how much we needed Mom. You know?"

"I know," Michelle agreed. "I know exactly what you mean."

"You are one odd little dude," Max said to Ellton as they climbed into the car later. His Southern accent made him sound so golly-gee, like Gomer Pyle.

"That's the way he's always buckled," Michelle explained. Ellton had long ago devised his own seatbelt arrangement, two of them crisscrossed over him as he sat in the middle of the back. Statistically, he'd let you know, this was the safest place to travel. Last year he'd taken to wearing a helmet whenever he left the house. It was only logical.

"You don't have to mention it every time we get in the car, you know," Ellton said. Not angrily, just observantly. "It's not like I'm going to stop doing this just because you talk about it a lot."

"Do *wha'*?" Max said abstractedly, pulling away from the curb.

Given a choice, Ellton would stay at home. Permanently. But Max wanted to go scout for animals on the roads around Portersburg, and Michelle knew she couldn't leave her brother home alone. Max wanted to visit the ghost town up the hill. Michelle had made the mistake of telling him about the annual litter of fox pups that cavorted in the empty fields just north of the town limits. The bears, the elk, the moose, the owls, the bighorn sheep—all of the Montana wonders. He wanted to experience everything, as if he were notching a belt or earning scout badges; he also wanted to help distract them from their uneasy sorrow, and the queer dark house that contained it. He was a practical man, Michelle thought. Excited by flora and fauna, kind, helpful. Why couldn't she love him anymore? Until tonight, she had gone through each of the ten days they'd been here understanding what would come next and how she would respond, as if the routine were a twenty-four-hour repeat performance she had merely to act her part in, as if there were an end to the show's run somewhere in sight. Each evening Max would finish washing dishes, fold the apron away over the towel rack, and clap his hands to rally his mopey co-horts as he promoted "taking a little spin." Michelle brought along a beer—no one in Montana was going to get fussy about drinking and riding—and Ellton his helmet and Game Boy. The dog followed them as far as the front door as if nervous to be left alone, but could not be enticed to join them, retreating once more as they slammed the screen. Max drove slowly along the dirt roads of town, small rocks pinging off the underside of the rental car. Only Main Street was paved; most of its shops were closed or vacant. The three bars were lit; the Elk Cafe was open. Soon they traveled into the hills and along the river, past the closed mill, past the abandoned mine, beyond the dilapidated barns and outbuildings of ranches that had failed. It was defeated terrain, under that famous big sky. Max would narrate blandly, querying about every brown lump, which Michelle would peer at and name: horse, rock, stump. The season of rampant wildlife was at least a month away.

"Don't they have animals in Texas?" Ellton had asked, the first night.

"Sure," Max replied. "But I like to get the lay of the land wherever I go. And we got unlimited miles."

"People must think they can do anything, in a rental car," Ellton said. "This road is four-wheel drive, usually."

"How 'bout you turn the sound off that Game Boy," Max said, "and listen to Mother Nature?" Ellton sighed, complying. Michelle poured more beer down her throat, grateful for its muffling effect. Outside of this amniotic sac of ale awaited panic, a peripheral force poised to strike. She thought she might never feel safe in a car again.

The first driver was dead, the boy who'd apparently swerved to miss the unknown animal. The trucker was dead, the one who'd come upon the little sportscar and then braked crazily, unleashing his load of enormous logs. His hitchhiker was dead, as was the hitchhiker's dog, but Michelle's parents, they who'd come last to the scene and skidded over the mountainside, dangled briefly in the tree, then fallen to the ground, lived, each in a separate wing of the Missoula hospital.

Michelle and Ellton visited every day. After the first day, Max waited in the cafeteria. They began with their father's room. Although he looked ghastly—like the Invisible Man, swaddled in bandages in some sort of torture device—he could now speak. It would have been funny, if it were in a movie, a man-shaped cast, a mummy in traction, weights and levers and hoists elevating legs and arms in suspension waiting to be puppeted about. "I can't hear a thing," he said loudly from inside this plaster form, cutting off Michelle's greeting. "You'll just have to bear with me, my hearing is temporarily gone. Kaput. And I've got the most odious melody running in my head; it would just figure that I'd get stuck with this song that I absolutely cannot stand but which I know every single damn lyric to. I wake up, can't hear a thing but Neil blasted Diamond." He breathed audibly through the two holes that were his nostrils. They had to lean over his face so that he could see them through his eye holes. "Song sung blue," he sang. One of his hands was free from the wrap, bruised, scratched, but there, and that's what Ellton held, gently stroking his father's swollen fingers. They looked purple beside the brilliant white, flesh like fat sausage links, dirt beneath the nails. "Son," said their father, "son, squeeze my thumb if your mother is all right." Ellton looked to Michelle, who nodded automatically. Let him receive simple, hopeful messages. Ellton squeezed as if making a wish. "Ahh," said their father.

"He's got a morphine drip," the nurse told Michelle, "and he knows how to use it! He's in no pain, is what I mean." He hummed his tune and laughed. "The deafness is temporary," she went on. "We expect he'll be fully conversant in a day or so." His room was like a hotel room: TV, easy chair, reading lamp, window unit, art bolted to the wall.

"Now Mom," Ellton said, once they were outside the door in the hall.

In the ICU he stood close to his mother's head. Unlike their father, their mother they could see and touch completely—arms, face, black eyelashes, slender body beneath the covers—yet make no contact. Ellton swallowed, pale, his clothes looking to Michelle suddenly filthy, ill chosen. When a boy stood beside his mother in a coma, nothing could look right. Their mother was diminished by her environs, at its mercy. She slept, it seemed; the tube in her arm was transparent, her new food source clear and pure. Aside from the bright light, the various monitors, the attendant who always sat at a console, the paging calls over the public-address system, the bing-bonging of elevator doorbells—aside from all of that mechanical racket and asperity, their mother looked normal. Simply as if she had decided to lie down in this active and acrid-smelling institution to take a very public nap. Ellton leaned in close to her face as if to whisper in her ear and instead pulled out a hair from her forehead. Then another.

"What are you doing?" Michelle asked.

"Watch her eyes," he said, pulling again. The eyelids barely moved as the hair gave. "She always wants me to get rid of her gray hairs for her. She can't see them so well."

Later, back in Portersburg, Michelle had stood in front of the bathroom mirror and wrapped a strand of hair from her temple around her finger. The yanking sensation made her eyes fill. The hair had a tiny bit of white flesh on the end, and the sight of that made her cry in earnest, great heaving sobs of despair. *Despair*, she had thought, watching her afflicted face contort in the mirror. It was rare, like a miracle, and real, like a law of nature.

"What's that?" Max shouted, pointing beyond the windshield into the gathering dark of the hillside, braking abruptly. A few grazing deer had stopped, still as lawn statues. Three were pregnant but extremely thin does. With them, a large buck, behaving as if he could protect them. Like everything else in these last ten days, they seemed no longer harmless nor beautiful to Michelle. It was one of their ilk who'd forced the first car off the roadway, an animal that no doubt still roamed about the forest, unscathed. A momentary heightened heartbeat, the spur of screeching brakes, and away it had bounded, whatever it was. These deer darted away suddenly, too, terrified, the buck last, as if making some point.

"Deer," Ellton answered Max's question, back to his Game Boy. "Haven't you ever seen deer before?"

"Of course I have," Max said, gunning the engine as he lurched forward.

"He didn't mean it sarcastically," Michelle explained. "He just didn't understand why you didn't recognize them."

"I did recognize them."

"Then why did you ask what they were?" Ellton asked.

This nit-picky argument—an argument that one of its participants didn't understand was an argument—felt at a numbed distance from Michelle. She would have to keep drinking beer, she thought. When she woke up tonight in a panic, rather than lie stricken and sweating, she would go straightaway to the kitchen and wedge open another beer. This would be what Max would call her "coping mechanism." Grolsch, with its elegant, masculine bottle and pretty lid apparatus. Her father probably preferred it for the ceramic cork and wire fastener. He liked old-fashioned things, wind-up clocks, typewriters, push mowers, his own long marriage.

"You should get back to school," Michelle told Max when he cut the engine in front of her parents' house. She put her fingers to his lips to stop his Doo Wop. Once more they'd forgotten to leave on the porch light. The place looked haunted. They'd never gone for typical upkeep, her parents. Instead, they did things like install bat habitats under the eaves or make a dog pen out of used tires, a greenhouse from reclaimed storm windows. The birdbath was a former sink basin sitting on a former engine block. As soon as the car had stopped, Ellton had unstrapped himself and hurried inside. "You don't want to screw up your semester," Michelle said vaguely.

Max didn't want to leave her—he didn't appear to want to get out of the car—but Michelle held firm. "I really appreciate your coming with me, but there's no reason for you to miss classes. And your plants will die."

"I will do whatever you need for me to do," he said sincerely. He was so keen to please her that Michelle wanted to hurt his feelings. None of his habits had bothered her—in fact, she'd been toying with the notion that she might marry him—until he had walked into her family's home. Suddenly he had come clear, like the solid human artifact placed in an otherwise unfathomable photographic image—the vast expanse of the moon, for instance, or the highly magnified body of a flea. Coming home had provided undeniable and inescapable scale. His handsomeness and his attraction to Michelle had blinded her to his essential missing qualities. Now she was sending him away on an airplane, back to Houston to finish the semester without her. To never see her again. In her mind she was busy saying goodbye to his apartment, wandering its rooms for the last time, leaving the tiny stovetop and the Murphy bed and the chair by the bare closet light where she read books when she couldn't sleep. That had been her previous insomnia, waking and then furtive reading in a crack of closet light while Max snored peacefully in bed. That had made her happy, his sleeping while she read. They'd had a pleasant domestic situation, she thought, recalling Max's elaborate collection of essential spices on the sill over the sink. Now she was packing away him and his life, as if in a box with a lid.

"I want to help," Max insisted. "Nothing is a higher priority than you, right now." Michelle patted his knee and climbed out of the rental car's bucket seat, staggering slightly. Inside the house, she flapped at the panel of light switches by the front door; only a few functioned, and she always forgot which. Ellton, long accustomed, had raced in ahead of her and gone upstairs in the dark. The dog's tail thumped from behind the chair. Michelle had to first call the hospital to see if there had been any changes. Her parents did not own an answering machine and she made this phone call every evening after their ride just to make sure no one had been trying to reach her. Next she needed to pee; so far as she could tell, that was the only drawback of her beer cure.

Max was still working to convince her that he ought to stay. Outside the bathroom door he asked who would cook, clean, drive? To hell with college, he claimed, while Michelle washed her hands. She stepped out of the bathroom to catch his noble sweeping gesture: with it, he smote the whole of higher education.

Michelle smiled; bladder empty, she still felt full up to her skull, wobbly and afloat on something turbid as molasses. "You have to go," she said thickly, patting his arm. He had been burrowing into her life, her family, her tragedy, with an enthusiasm that made her queasy. She knew he would go—he wasn't secure enough in his duty to her to stay—but she also knew she would have to have sex with him tonight. It was an unspoken part of the deal she was proposing.

He snuggled close when they got into bed.

"Are you sure you want me to go?" he said, kneading her breasts.

She found it difficult to feel erotic in this house, in the place where she'd grown up, in the bedroom and the very bed where her parents, each night—until in a fit of peevishness at age fourteen she asked them not to—had come to tuck her in, to murmur shyly their love for her. Her father was a wry person, droll, analytical, typically prickly in matters parental. He was such an oddball, he'd always claimed, that he couldn't believe his luck in finding another oddball to marry. His wife, he understood. But his children continued to confound him. He assumed that they knew without requiring spoken proof that he of course loved them. Yet when he leaned over Michelle in her bed, ran his large, rough hand over her cheek, all restraint and mockery fled, leaving his eyes damp with surprise at the feeling he had for his children. Every night he gathered the force of his gratitude and kissed Michelle squarely on the forehead as if to infuse her slumber with it. Then he traded places with her mother, who had been saying good-night to Roxanne across the hall.

In her bed with the rosebuds and winding vines hand-painted along the iron headboard Michelle had waited. Her mother rested her weight gently beside her in the dark and began her nightly performance of folk songs. Max would have found these alarming—the wife who convinced her husband that her lover's head on the pillow was nothing more than a cabbage, the maiden whose virginity was wagered for five hundred pounds, the tree in the forest where the rifles were stored—but these were the songs Michelle sang to herself when she courted sleep, the ones guaranteed to turn her mindless. Sleepy, limp amnesia.

She'd not shared her childhood bed with any man before Max. "You have to go," she told him gently. "Really, I insist."

A shadow, like death, stood mutely at her side as she woke suddenly that night. She rolled quietly from beneath Max's hot, possessive arm and followed Ellton down the hall.

They climbed into their parents' bed, which was cool and smelled like hand cream, her brother on their father's side, Michelle on their mother's. "This is cozy," Michelle whispered, having felt tears on her brother's cheeks. *Cozy* was his favorite word. That was how he described the cave he'd made of his own lower bunk bed, blankets and flashlights and a drawing pad at hand. Stuffed toys and a box of crackers. A small television at the foot, a smoke alarm at the head. "Bunker bed," her parents had named it. When Michelle had lived at home, she'd taken turns with her parents beside Ellton in the dark until he fell asleep, assuring him that all was well, humming to him the songs she'd once been sung. Every night he had dangerous propositions to explore before he drifted off, crafting them in the stuffy space between his face and the bottom of the bed above. The plight of the ozone layer. Sharks. Toxic mine tailings. Escaped felons. The wail of a rare siren, the rumble of thunder, the screaming headlines of the evening news. His child's mind, that genie in a bottle, turned toward spectacular, wide-ranging disaster. This disposition might suggest he'd be prepared for his parents' car crash, the accident he'd been anticipating all his life. But no.

Michelle held his hand, which was the size of her own, and they looked out the window at the moon, which shone through the bare branches of the aspens and broke into faint, elongated quadrants on the blanket pulled over them. Chenille, old as Michelle, older, no doubt.

"Isn't it weird that the moon is mostly shadow?" Ellton said.

"Yes," Michelle said. Was it mostly shadow? Was it weird?

"When I can't sleep, I pull these little dots off my pajamas."

"People call those *pills*."

"Pills bother me."

She heard something. They both sat up.

"That's Leroy," Ellton said. "Coming up the stairs. Do you remember BoBo?"

"Of course." BoBo was the dog before Leroy, the one who'd died when Ellton was three or four, buried now under a brick out back.

"No one was nice to BoBo until he got sick. Then everybody started being nice and quit yelling at him."

Like Leroy, BoBo hadn't been a dog you'd feel charitable toward. It was true, what Ellton said. No one was good to a bad dog until he was dying.

"Leroy hasn't come upstairs since I got here," Michelle said. The dog moved slowly, one step after another, and then clicked limpily, as if three-legged, down the hall into the room where they lay. "Hey Leroy," Ellton said. The dog ignored the greeting, simply sighing in disgust as he crawled under the bed, moving in a circle beneath them, settling, wheezing once more very deeply, as if he'd been waiting for a long while to have reason to do so. "That's where he usually spends the night," Ellton explained. "Here close to Mom."

"Poor dumb dog."

"He's eighty-four, in people years. Actually, eighty-six or so, if you count half years." Michelle guessed it was just about time to start being nice to him. Ellton went on, "Maybe there has to be someone *in* the bed before he'll crawl under it?"

"That could be," Michelle agreed.

Ellton fell finally to sleep, his hand balled beside his cheek, and Michelle waited for dawn. This was her mother's view, day or night she lay appraising this square, divided exposure to the world. She looked at it over her husband's sleeping form, she viewed it alone, she listened to her old dog sighing beneath the bed. She thought her thoughts, here, watching the trees grow larger, sway in the wind, fill with leaves, lose them, the moon beyond getting fat and thin as the world spun itself between it and the sun. Michelle attempted some version of her mother's voice, recalling the cuckolded character and the virginal one, all the Irish songs, wondering if she could sing herself to sleep, but she couldn't. Her mother's deep slumber, seventy-five miles away, was vast enough for them both, she supposed. Instead, Michelle would lie awake, holding her mother's place, under the window, wrapped in the chenille spread, next to the boy, above the dog.

She lay there as daylight broke, as she heard Max rising, his sounds and the house's as he moved through it: his elaborate honking nose-blowing, the clanking blustery shower, his solid thunking feet as he sought her out in her parents' room, where she pretended sleep, and of his next taking the creaking stair treads two at a time, running water in the kitchen to fill the ancient percolator on the stovetop, and then the ringing bell of the phone call that she had been awaiting. Like the rest, it felt predictable, the second—or was it the third?—act of this strange drama she'd been living for ten days. Eleven, now.

She had to leave her parents' bed to take the call, since there was no other telephone in the house.

"The hospital," Max mouthed.

"I'm sorry," the doctor said, speaking his part as Michelle's inner organs began dissolving, slipping formless inside her assemblage of bones, messy, confused. "Is there someone with you?" the doctor asked.

"Yes," she said, thinking not of Max, before her, studying her with his slow-moving, big brown eyes, but Ellton, upstairs asleep, still dreaming, still under the spell of hope and a happy ending.

"We're waiting to notify your father," he said. "His hearing remains compromised. I don't know if we want to risk further strain, at this point."

"I don't know either," Michelle said. Now her bones were going, entitled to also succumb, given that she'd been drained of vital substance through the soles of her feet. Even her breathing seemed affected, as if someone had snipped the wires and left her powerless. Powerless but not mindless. She was imagining how to break this news to her brother. If only Max would disappear. She should have sent him away days ago. He would refuse to go, if he knew her mother had died. "Passed," he would say. He'd brought home yellow-frosted cake from the grocery yesterday. "Yellow is the color of friendship," he'd told Ellton.

"Yellow is the color of urine," said Ellton.

"Do *wha'*?" Max said.

"Thank you," Michelle told the doctor, who had expressed his sympathy repeatedly during her long silences. She hung the receiver up and sat at the sticky kitchen table. Fortunately, her shock was profound enough that she did not think Max could guess what was wrong.

"My flight's at eleven," he said, bringing her coffee. "If you still think you'll be all right?"

"Fine," she said.

"'Cause I can definitely stay. I can stay indefinitely." But his bags were packed, she noticed. "You okay?" He reached to push her hair back from her cheek.

"Tired. Ellton had nightmares."

When Max pulled open the kitchen curtains he exclaimed; it had snowed and the ground was an alarming bright white, reflecting in the sunlight for miles and miles. The heater, Michelle noticed, had kicked on, providing a dusty, dry warmth. A burst of wind made the shutters creak, and a gate outside slammed. Some time between the clouds rolling in yesterday afternoon and the moon beaming down late last night, a load of spring snow had been deposited onto the hills.

"Wow," Max said, staring in wonder. "That is just about blinding. What'd the hospital have to say?"

"Nothing," Michelle said, burning her mouth with a hot swallow of coffee.

"Just a wakeup call? Weather here is *nothing* like Houston, is it? Geez Louise. So, we should leave pretty quick." He was always cheerful the morning after sex. Cheerful and industrious, two more character flaws. His bags stood already at the front door, lined up in descending order of size: one duffel for clothes, one for toiletries, one for his laptop. "You think old Ellton would lend me a computer game for the flight?"

"Sure." Ellton would hand over the disc without thinking twice. And Max would forget to return it.

Leroy's feeble descent down the stairs now began, the skitter and hop and pause, and behind him the patient sound of Ellton, who would wait for the dog to take the steps as slowly as he needed to. In between depositing Max at the airport and their visit to the hospital, she would tell her brother what she had to tell him. It would be far,

far worse than receiving the news herself, having to hand it to him. He was special, she knew that. But however special he was, however peculiar Michelle felt her upbringing had been, despite how oddly shameful and wonderful her family seemed to her, and no matter the resplendent, bizarre morning, in its dizzying white ground and radiant blue sky—no matter how extraordinary this day and how it had arrived seemed—she was soon going to have to bear some very ordinary bad news. Every day somebody's mother died.

Max began singing a silly song, putting on a sappy, falsetto voice, rocking his head and shaking his fists as if they held maracas. "Ellton Ellton, fo fellton, be bop bo-bellton, tree top tellton…," and Michelle's brother ignored him, rubbing his eyes and leading Leroy to the door to let him go pee, tapping his rear end gently with his foot to hurry him along. Why, when the cold wind blew in, the snow so bright she could make out as if in an x-ray her brother's thin limbs through the light pajamas, did Michelle think of fences?

Those falling-down fences that you saw all over Montana, those crude, elementary dividers criss-crossing the land. They required no hardware, no nails or post holes or wire or notching; that was supposed to be the beauty of them. Along every road and river, up and down the hills, ran the pine-pole fences, structures that looked like tent skeletons, great long rows of them, sturdy triangles set one after another and in constant need of repair. One of the pieces of timber was always crooked or down or busted or missing; livestock was forever wandering off, stepping through or over, unaware of their own escape. These fences tempted you to stop and park your car, jump out and set them right. They seemed just that obviously and simply broken.

My dad and I, a long time ago.

Deborah Tarnoff lives in Greenwich Village and New Paltz, New York. She received an MA in Modern European History from Columbia University and a degree in law from NYU. Her work has appeared in a number of literary journals including *The Quarterly* and *McSweeney's*. A finalist last year in *Glimmer Train's* Very Short Fiction contest, she won her first writing contest at age twelve when she was awarded first prize in a Hebrew language national contest for an essay on the biblical character most likely to bring about world peace if alive today.

CRAZY UKRAINE GIRL

Deborah Tarnoff (signature)

Deborah Tarnoff

In Kiev, the shtetl is a cemetery. Jews who had been up all night waiting for exit visas stand pitiful like birds, blue, unshaven, in vests without socks. Me, Fevora, I'm not five years off the boat and I get a deserving-poor scholarship to a famous American law school. By the second week, precedents sprout out of me like buds and shoots. Weighed down with buds and shoots, maybe even a few leaves, I feel unhappy. Otherwise, I would not have wiped my nose on Ada Belle Rive. I never held a job. My mother refused to give me carfare to even get to the law school. She said I'd be better off as a bank teller because banks are clean. I knew nothing about banks or law school. All I had was the beautiful American dream glittering before me like the sea beneath the sun, beautiful and empty. I did not wipe my nose on Ada Belle. No, Ada Belle wiped her nose on me. What was the reason? The reason was intoxication. Ada's beauty intoxicated everybody. In law school she sat in the last row so people wouldn't get intoxicated. In real life, her presence so intoxicated Freddie Bananas, architect of the Ground Zero freedom towers, that instead of designing buildings that would bring the dead back to life, he designed buildings that led the living to their death.

Ada Belle Rive, the only child of Tuckey Revlon, the lipstick king, lived in a townhouse with fourteen-karat-gold fixtures in the bathrooms. Stuffed chairs in the style of Queen Anne flanked the marble fireplace over which hung works by the Old Masters. On the mantel stood two fans owned by Madame Chiang Kai-shek's sister Rhoda. What more can you want? Can you want more? And yet Ada chose, almost casually it would seem, loyalty to a married man, and a refusal to do anything except wait for him to leave his pregnant wife. Thinking about it, even now, makes my nose itch. I give you my word of honor, there was nothing more to want. But I'm not going to send my story down side streets, even if on those side streets chestnuts are blossoming and lilacs are in bloom. So I will tell you about Ada, then go on to Freddie Bananas, and that will be that. Then I can say I put the period where it belongs.

It was early afternoon. Ada and I were sitting on her balcony watching the stale winter light moving slowly along the branches. I was about to nod off when Ada swung her head and her diamond earrings hit me right on the bridge of my nose. God, were those earrings. Three times the size of normal diamonds. Thick, glittering penises. I tried not to stare. Ada licked a sliver of chocolate icing from a knife and watched me try. Then she spoke.

"Tell me, Fevora, how much weight do you think I've lost on my chocolate-icing diet?"

"Well, now that you ask me, I have to tell you my honest opinion. If you ask me, you've lost at least four, maybe seven pounds."

"That's great," Ada said. "I thought it was between two and three, myself." Then she removed the earrings from her earlobes and said I could have them in exchange for my torts notes.

"And there's a reason why you can't take your own notes?" I asked, trying to affect a tone of ironic detachment.

"I'm depressed. You didn't notice?"

"I'm sorry. In Ukraine everybody is depressed so it is not something you'd notice."

Ada's face was smiling, gentle, a radiant white. "Listen to me, Ukraine, and listen hard. Each of us gets one true love in this world. Unfortunately, mine has a wife who got pregnant the day before he was supposed to leave her."

"And that's why you can't take the notes?"

"I know how it sounds," she said. "The love I share with Big Al few people on earth would understand. I barely understand it myself. Then, last night I had a dream in which he said, 'All this is very sad, I know. But there's nothing I can do, because I don't love you.'"

"So you just want the torts?"

"A bad dream," she added, "but who knows? Maybe because it's bad, everything will turn out well, and his wife will miscarry. You were saying…?"

"I asked if you just wanted the torts?"

"Sybil Gross is giving me contracts and crimes for my old clothes."

"Sybil Gross has no nose. What did you see in me?"

"Oh, this is utter rot and nonsense. I like you, Fevora. More important, I respect your gumption, trying to make it here all on your own. That is what this country is all about. My uncle, Doctor Sergei Fleck, lay under a pile of corpses in Babi Yar three whole days. And now he is a big pain doctor on the Upper East Side, specializing in the pains that don't show up on x-rays or tests.

Blah, blah, blah. That day there was only one subject between us, the notes.

"Yes. Making your own way in America is a very worthwhile endeavor." I said. "We learned about it in Kiev. 'Give me your tired, your poor…yearning to breathe free…the wretched refuse…'"

"Take the earrings and shut up, okay?"

"Okay, whatever."

"Maybe I'll go see his wife," Ada said, pacing excitedly back and forth. And I'll tell her about us, ask her why she wants to stay with a man who doesn't love her."

The first time I wore the earrings I felt as if there was more of me. So much more, I was bursting with passions, all runny and liquid, looking for a container to hold them, trying this one, then that one, looking for a perfect fit. But my deserving-poor scholarship advisor said there was too much Fevora to take, and I should hold something back. Back where? I wondered, until I saw Bush the Senior talking on TV in that chokey way of his and I knew—it was back in the throat. His throat might have been as dry as a grasshopper's from all the holding back, but choking was a risk I was willing to take, because who, after all, knows more about making his way in America than him? So now when people ask me, "How ya doing, Fevora?" instead of telling a big sad life story, I say, "Very well, thank you for asking." But when I spotted Sybil Gross in Ada's apple-scented silk tunic, I was again bursting with desires all runny and liquid, and ran right over to Ada's, and before Sybil got there I offered up all my notes for her worn-out Chanel purse.

"Fevora, have you no pride?" asked Ada.

"What for I need pride?" I said, nervously lapsing into my old, worn-out speech patterns, again. "Pride is important to people with cloudy identities. Me, I know who I am."

"Who are you?"

"I'm me, Fevora. That's the one thing I insist on. Being me, Fevora."

"Give me a break."

"You have many breaks. Me, all I have is myself."

"How many times do I have to tell you that without Big Al I have no life?"

"No life," I said. "That's not good."

Her eyes narrowed into slits. "Even you have a life," she said.

"I might," I said, "I might very well have a life. Who made me so rich that I can throw away the life, who gave me the right to run the risk? After the scholarship dealer came to see me, didn't I see him drop by on Sybil Gross? To make long story short, I whispered a little warning about Sybil in his ear. And that was that."

"You want something to eat?" she said.

"Later. Now, I'm going to see *Schindler's List*. Come with me."

"What for?" she said, "It. Is. Stupid."

"It is not stupid. It is *Schindler's List*."

"Whatever. I can't be bothered."

Can't be bothered was her favorite expression. Perhaps she was holding out for something better. Maybe I was wrong and there was something more to want besides beauty and furniture and clothes and love.

Each spring, Ada went through her closets and made piles of discards, grades A through D. Grateful Sybil got only the C and D dregs. The stuff less than a year old went to Ada's cleaning lady and to cousin Bette in Nairobi. This year, among the discards was a certain white-satin pantsuit that I'd worn to a bar and and soiled with menstrual blood. I used eighteen cleansers to get it out, and still there was something there. But if Ada noticed it, she didn't say a word. "Ada." Darling Ada. To this day, saying her name aloud makes me ache and yearn.

It was not her fault. Yearning and aching is very big in Ukraine. Once I'm in somebody's vicinity, anyone's vicinity, I get lonely. Lonely for that person, I ache. I ached not only for Ada, I ached for her lovers, for the ones she had, for the ones she didn't have, the ones I would have had, had I been Ada Belle Rive. I ached for her hand-stitched underwear, her imported face creams, her pills for sleeping, her pills for waking—don't get me started. In any event, I was not on her discard list, so you can imagine my shock when, right in the middle of our *Schindler* talk, she shoved seven cartons of clothes at me and said, "Choose anything you like. Just leave a little something for the others."

"*Is this a joke?*"

"Just as I thought. You're not used to having people do nice things for you."

That was it. Pity tore my heart into a thousand pieces. I let her have it. "Freddie Bananas tells everybody your breasts are fake," I said.

"Freddie? You sure it is Freddie?" she said. Then, jingling her loose breasts in her hands as if she was looking for change, she went back to her chair by the window to mope. And I was free to paw the discards to my heart's content.

But there was too much to paw. It reminded me of the seven hundred cable TV stations. If there were nine, maybe even twelve stations, people would feel as if they had a real choice. But seven hundred is too many. So you keep switching the remote faster and faster, until you can't stop. Looking, I suppose, for the perfect channel. But there is no perfect channel. So you get frenzied and disgusted, shut the TV, and enroll in creative-writing classes at The New School with all the other frustrated lawyers.

I was already enrolled part-time in The New School when I wept my way through her delicate lovelies—stroking the bunched-up silks, sniffing the leathers, romping around in a straw hat festooned with fake cherries she picked had up in the 23rd Street flea market. Finally, I started to make a pile of the clothes I wanted—the hat, a black-leather gestapo coat, tennis shoes from France. But the enterprise was doomed to failure. Each time I chose one item, I ached for another. I thought perhaps I should take everything, but the thought made me ache even more. Over coffee and cigarettes I told Ada about it.

"What are you aching for?" she asked, and blew cigarette smoke in a thin viper's blue line straight at me.

"I don't know, exactly, all I know is that I ache."

It was the same with the earrings. The first time I wore them I felt more like me, Fevora. The second time they felt cold, alien, and depressing.

"A pity," she said. "With the right clothes, you wouldn't be half bad looking."

Salt choked my throat. There seemed to be nothing to do but hurt.

Ada sat there. Twirling her hair with those dainty fingers of hers, she drank up her coffee and said, "Why not choose stuff that will make you more Fevora? Didn't you say that was all you have, being Fevora?"

Out of her mouth the *more Fevora* sounded ridiculous. What kind of presumptuous jerk says, "All I have is being me, Fevora?" "I'm going," I said, without moving from my chair.

"Where do you have to go?"

"I have to go, that is all."

"So go."

"I don't really have to go," I said. Then I got up and left.

Outside, the dirty winter light was getting ready to make way for the new season. The spring sun was like a party; it was music. It was bursting at the seams. Tenth Street, where I lived, lit up first. Then 17th Street, then the streets going down to the river. Within seconds, sunlight, like long tongues of fire, flooded the wide avenues in Tribeca, the tall buildings lining Park Avenue, the Central Park trees stiff and bowed from the long winter. Why are you afraid? I asked myself. You're free, you crazy Ukraine. Free in America. You don't need her *shmattes*. Just take the stained satin. Isn't that all you ever wanted? Otherwise, why wear it on the first day of your period?

That night I could not fall asleep, and when I finally dozed right before dawn, I slept badly and dreamed she gave the white satin to the Salvation Army. I opened the shades. The light was as intense as a love affair. I went outside, tripping over slabs of sunshine as large as cities, pouring out without regard to my feelings. That indifference pained me.

I used to be a fanatic optimist. I still was, and I expected to end up with the one thing that was mine, that I'd made mine, the stained satin. I felt whole just thinking it.

Ada served coffee that day. Thick coffee with de-icinged slabs of Sara Lee chocolate cake.

She lifted a cup, "In celebration of your new wardrobe." She smiled, stood up, came into the sunlight on her balcony. Something had changed. Perhaps it was the light on her face. I thought I recalled her from way back down, from the light at the bottom of the sea. In the hushed tones of a shy lover I told her all I needed was the satin. "Let Sybil and Bette have the rest."

"The satin is not up for grabs."

"But that's all I want."

"Something ruined?"

"I don't see it that way.

I thought you loved all my clothes."

"I don't care about the clothes."

"What are you, then? Some kind of thief?" she said, her dark eyes glittering, the lines around her mouth almost mean. "Sybil told me you've been wearing my stuff behind my back."

"I'm no thief," I said in a cracked voice. "I pay my way."

"Humor me then. Take the vest. Take the jacket. The red shoes, take the shoes."

"I don't want the shoes."

"Take the shoes, for chrissakes, and I will go with you to see *The List.*"

"*Schindler's List.*"

"Whose ever. It's still a sentimentalist's movie."

"He saved lives."

"He saved himself. Became himself. Before he saved Jews he was no Oskar Schindler. But you, my pet, you will always be my little Fevora."

Can you toy with someone like that and still care for them? I thought you could. I knew that whatever happened that day, whether I took the clothes or left them, it hardly made any difference. I had a feeling of someone in a play; there was the story of a not-so-wicked witch who gave me handouts so I'd be less Fevora. Or perhaps there was no such story, and she just wanted the junk out. And what about the scholarship advisor who told me to be less Fevora?

Didn't she know?

You take the life away and only the shell is left?

And why did I need the soiled satin? The answer is contrariness. To keep alive what made me Fevora. *Contrariness.*

"For the white satin, I'll take notes for you forever," I said, knowing she'd never last out the year, relying on Sybil Gross's notes—a big mistake.

"Forever Fevora—I think that's what I'm going to call you from now on."

"As you like."

"Oh, don't sulk. Take the satin. I was going to let you have it all along. What kind of monster do you think I am?"

I took the satin home and cut out one small piece for a wedding hat for my niece's doll. The rest I tore into shreds and threw out the window, expecting them to be carried off by the wind. Instead, they landed on our front stoop—to the unabashed delight of Corrigan, the super.

"You crazy Ukraine," he said, "you pick up every last piece here, kapeesh?"

After picking up the pieces, I put them in the bottom of a large flower pot. Then I covered them with dirt and planted irises and gladiolas. Soon, buds and leaves started sprouting out of the pot and I forgot about the satin pants.

Listen: forgetting is no trivial matter. All over the world people are preoccupied with building memorials to help them remember. But the smart ones are busy forgetting. And that is a valuable trait in a person—being able to forget. And with that a sudden peace descended on my wandering soul.

This is my first story. Who was to blame here, and what was the reason? Was Ada to blame? Let us not pull the wool over each other's eyes. There is no other like Ada Belle Rive. She was able to overcome the misfortune of a lost great love, and go on to make Sybil and Bette's hearts soar with gratitude. But what can you do when everyone else is not as grateful as Sybil or Bette? Most people don't yearn for handouts, and don't look for them, which is even better.

I recovered, escaping from Ada's web only to fall into Freddie Bananas.' I have told you about Ada, and will tell you about Freddie. But let us stop here. Then I can say I put the period where it belongs.

SILENCED VOICES:
HRANT DINK

by Sara Whyatt

Hrant Dink

On Friday, January 19, Hrant Dink, editor of the Armenian-language magazine *Agos*, stepped out of his office into a busy Istanbul street, to be shot dead by a teenage nationalist. Dink's murder has left Turkey's vibrant literary and academic community in profound shock. As triumphant ultra-nationalists celebrate the murder, fears for the safety of other writers and intellectuals are acute, and many are now living under police guard.

The pavement upon which Dink died has now become a shrine where people come to stop for a moment, to leave flowers and messages, and to light candles. They come to honor a remarkable man, killed for his belief that there could be reconciliation between Turks and Armenians through coming to terms with the past.

Glimmer Train Stories, Issue 64, Fall 2007

In the days following, Dink's alleged killer had been arrested, along with four accomplices, and a hundred thousand mourners had taken to the streets. This was a show of mourning that would have been remarkable in any country, but especially so in Turkey, where Armenians are discriminated against, and where to write, as Dink had done, on the mass killings and deportation of his ancestors at the turn of the last century, is taboo. He did this despite constant death threats and being hauled before the courts on dozens of occasions to face charges of "insult to Turkishness" under the now infamous Article 301 of Turkey's Penal Code.

Elif Shafak, a novelist who herself was tried and then acquitted last year under Article 301 for her novel *The Bastards of Istanbul*, describes how important a figure Dink had been: "Hrant was a dreamer, and as relentlessly as he was misunderstood, mistreated, and downtrodden because of this dominant aspect of his personality, to the end he knew very well that dreams are contagious. He gave us hope and faith, but most of all, he passed on his dreams to us." (www.opendemocracy.org)

Article 301 is a new law; introduced in 2005, it penalizes "a person who explicitly insults being a Turk, the Republic or Turkish Grand National Assembly…the Government of the Republic of Turkey, the judicial bodies of the State, the military or security organization…" It carries with it a maximum three-year prison term. Its reach is broad.

Within two weeks of Article 301 coming into force in, Orhan Pamuk, one of Turkey's most well known writers, and later Nobel laureate, became its first victim. He was tried for an interview he gave to a Swiss newspaper in which he referred to "300,000 Kurds and a million Armenians" having been killed in Turkey in the last century. Dozens of other trials against writers and journalists followed. Among them was Elif Shafak, accused for comments made by characters in her novel. Publisher Ragip Zarakolu is on trial for books by Armenian writers who wrote about the mass killings of the early 1900s. Hrant Dink was appealing a six-month suspended prison term to the European Court on Human Rights when he died. His crime was to write an article calling for reconciliation between Armenians and Turks. Two other trials were also under way against him for similar articles.

Pamuk's trial was closed on a technicality in February 2006. Elif Shafak was acquitted in September. Ragip Zarakolu's trials were dragging on in March 2007. Hrant Dink, the peacemaker, is dead.

In his final article, published the day he died, Dink wrote that since being charged with insult, death threats against him had intensified, and that his computer hard drive was full of messages of "rage and threats." He told of his fears for his family, and questioned whether he should stay in Turkey, concluding that he owed it to his friends and those campaigning for democracy to stay. Anyway, to leave was "not my style…I know myself. After three days abroad I'd miss my country. What would I do there?" He spoke of the "psychological torture" his unwanted fame had brought him, of passersby nudging themselves as he passed, saying, "Look, isn't it that Armenian?" He described himself as like a pigeon, constantly nervous: "My eyes dart everywhere, in front of me, behind, to the left, to the right." He pointed out that prison is not the only penalty, that his life of fear and nervousness was a prison in itself. "Just look at the price. This is the price."

Now that price is being paid by others, as threats against those who have raised the ire of the ultra-nationalists have escalated. Right-wing groups have reportedly issued "death lists" against writers, academics, and activists. Some are under twenty-four-hour police protection. Among them is the eminent journalist and academic Murat Belge, who was acquitted of "insult" under Article 301 last year, and who told the BBC in February, "Everyone is in danger. This is very savage… All around there are similar groups aching to murder someone for their country. This is shocking."

Dink's murder has exposed what some in Turkey refer to as the "deep state"—a seam of extreme nationalism that runs through all levels of authority, even, it is said, within the judiciary. Yet in the days following Dink's death, an estimated 100,000 mourners took to the streets, many bearing placards saying, "We are all Hrant Dink. We are all Armenians." Others proclaimed, "301: Murderer." Orhan Pamuk, in paying homage to Dink at the *Agos* office on the day of his death, spoke of a collective responsibility for the tragedy: "We have killed a man whose ideas we could not accept…We are responsible for his death, but above all, those who still defend Article 301 and insist it should stay are guilty."

The government has said it is open to suggestions on amendment to Article 301. Some in Turkey are suggesting that the term "insult" could be changed to "debase and deride," and that the concept of "Turkishness" could be more clearly defined. Others, including the writers association, International PEN, are calling for its repeal believing that "insult" (and indeed the alternative suggested wording) is a term that is too amorphous, too vague to stand up to legal scrutiny. Article 301's very existence in any form is a clear threat to the right of writers to question and to debate taboo topics without fear of imprisonment, harassment, or, as in the case of Hrant Dink, death.

Please write letters calling for abolition of Article 301 to:

Prime Minister Recep Tayyip Erdogan
Office of the Prime Minister
Basbakanlik
06573 Ankara
Turkey

Sara Whyatt is Program Director of the Writers in Prison Committee of International PEN, the writers' association, in London.

Despite what my family might say, this photo is proof that I did indeed have moments of quietude when I was a child.

Susan Petrone holds an MA in English with a concentration in Creative Writing from Cleveland State University. Her plays have had productions and/or staged readings at the Lamb's Club (New York, New York), St. Johns College (Annapolis, Maryland), and the Cleveland Playhouse. Her fiction has been published in *Whiskey Island*. She is currently fine-tuning one novel and completing another. She lives in Cleveland, Ohio, with one man and three dogs. By the time you read this, one child will have been added to this mix.

THIS IS HOW IT HAPPENED

Susan Petrone

M arch 8, 1998.
Dying of cancer can make you feel very popular. Everyone you know—practically everyone you've ever met who had any strong feelings about you in any way—feels the need to come and see you one last time. You are Mecca. You are the Wailing Wall.

I was diagnosed with Stage IV squamous cell lung cancer five months ago, and since then I have entertained—for lack of a better word—a steady stream of visitors. Today it was two former work colleagues, Marguerite and Betty. My youngest child, Emma, who just turned thirty and seems to think this makes her ancient, was here when they arrived. One of my children is always here when I have visitors, as though they think I need a bodyguard or a valet. I'm not sure why.

Unless the visitor is one of my closest friends or immediate family, visits always follow a remarkably similar pattern. First there is the forced jovial greeting—a hale and hearty "Well, hey there. You look great." This is followed by a moment of awkward silence. Marguerite and Betty were no exception. Emma let them into my apartment and both immediately descended upon me. Marguerite got to me first. She's younger than Betty and moves faster.

"Shelley!" she said, going in for what looked like a bear hug, but which was clearly aborted when she got about six inches away.

"You're not going to break me if you hug me," I said. I've lost a lot of weight and know I look much more frail than I used to. I had stood up when they arrived, but I'm not always steady on my feet. I got two gentle hugs, one from Marguerite and one from Betty. Then we all sat down—me in my standard spot at the end of the couch, Betty in the easy chair across from me, and Marguerite in the booby-prize seat—sharing the couch with the cancer patient. Emma hovered on the sidelines like a border collie watching its flock, watching and waiting to fix anything that needed fixing.

Marguerite and Betty did the "Hey, you look great" thing, and then came the next predictable moment. Betty asked, "How are you?" This question is always asked in the most sincere manner possible, and I know everyone who asks it is sincere and well meaning—I'm just never sure how to respond.

"Fine," I replied. Generally all I can say is "Fine." Considering I have cancer, I am fine. I don't feel cancerous. I don't feel particularly bad or sick. I just feel weak.

"That's good," Betty said, and I know she meant to say more but didn't have the words. She is a kind soul.

"You know," Marguerite said, "everybody down at school misses you. They all send their best." Marguerite, Betty, and I used to work together at the local state university until I retired last year. I wasn't more than a glorified office manager there, but the job saved my life years ago when my husband moved out and I still had kids at home. I liked the people I worked with, and they liked me. Many of them have sent cards of support or telephoned. A brave few, like Marguerite and Betty, have made the journey to visit the dying.

Perhaps they aren't brave at all. Perhaps they drew the short straw when the old gang decided that someone had to come and visit. I know that I make some people uncomfortable now, but let's face it, we're all dying. Some of us are just going about it faster than others.

"You know," Marguerite said, "my uncle was diagnosed with prostate cancer four years ago, but they caught it and zapped it out of him. He beat it. You'll beat this, too," she added with startling surety.

"She's right," Betty said. "You'll beat this, you're strong."

"Thank you," I said. I didn't want to be rude, so I didn't tell them the truth. I won't beat this. That is the unfortunate fact of my existence. It's too late to zap it out of me—it was too late to zap when they discovered I had cancer, and even so, they zapped for a couple weeks anyway. I think the doctors just wanted to feel they were doing something. At first, I wanted them to do something, but their zapping didn't seem to have any appreciable effect on my tumors. It did, however, cause my hair to fall out and actually make me feel so sick that I finally could believe I was dying. That's when I decided enough was enough—no more zapping.

Don't get me wrong—I'm not giving up. I love living. I have had a good life and desperately wish for more of it. But not as a cancer patient. Not taking treatments that make me so weak and sick that I don't feel I'm living.

Betty and Marguerite stayed a little while longer, then made a polite exit. It was good to see them, but my stamina for socializing isn't what it used to be. Emma let them out while I made my way to my bedroom for a nap. Emma came in and sat down on the bed next to me.

"Do you want me to stay while you sleep?" she asked.

"No, that's okay. You go home and take care of that nice husband of yours." Emma was married a little less than two years ago to a lovely man named Aaron. I know I'm leaving her in good hands.

"I hate leaving you."

"I'll see you tomorrow." Her face looked unsure. "I'll be here tomorrow," I said. "I'm not going anywhere." Emma's face screwed up slightly in the same expression she would get when she was a tiny girl and would get frustrated. "What's wrong?" I asked.

"I don't like thinking about the day when you won't be here," she said.

"I know," I replied.

"Are you afraid? Of dying?" she added, as though she wasn't sure if she was allowed to actually say the word. This is something I have thought long and hard about, and I can honestly say that I don't think I am. And I told her so. "What's it like?" she asked. "I mean, what goes through your mind? Do you think about it all the time? Do you still think about mundane things like, 'I have to do the laundry,' or, 'I should call so-and-so?' I just can't imagine…" She paused. "I just… I'm scared, Mom."

"You don't need to be scared for me or for you. You'll be okay." Even as I tried to reassure my youngest child that she would survive my passing, I thought back to when I lost my own mother, who died far too young. All I can remember from that time period is devastation. That's when I decided to start taking notes, to chronicle what I'm going through and what I'm feeling. Perhaps it will save my own children from devastation.

March 9, 1998.

My cancer started in my lungs. I've never smoked, but one of the wonderful ironies of being an organic life form is that you don't need to smoke in order to get lung cancer. I don't cough any more than the next person, and chest x-rays are not typically on the list of annual physical exam items. By the time they found it, it was too late to zap it out. It's funny; when I say this, I feel as though I'm making excuses, as though it's somehow my own fault that I have cancer. But there is no blame lurking in the wings waiting to be assigned. Things, despite our very best efforts to prevent them doing so, happen.

I liken cancer cells to a very persistent band of evangelical missionaries. They move in with a single purpose—to increase their numbers. Using my lungs as a base, they have thus far converted my pancreas, my liver, and my brain. I don't mind the pancreas and liver so much—I never thought much of those organs anyway. I am, however, disappointed in my brain. It's served me well over the years, and I suppose I expected more from it.

Sometimes I feel bad when visitors show up because I don't have any great insights to offer them on the nature of human mortality, and I think they're looking for something—some word of wisdom. Every meeting is fraught with the knowledge that it may well be the last time they ever see me. I'd really like to say something profound, something that the person can look back on years from now and say, "You know, the last thing Shelley ever said to me was…" I think I disappoint, as my thoughts are primarily occupied with more immediate issues: Will my bowels move today? Will it be terribly painful if they do? Will I feel well enough to eat something? How many calories will my children attempt to push down my throat today? Can I make my body move in the right way at the right time to get to the bathroom before I pee all over myself? This is more than enough to occupy anyone's day. Contemplating the issue of my own mortality just doesn't fit in.

I did spend a lot of time thinking about death when I was first diagnosed. At first I couldn't believe it. It was the quintessential surreal moment when you're positive you must be dreaming. But it's five months later and I haven't woken up, so I can only assume this is my real, waking life. It's there and I've accepted it: I'm going to die. This is inevitable, and I will not waste my last precious days worrying about something I can't change. I may not have any insightful, profound thoughts on the nature of death and dying, but I like to think that I'm at least setting a good example for what to do when you are dying.

March 10, 1998.

My children are accepting my illness with varying degrees of maturity, anger, sadness, and efficiency. My oldest, Janie, is taking over. Although I'm still living in my apartment—the second floor of a garden apartment complex where I've been happily ensconced for over ten years—she's made a schedule for all my visitors. They must now call ahead and make an appointment. When I tell her I feel like a trendy New York restaurant, she doesn't laugh. She does have a marvelous sense of humor—really, she does. She has a PhD in anthropology and I think my illness has thrown her for a loop—it's the first thing in her life she hasn't been able to fix by sheer will or native intelligence. Her husband, Jason, helps keep her in balance. He's been part of the family for so long, I feel as though he's my second son.

My actual son, Jerry, seems to swing back and forth between his standard laid-back, semi-ambivalent exterior facade and an interior of mush. He waits until even his wife, Beth, is out of the room before he shows the mush. Then he cries and tells me how much he loves me and how brave he thinks I am. When I tell him I don't feel particularly brave—this is simply something I have to go through—he says facing the unknown and not running away is the definition of courage. He seems to believe that I have somewhere to run. I feel privileged that he shares his fears with me. I suspect that he shares them with Beth, too. Somehow she understands and accepts these two divergent sides of his personality. He's lucky to have found her.

Karen is my next child. She's the only one of my kids who isn't married. When she was younger, she liked to pretend that her family—especially me—was unaware that she prefers women to men. When she turned thirty, I finally said to her that she didn't have to pretend. I don't know why she felt she couldn't—I believe the term is—"come out" to me. But she couldn't, so I'm glad I said it—it did bring us closer. She ended a long-term relationship shortly before I was diagnosed and thus isn't sharing my illness with anyone. I'd like for her to have someone to lean on.

And then there's my baby, Emma. I'm not sure how we managed it, but sometime in her late teens, we became friends. I am still her mother and she still (occasionally) acts like a daughter, but we're friends. Although she is my youngest, I often feel she's the one I need to worry about the least. As my former father-in-law always said about Emma: She's got her head on straight.

These are the people I'm leaving behind.

There is a former husband in the mix, too. Jack. I'm not sure how to describe him. How do you objectively describe the love of your life who broke your heart? We've been divorced for sixteen years? Seventeen years? Long enough to forget the exact amount of time. I've accepted the divorce, his infidelity, my life without him. In fact, I've loved my life without him. He isn't a part of my current life, but he is a part of my past. He's the father of my four wonderful children, grandfather to three beautiful grandchildren. For that role alone, I have to mention his name. I suppose I'm leaving him, too.

March 15, 1998.

Jack came to see me today. This was his first visit to me since I was diagnosed. Really, his first visit to me ever. We've seen each other at weddings, funerals, and occasionally at birthday parties for the grandchildren, but this is the first time he's paid me a social call, if you can call visiting your ex-spouse who's dying of cancer a social call.

I opened the apartment door and saw Jack standing there with this little grin in which only half his mouth moves. It used to make me melt, but I'm proud to say it hasn't had any distinguishable affect on me for years. "Hi, Shel," he said. "Sorry I didn't call first, but I wasn't sure if you'd want to see me."

"Why do you say that?" Even as I said this, I realized it was a loaded question, because there are so many answers to it that are just downright nasty. I figured he was old enough to know to close the apartment door behind him, and headed back toward the couch to sit down. Even with a quad cane, at this point standing up for too long is difficult. Out of the corner of my eye, I saw him move toward me, as though he wasn't sure whether I needed help walking or not. It was a sweet if awkward gesture. Funny how I used to think he was so smooth.

"There's a lot of reasons you might not want to see me," he said.

"Don't I know it," I answered. I know he caught the glint in my eye because he just gave me another one of those Jack grins and mumbled something about everybody making mistakes.

He hung around the entrance hall for a second, so I told him to come in and sit down. My apartment is not large, but for a moment he looked very small and far away standing there by my front door. He walked over to the couch where I had managed to plop down. He was still looking nervous and ill at ease, then at the last instant chose to sit in the easy chair opposite me. That was when I realized the visit was not about me, but about him. It was actually a relief. I don't like visits about me. I feel put on display. People want something—wisdom, insight, comfort—that I don't feel equipped to give. But Jack, Jack I can handle. I'm over losing him. If he needs forgiveness, that I can give.

We started out with the safe topics: How are you feeling? Which of the kids have you spoken to lately? Which grandchild did or said what adorable thing? Then there was a pause. My children have always referred to it as the twenty-minute lull. Supposedly, approximately every twenty minutes there is a lull in every conversation—that moment where the conversation dies down and people either start a new topic or decide to grab their coat and go home.

Jack looked at me and smiled a halfhearted what-do-I-do-now kind of smile. Then his expression changed. "The twenty-minute lull," he said triumphantly.

"I forgot you were around when the kids started espousing that theory."

"I was around. It was Janie's freshman year in college."

"I seem to remember her timing the conversation at the dinner table," I said.

"Remember how after one semester at college she kept spouting off every theory she had heard like it was the gospel truth? She was so intense and serious about everything, and she treated you and me like we were morons."

"I didn't realize you had noticed that."

"How do you not notice your daughter treating you like you're the village idiot?" he said, picking a scented candle off the coffee table and sniffing it. The candle was a recent gift from a friend. It's an aromatherapy candle. The fragrance, when lit, is supposed to soothe and relax. I suppose that's a handy thing to have around. "Have you noticed that all our daughters start thinking we're stupid the minute they begin college?" Jack added.

"Just our daughters?" I said. "I think they all thought we were stupid before they started college. Teenagers are surly. It comes with the territory."

He put the candle down. "You weren't."

"That's true," I said with mock coyness. "I was always the nice girl."

"You still are," Jack said, with no trace of coyness or mock anything. "You still are the nice girl."

Well. Wasn't that sweet? If I didn't know better, I would have thought he was flirting with me, but I know what I look like these days. I've decided that one of the symptoms of a terminal illness is forced androgyny. It's not just the weight loss or sunken eyes or hair loss that makes your appearance start melding gender lines—it's the way you're viewed by the rest of the world. One morning you wake up and you've moved beyond female or male and become a third, genderless gender. I don't think I look male or female anymore—just human.

"Thank you," I said.

Jack kind of shrugged in a it's-the-least-I-can-do way. "Well," he said, standing up. "I suppose I should be going. I don't want to tire you out. I'm sure you need to rest."

"Thank you for stopping by. It was good to see you."

I stood up, a little faster than I should have; my head started spinning the instant I was vertical. I think I must have started swaying because Jack quickly took my scrawny arms in his hands. "Are you okay?"

"Sure," I replied. I was momentarily embarrassed to let him see how weak I had become, but that moment passed.

"I can see myself out," Jack said, and gently helped me sit back down.

"Well, considering the circumstances, I won't stand on ceremony," I replied. "In fact, I won't stand at all."

He gave me a little smile. It was a tired, sad smile. "Considering the circumstances, you have been the perfect hostess."

"Thank you."

"Um, do you need anything before I go? A cup of tea, juice, something?"

"No, that's okay." He paused as though he was going to say something else.

"What is it?" I asked.

He looked at me and his face was wide open, like I hadn't seen it in years. "I love you, Shel. Always have."

A part of me had actually wanted this—or something like it. Some sign that this man who had been my husband hadn't wasted twenty-five years of my life in a marriage that meant nothing, that my children had been conceived out of love rather than obligation, and that ultimately some small part of my ego could be vindicated. But another part of me didn't want to shed a tear in front of Jack.

"Likewise," I said. That was all I could manage.

He ran a hand through his hair as though he was trying to gather up the nerve to say something else, but all he said was, "I'll see you," and that was it. That was our visit. But it was enough.

Susan Petrone

March 21.

I'm moving. Or rather, I'm being moved. This apartment is getting to be too much for me. I hate to admit it, but I need help. The tumors on my brain have affected my motor skills—I can tell myself to stand up and walk to the kitchen or the bathroom and it simply doesn't happen. Sometimes I forget what to do with food once it's in my mouth. The other day, in one of my few solitary moments, I nearly choked on a piece of toast because I couldn't remember how to swallow. I knew I had to swallow, that the food wasn't supposed to stay in my mouth all day, but I couldn't quite remember how to get it out of there. The lack of reliable motor skills brings up other issues, too. Getting to the bathroom is difficult. I realize I keep harping on this, but it's become an issue. I'm not incontinent. I am not unaware of when I need to go, but I can't always make my legs walk where they're supposed to when I need them to. I can't keep both the apartment and my dignity—one of them has to go.

March 23.

I've moved. I'm at Hospice House. It's a very nice facility—clean and modern yet cozy, set on about five acres of land so every room has a beautiful view. And I'm not the only one sitting around in a wheelchair, which is somewhat refreshing.

Janie and Karen moved me in. They packed for me—rather, I sat on the bed and told them what I wanted to bring. This move wasn't like any other in my life. Just about all my possessions are still in my apartment. I'm only bringing with me what I truly need—some photos, some books, some clothes. I read once, many years ago, that Mother Theresa could carry everything she owned in one bag. She had reduced her material possessions to the absolute necessities. At the time, I couldn't comprehend owning so little. Now I wonder how I ever accumulated so much.

We don't say, although we all know, that I am going to the hospice facility to die. It's like moving into a very exclusive co-op—except in this case, the only criterion for admittance is that your doctor must agree that you have less than six months to live. In all honesty, I know that I have much less than that. I haven't told anyone this—they'd think I was being pessimistic or morbid or giving up. I'm not. I just know that I can't keep this up much longer. My body is breaking. I've resisted the idea of moving to the hospice facility because I want my independence and my space. So many choices have been taken from me; I don't have many left. The choices I am still allowed to make for myself I will hold on to.

My daughters and I pretended that I was packing for an extended vacation. My children seem to be pretending a lot—that I am still who I was, that I will be around for a long while yet, that miracles are possible and that I deserve one. I don't think any of them are in actual denial: they understand that I am dying, they're just getting used to the idea in incremental fashion.

March 26.

I thought the point of moving me to the hospice facility was so that I would have professional care twenty-four hours a day, and yet my children won't leave me alone. One of them is almost always here. I adore them—I adore listening to them, seeing them, holding their hands, even simply breathing in the same room with them. But I miss my privacy and my independence. I don't think I've slept more than four hours at a stretch since I got here, since a nurse or an aide is always checking in on me. Not that they need to, because one of my kids is almost always here. Don't these people realize that I'm sick? I need rest.

April 5.

While my personal decision-making has been reduced in quantity, I accept the fact that it remains strong in quality. There really are only a few things about which I can even make decisions at this point. I can still choose what and when I want to eat and drink. I can still choose when I want to sleep. I can choose when—more or less—I want to die. And I can choose who—if anyone—I wish to have present at the moment of my death.

These last two decisions are not to be taken lightly. Knowing my kids, they'll try to read all sorts of things into the day I choose. Easter is coming—or maybe it's already been. I have become forgetful. Easter might have been an appropriate day. There is an Easter basket in my room. I thought it was a flower arrangement, but when I focused on it, I could see it clearly. An Easter basket. It must have come early this year. So it won't be Easter. I know that none of my children or grandchildren have birthdays in April. I can remember that and that is important. I would not die on, or near, any of their birthdays. That isn't fair. Somebody was born in May—a grandchild? Kaitlin. Yes, Janie's oldest, Kaitlin, was born in May. The end of the month, I think. May is out. So I will die in April.

I had considered trying to hold out until June, until my ex-husband's and my wedding anniversary. I thought that would have been an amusing final touch, but decided it was too mean spirited. And I know I couldn't make it to June. I'm tired. This has been a long journey. Fortunately, nobody gives me the "Rah Rah Rah" football banter anymore. It is quite obvious to even a casual observer that I won't be around much longer.

So the date—more or less—is decided. The more important question is: who will be with me?

April 10.

I'd like to think I'll face the moment of my death courageously. The problem I think most of us have regarding death is that we fear pain. We fear that death will be painful. Therefore we fear death. The hospice will not do anything to keep me from dying when I'm in the process of doing so. They will, however, work to keep me as pain-free as possible. If this is true, then I have nothing to fear. And truly, I'm not afraid.

I believe in God. Not because someone at school or at church told me that I should. I believe in God as I believe that I need to take another breath in order to stay alive. To me, the presence of the divine simply is. I'm curious to know what the divine is. I think I shall soon have my chance to find out.

When I think about who I want to be with me at the moment I cease to be, I have a number of options. There are plenty of nurses and social workers running around, some of whom I've grown quite fond of. There are friends who visit regularly. But somehow none of these people seem right. This—dying—will be my last act in this life. It's too intimate a gift to give to someone who isn't flesh of my flesh, blood of my blood.

But which child? I have to rule out Emma. They will pump me as full of drugs as possible so that I will not feel the pain—whatever pain may be present. But I don't know what will happen. It could be ugly. I know I've said that I don't have to worry about Emma, but I don't want her to watch me die. She is and always will be my youngest, my baby. Therefore, Emma is out.

Jerry would like to pretend that he's a stoic man's man, but I know how deep his soul goes. I wouldn't put him through it. Thus Jerry is out.

Karen...maybe—if she had someone to hold her hand. A significant other to put an arm around her and ask, "Are you okay, sweetie?" I don't care whether that someone is male or female. I'd just like to leave her with a source of unconditional love. To the best of my knowledge, she is alone. And I won't make any child of mine go through this alone. So Karen is out.

Janie would seem the logical choice to be with me—there's a certain symmetry about having my oldest child present, plus she's pragmatic and levelheaded. And yet...something tells me that the efficient, grown-up front she's putting on is just that—a front. She has always willingly shouldered any responsibility asked of her without complaint. That is one of her finest qualities and one of her worst. I'm never sure if I'm asking my oldest child to do something she truly doesn't want to do. This time, she should be relieved of the responsibility of being the oldest. And thus Janie is out.

That's it. I don't have any other children and I'm not going to die in front of my grandchildren. And I sure as hell am not dying in front of my ex-husband. It looks like it's me, myself, and I.

April 12.

Here we are again. Another day. When Jerry and Beth came to visit this morning, he asked how I was. I told him, "Despite the catheter in my bladder, my inability to feed myself, and a sharp pain anytime anyone tries to move me out of my bed, today is a gift. I'm still alive." Jerry replied that, "All this time, I thought the hearing was the last thing to go, and now it turns out it's really sarcasm." I love having my son make me laugh.

April 13.

I can't escape the notion that because we come into this world alone, possibly we should leave it in the same manner.

April 14.

My children watch me while I'm sleeping. They watch me breathe. I think they want to reassure themselves that I am still breathing and have not—yet—died.

April 15.

I'm starting to think that it's time for me to go. I don't feel like eating or drinking anymore. I don't feel like talking. I don't want to get out of bed. I'm starting to think there really isn't a point to staying here much longer.

April 16.

I haven't spoken since yesterday. I haven't eaten or drunk anything since yesterday either. At least I think it was yesterday. I haven't felt much like speaking, but Jerry was right. The hearing really is the last to go. I can still hear them talking about me, the hushed tones from the other side of the room: How much longer do you think she has, Janie? What does the nurse think? What does the doctor think? How much longer? When do you think it will happen? Should we spend the night here? My dear, sweet children, it will happen soon. I'm too tired to open my eyes at this point, but I can hear in their voices how worried they are. I hate doing this to them. If I could hasten this process at all—essentially, if I could die faster—I would.

April 17.

My own mother died quietly in her sleep. I'd like to die in my sleep, except I don't know that I really sleep anymore. You know the feeling you get on a Sunday morning, when you know you're going to the late mass and you don't have to get out of bed for another half an hour and you can just lie there and luxuriate in the warmth and comfort of that space between sleep and wakefulness? That's where I am.

April 18.

I think I'm ready now. I just need one moment, one moment of calm and privacy to take this final step. I hear my children's voices, mixed with those of hospice workers or friends. I love them all, but I want them to leave me alone just for a minute, just long enough for me to finish this. I hear Emma and Karen's voices. I know they're here. Emma said something about flowers blooming and birds singing. It sounds like a lovely day to die. I just need to wait for the right moment, a moment when I'm alone.

I can't tell them I want to be alone. The other me, the me before this illness, would have done her best Garbo imitation and cleared the room. Here I am on the day I'm going to die thinking about Greta Garbo.

There's a new voice—Jerry. And his wife, Beth. More voices. Janie. The sons-in-law Aaron and Jason. These children of mine who will not let their mother alone. I want peace. I want perpetual light to shine upon me.

Every voice in the room is familiar. The nurses have gone—it's just me and the kids. There is a silence and I know they're all staring at me. Waiting for me. I hate being put on display. The only thing left in my bag of tricks is dying—I can't do anything else.

After a while, I hear two of my daughters start singing to me. "Summertime." It's a song I used to sing to them when they grew too old for lullabies. Their voices are soothing.

Really, when I think about it, I don't know any better than they at what moment death will come. If they all were to walk out en masse and leave me alone, would death really come at my command? Perhaps they aren't waiting for me to do anything. Perhaps they're merely waiting with me. We're waiting together. I'm not alone after all.

This isn't so bad.

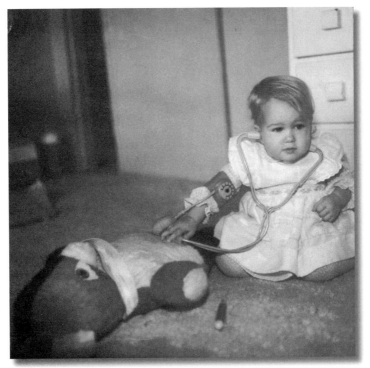

*Someone should have told me back then that
medicine was more lucrative than writing.*

Elissa Minor Rust's stories have appeared in the *Baltimore Review, The Ledge, Crab
Creek Review, Carve Magazine, Honolulu Magazine, Peregrine,* and the *Beacon Street
Review,* among others. Her short-story collection, *The Prisoner Pear: Stories from the
Lake,* was published in December 2005 by Ohio University Press/Swallow Press. She
is the recipient of the Peregrine Prize for Fiction, the National Society of Arts and
Letters Cam Cavanaugh Literature Award, a Honolulu Magazine Fiction Award, the
Swarthout Fiction Award, and the Leslie Bradshaw Fiction Fellowship from Oregon
Literary Arts. She lives in Portland, Oregon, with her husband and two children.

IN MY MOTHER'S TRAILER

Elissa Minor Rust

My girlfriend's son, Charlie, is watching a boy about his age resuscitate a frog on tonight's news. To be fair, the boy is only *pretending* to resuscitate the frog, a re-enactment of the actual event, which happened earlier in the week. According to the news anchor, the pudgy boy ran outside to play one sunny afternoon, only to find the frog caught in the perilous jowls of his dog. It was then that he took the creature inside and proceeded to save its life.

I call to my girlfriend: Martha, you really must see this. On the television, the boy's chubby, ten-year-old fingers are pressing into the chest of the frog, which is no larger than a potato chip, flipped upside-down in his palm. Charlie laughs hysterically.

Really, Martha, I call again, come see this.

Stop calling me Martha, Claire says. She breezes in with a tray in her hand. The tray is peppered with mushrooms, stuffed to bulging with God knows what and sitting on little leaves of lettuce.

I say, Seriously, Martha, this frog should be part of your group; he's cheated death; he's beat the odds. It's a miracle.

Claire glares at me and walks back into the kitchen after leaving the tray on the table. I hear the heavy-duty mixer blend, whirl, and pulse, the one I bought her for Christmas last year. She calls out over the noise, It's your group, too. Mock it all you want, she says, but you're one of us now.

I know that any second she'll be on me for not helping, so I turn off the television and get Charlie to set up chairs and tidy up. Soon, the mushrooms have company: within minutes the table is swimming with trays. I'll admit it, sure: they're really something. She's got a dip with artichoke hearts and jalapeños spilling artlessly out of a bread bowl, exotic fruit sliced thin and rolled to look like sushi, a duck-liver paté that took her three days to prepare. She's quite a chef, my Claire. Used to be she'd sit in front of Martha Stewart every day, nine a.m. sharp. But now she watches less and cooks more. Not too long ago she was throwing her pencil at the television, cursing Martha and demanding she explain what creme fraiche was. By now, though, I'd bet you money Claire is using it like a pro, whatever the hell it is.

Martha, you've come a long way, I tell her as she passes, slapping the back of her pants. She grabs a mushroom from my hand before I can get it to my mouth and returns it to its cozy lettuce bed. The doorbell rings and I see several silhouettes through the frosted glass on either side of the door.

I say, The Miracles are here. Charlie laughs.

You watch it now, she tells me. I mean it.

Seriously, I say over my shoulder as I head to the door. The frog, he's a Medical Miracle, too.

She says, Behave.

Claire's making me sit in on her group meeting because it has been recently brought to my attention that as a baby I cheated death. The group is called Medical Miracles, made up of those who are alive today despite harrowing circumstances. Claire found the group herself four years ago, after a boating accident off the Florida coast where she was vacationing with her mother. The doctors told me not to hope, that she'd be dead in days, that to hop a plane and get to the hospital would be a waste of time.

She came out of it all right, but she was changed. She walked around in a daze, day after day, her skin stretched tight and thin as if it had to fight against some unseen substance underneath, trying to break its way through. Then she found the Medical Miracles. I'll give credit where credit is due: they gave me my girl back.

It's Eben, Scott, and Delores at the door. I can see by the three cars in our driveway that coincidence, not carpool, has brought them all here at the same time. Eben (car accident, forty years ago) walks in first.

Hey, partner, he says to me. He's looking straight ahead when he speaks, which is unnerving. Eben's a tall black man in his late sixties, who is blind in both eyes and walks with a slight limp. I nod in reply, which is rude, I know, since he can't see me, but I can't seem to help myself. He seems satisfied, though, somehow, and finds his way to a chair. Scott (head injury on the football field, last year) wheels past us and heads straight for the food table. There, I think to myself, is a boy after my own heart. Claire perks up so much when she sees him that if he weren't only barely past eighteen I'd be jealous of the kiss she plants on his cheek. She has to bend over to do it, and sue me if I can't help but admire the way her skirt clings to her thighs. She's delicious, my Martha.

Delores (liver cancer, remission, six years) comes in last. She ignores the food altogether and stares at me blankly when I offer to take her coat. This is not new; she's been wary of me from day one. Claire claims she is just wary of men in general, since her husband of thirty years left her just months after her diagnosis, but I tend to think it's just me who unnerves her.

Claire says, Is that everyone?

Eben says, No, we'll have a new member tonight. Should be here any minute.

Claire nudges me with her elbow. Two of them, she says.

Two what? Two what? Delores asks suspiciously, her eyes going from person to person as if we've all purposely kept something from her.

Claire says, Two new *members*, Delores. Steven's joining. The room is silent for what seems like an eternity, then everyone begins to speak at once.

Eben says, Something happen to you?

Scott says, Him?

Delores says, No one tells me.

And then nobody moves, waiting for me to explain. I offer: I'm not really joining; I'm only sitting in.

Oh, he's joining, Claire says in her I-mean-business voice. He belongs here. She proceeds to tell them about the hellish month I've had, how the fat woman with the orange hair and chipped tooth appeared on our doorstep a few weeks ago declaring she was my birth mother; how she told the outrageous story of my "miracle birth;" how the doctors supposedly had to bring me back from death's very hands three separate times in my first two days of life.

I'll be damned, Eben says.

Claire says to the group, as if I'm not there, Really explains a lot, don't you think? The room is silent again, and still all eyes are on me. I plunk down into one of the chairs and put my hands up in a gesture of mock defeat.

Eben is not amused. Mock it all you want, young man, but you have obligations now, he says. How he knew what I'd just done is beyond me. Sometimes, I swear to you, I think this man fakes his blindness, though I'd never suggest it to my girlfriend.

Claire says, He's right, you know, about the obligations.

There's this to consider, I'd like to say, about the fat woman and her outrageous story: I didn't ask for any of it. Because if it's true, let's face it: I come from trailer-park dwellers of the worst kind. It's the kind of thing a man's better off not knowing.

The bell rings. Before I can get there, Charlie's answered it, hoping maybe for one of his friends. When he sees the woman standing on our porch—early thirties, well dressed, carrying a soft attaché case—he turns on his heel and returns to his bedroom without saying a word, leaving the door wide open. For a second I think she must be a saleswoman, until Eben calls out from behind me, That's Celeste. Show her in.

She walks into the house and removes a dark scarf from the top of her head. I'll admit I'm taken aback, if that's a term people still use. Who wouldn't be? The woman's got a monstrous scar on top of her bald head, spanning from one ear to the other in the perfect shape of a cut fingernail. Damn shame, really. A fine girl everywhere else and then this?

The first thing Celeste says is, Brain bleed. Hit by a car, six months ago. She sits down in an empty chair, and, after a slight hesitation, I join her. We spend most of the meeting (in light of the new members, Eben says) discussing the Medical Miracle's three basic tenets, all of which I've heard Claire talk about to no end. Scott looks bored, Delores annoyed. Only Celeste is intrigued, listening as if to the voice of Truth itself as Eben goes over them: first, that miracles bring obligations. Second, miraculous survivors are given the gift of the Miracle Ear, an ability to hear beyond this world. And third, survivors aren't free until they find their Miracle Reason, the one thing they were meant to survive for, the one thing they can't leave this world without having completed. I try to think of something else while he talks, anything else (Claire's fruit sushi, waiting for me on the dining-room table, the pudgy kid performing mouth-to-mouth on a dying frog, the even pudgier woman—my mother?—with her red press-on nails). It's no use. Eben's voice carries, even above my own thoughts, so I listen.

Claire has invited the fat woman over for dinner. And it's a pulling-out-all-the-stops, no-holds-barred kind of dinner. She's been cooking all day, leaving Charlie and me to fend for ourselves.

Steven, she says to me, peeking her head out from the kitchen, Josie will be here any minute. Could you set the table? I nod. Five minutes later, Claire's in the dining room, frantic, telling me I've put out the wrong plates.

She says, We're using the china, Steve. For God's sake, she's your mother. Use the nice china.

I say, What's the big deal? And then: This woman has probably never even seen china in her life. Charlie walks in the room.

I've never seen China either, he says.

The plates, not the country, I say. I feel like adding to Claire that nice china might even make this woman more uncomfortable, but instead I do as I'm told. As I set out each piece, Claire breezes by with a new dish of food to place in the center of the table. She's made a fabulous chicken thingy with capers and marsala sauce, braised squash with Moroccan spices, some spinach dish with cumin and garbanzo beans. When I try to move some of her food over, she tells me to leave a space open near the center.

She says, We'll put Josie's dish there.

She's bringing something?

Claire says, She insisted.

This will be a disaster, I say.

Stop it.

It will be, I tell her, just remember you heard it here first. She'll come in here with some white-trash food and we'll all be uncomfortable. It won't fit in.

Charlie laughs from the other room and says, She'll bring Spam! Now I can't help but laugh at that, can I? But Claire makes it clear she doesn't find it funny, not in the least. Her face gets red and she mumbles something like *Look what you're teaching him* as she walks back into the kitchen.

Over her shoulder, she says: You really are an S.O.B., aren't you? I laugh again and follow her to the kitchen, put my hand on the small of her back to lighten things up, to let her know I'm just kidding around.

I'm doing this for you, you know, she says, softly, so Charlie can't hear. I nod my head, but really I'm thinking about the real reason for this show of food and hospitality: she told me the night before that this fat woman is finally my chance to find my roots, to ground myself. That if I can ground myself, there is hope for a future for Claire and me. It's not that I don't agree with her. God knows I am not so great at relationships. Claire and I are coming up on five years, which is the longest I've ever been faithful to one woman. Claire knows it.

Besides, Claire says, in a funny way, I like her.

Martha, you have a big heart, I say. I think I mean it.

She says, Don't call me Martha.

You're right, I say, you're a much better cook.

And I have better hair.

Yes. Yes, you sure do.

The fat woman arrives about ten minutes later. Claire gives me a nervous smile while Charlie goes to answer the door. I squeeze her hand. Before Charlie can escort our guest to the dining room, I think to myself what a lucky guy I am. Claire's all class, really. She's wearing a black cotton number that barely hugs her figure and stops just below her knees. Even her son has on a nice dinner coat, one his grandmother bought him for his latest birthday.

Our guest, on the other hand, is wearing blue jeans and a white T-shirt with naugahyde fringe hanging in rows from the bottom seam. It floors me that this woman might, indeed, be my mother. She hands Claire the rectangular casserole dish she's carrying and Claire lifts it up, smiling, and places it ceremoniously in its reserved spot at the center of the table.

Whadya bring? Charlie asks quickly, then smiles at me.

Corned beef and potato casserole, she answers. I hope it's all right?

Claire says, before either Charlie or I can respond, It sounds fabulous. She peels back the tinfoil, revealing only a top layer of crumbled saltine crackers, and we all sit down to eat. Charlie giggles a bit as he sits down, his eyes still on the fat woman's casserole dish.

What's on your lap? Claire asks him.

Nothing, he says.

Charlie? Claire's using her this-is-not-the-time-to-mess-with-me voice now, so Charlie folds. He says, Just Harold, Mom.

Claire says, Take him in the other room, *now*.

Charlie lifts a small plastic aquarium off his lap. Inside sits a tiny frog, the size of a fun-sized Snickers bar, that he purchased last month at the local pet shop after the news story aired about the pudgy kid's life-saving efforts. Charlie begs even as he walks from the room, What if something happens to him while we eat? Claire says nothing, so he kicks the bottom of the doorway and stomps dramatically into the living room.

Our guest asks, The frog sick or something? The room is silent for a minute because Claire wants me to answer her.

He's hoping to save it, I tell her. With CPR. Thinks it will get him on television.

The fat woman laughs, a full, hearty laugh, while Claire dishes the marsala chicken onto our plates. It's the kind of laugh that's mostly air from the back of the throat. By the time Charlie's back, though, the laugh has sort of morphed into a sob and she's dabbing her eyes with Claire's best table linens.

I'm sorry, she says, I'm sorry. She says, That's just the thing I missed. With you, I mean. She doesn't look at me, but we all know who she's talking to. I say nothing. Charlie waits for her to dab her eyes again and runs his finger in a circle around the side of his head, indicated that this woman is (in his favorite word) loopy.

He's right, though. I'll tell it straight: the woman is off her rocker.

We sit awkwardly for a few long seconds while she composes herself, and then we all dig in. There's one place the night isn't a bust—my girlfriend is a tremendous cook. We all eat, and then we all eat seconds. The food is so good, I almost forget the occasion. Even Charlie, who is normally a very picky eater, takes seconds of the spinach after he leaves the room to make certain Harold isn't in need of rescue breathing.

The doorbell rings just before dessert. Charlie runs to get it and screams from the front room, It's one of the Miracles! For the second time that night Claire gives me her see-what-you're-teaching-him look. Within seconds, Eben enters the dining room with Charlie at his heels.

Thought I should stop by, he says, but I see you're busy, so…

Claire says, Don't be silly, Eben. We're just about to have dessert; take a seat. She leads him to an open chair. As he sits, he tilts his head sideways, as if sensing the extra person in the room. Oh, Claire says, this is Josie, Steven's…

I interrupt before she can finish. Sweetie, I say, go grab the dessert.

While she's in the kitchen, Charlie leaves again to check on Harold, and Eben says, again, Just thought I should stop by.

Hear a voice? I ask him. I'm smiling, but I know he can't see that.

He says, The Miracle Ear is nothing to mock, son. You should know that, especially now.

The fat woman says, Miracle Ear? The way she says it makes me think of those hearing devices you see on late-night television, where the old man uses a device that resembles a walkman to listen to a couple conversing on the other side of the room. Eben answers her question.

The gift bestowed on miraculous survivors, he says. An ability to hear things no one else can. I can't discern from her face what she thinks of this. She furrows her brow a bit, her mascara smudged under her eyes from her earlier breakdown. As Claire returns with plates of scrumptious-looking crème brûlée, the woman says, You all got this? This ear thing? All of you?

Claire says, Just Eben.

Eben says, We all got it. Just I'm the only one knows how to use it.

I say, Let's eat. But before I can get my first bite to my lips, Eben is handing this woman—this huge, strange woman—a business card.

I do readings, he says. First one's free.

You've got a business now? I ask. This is a money thing? This card of his surprises me—and believe me, I am not a man who is easily surprised.

Not a business, he says, a service.

Charlie slinks back into the room, looking dejected. Frog still alive?

Yes, he says. Dumb frog.

Don't you worry, little man, I tell him. Somewhere in the world are a pair of frog's lips waiting for your own.

He glares at me from across the table, his mouth already full of crème brûlée. Beside me, I can tell without even looking that Josie is crying again, which I'll admit might bother me, just a little. It's momentary.

Mmm, mmm, I say. Martha, this is some good dessert.

Two months after my official membership with the Medical Miracles begins, something happens at a meeting that throws us all, as they say, for a loop. Celeste announces that she's found her Miracle Reason, the one thing she was meant to survive for. There's a moment of silence after her announcement in which she adjusts her scarf around her shoulders, and crosses and uncrosses her legs three times (this woman, if you'll forgive me adding, has fabulous legs). Pandemonium ensues.

Delores says, It's not possible. You just joined.

Scott says, Way too soon.

I say: Bravo, girl.

Eben raises his hand to quiet us. Let her talk, he says.

But Eben, Delores says, we can't start letting people march in here and not take us seriously. She ends her statement with a pointed glare in my direction.

Let her talk, Eben repeats.

She talks: seems that earlier in the week, Celeste started out for her morning walk as usual. The walk took her, as it always does, through the far side of Privet Park, past the bathrooms that have been chained closed since last winter, past the fountain with the giant bird statue in its center. The sun had just come up, so everything had a strange glow about it. Along the path where she usually walks, students from the local college were just beginning to assemble booths for the annual fall arts festival, so she stepped off the path and into the bordering neighborhood to avoid the confusion. A few streets in, as she turned the corner to head back home, she thought she saw something flicker in the top story of a house. But, as she said, the light was strange, and she assumed her eyes were playing tricks on her. Soon, though, she heard a voice, a strange, light voice, airy almost, calling distinctly to her, saying *her* name, asking for help. She ran back to the house and noticed through the window a fire was burning inside, growing steadily larger by the second. She broke a window, shielded her mouth, and from inside opened the front door of the house, without knowing why. Within seconds, at least six dogs were crowding her, pushing through the doorway and outside of the house.

And? Delores says.

Celeste says, The dogs would have burned to death if I hadn't been there. And a person, too. When I broke the window, it woke the old lady up from the back of the house.

Delores says, You get this from some tabloid?

Celeste doesn't answer her.

Eben says, The voice, was it…?

Yes, she answers. A dog. I'm sure of it.

And he: The Miracle Ear.

I roll my eyes.

We spend the rest of the meeting celebrating her find. Candles are lit, hands are held, the whole nine yards. I can't help but think to myself, This shit is not for me. But when I look at Celeste, it's clear that regardless of what Delores says, she's taking this quite seriously. She isn't crying, but she's close. Her head is slightly bowed, revealing again the outrageous scar shaped like a crescent moon that runs across its top, the only place on her scalp without fuzzy growth sprouting like newly planted seeds.

Honestly, her solemnity unnerves me a bit. Staring at that map of hair and scar, I actually can see how one might believe she's found her Miracle Reason, her One Thing. More than that: I can see how one might actually believe there was a reason for her to find. She lifts her head and looks at me as she shifts slightly in her metal folding chair across the room. Delores is speaking, but all I see is Celeste, her scarf now falling from her shoulders, defeated by gravity, her face like a question mark. Claire clears her thoat from beside me and gives me a look. She holds up her right hand, shakily, all five fingers pointed straight as matchsticks toward the ceiling: *Five years*, her hands are saying, *five years without cheating. Watch yourself.*

So clearly I'm caught off guard when Celeste stops by our home a week later, looking for Claire, who isn't home. She stands in the doorway, a perplexed look about her, her jacket pulled tight around her body.

I invite her to come in, and she nods her head in reply. We pass Charlie on our way to the living room, lying on the rug in front of the television with Harold's aquarium perched haphazardly on his stomach. Celeste pays him no attention, and once we reach the living room she sits down on the sofa without me having to ask. I'm not quite sure what to say.

Claire should be back within the hour, I say. And then: She's at her cooking class. Celeste doesn't respond, doesn't even lift her head. Looking at her, it occurs to me that I should have offered earlier to take her coat. She still has it wrapped tightly around her, cocoon-like, each button closed, the collar snug around her neck like a moat. It also occurs to me, though (I swear it!) I try to keep it from my mind, that I'd like to get a closer look at what that moat is guarding. I find myself wishing she'd remove her hat as well, longing in some strange way for just a peek at her fuzzy head, at that moon-scar looming above her face. The thought of that covered red line is appealing now, in an unsettling sort of way.

She speaks abruptly, as if answering a question, though I've posed none. Yes, she says, I'm a mess, I know.

I say nothing, waiting for her to go on.

I'm just waiting for it to happen, you know? she says. Every day, every minute.

I say, For your One Thing?

No, she says, for death.

Death?

Death, of course. I've found my Miracle Reason. It's just a waiting game now. The rest of you, you're safe, because you haven't found it. But me?

I don't know what to say to her, so I reach out my hand and place it just above her knee. What I want to say: I know nothing about life or death, but you sure seem okay to me. And this: Forget this miracle business—it confuses things. But I can't. I can't say anything. Truth is, there's something about Celeste that makes my head clear, that makes me want to believe we're both Medical Miracles, saved for something, the way she does. It might be the way she speaks so frankly, takes it so seriously. But it could just as easily be those legs of hers. I will not kid myself. I am a man known to be thrown all off-kilter where a beautiful woman is concerned.

I hand her a kleenex from the box on the side table just as Charlie walks in. She dabs at her eyes silently and doesn't seem bothered when the kid plunks his frog down next to her on the couch, smelly aquarium and all.

Good going, Charlie says to me, this is the second woman you've made cry lately.

Celeste says, He hasn't made anybody cry. I was crying when I got here.

He made that strange woman cry.

What strange woman? she asks.

His mom. The funny lady with big hair.

134

Charlie, I warn him with the tone of my voice, that's enough.

It's okay, Celeste says. Hey, kid, she says to Charlie as he leaves the room, I used to have big hair, too. No shame there.

She's smiling now, but the damage has been done. Thanks to Charlie, when I look at Celeste, I see only Josie. I hadn't noticed before, but when Celeste looks at me, there's something hidden, penetrating, in her stare: it's a look she shares with Josie that eats you all the way through, the sweetest plumbing acid there is. Makes you think if you'd only let go for the slightest of moments it'd be the end for you, makes your whole person feel warm and tight at the same time (for better or worse, who knows?), like a plaster mold from the outside, like a freshly eaten hot meal from within.

I move my hand from her knee.

When Claire gets home an hour later, she finds me sitting in this same spot, alone in the living room except for Harold, abandoned by his boy, sleeping the day away in his little bowl of water and sheltered by glass walls on each side. Claire sits between me and the frog, where Celeste had been not too long before. She looks at me and then pulls the rubber band from her ponytail, letting her hair fall in flat hanks around her face. I can tell by the miniature droplets of water in her bangs that it must be raining outside. She's beautiful. Heaven help me, I really do want to do right by this woman.

She says, Charlie says Celeste came by. The inflection in her voice makes it sound like a question.

I say, She was looking for you.

Didn't find me, Clarie says. She shifts uneasily. I want to tell her that she has nothing to worry about, that I'll behave myself with Celeste, with everyone. But I can't. Instead I cough into my hand and look over her head, into the china cabinet behind the couch.

What happens next is a mystery even to me. I hear something in the room, clear as day, but so unusual, with such an of-the-air quality to it that I know I'm the only one who's heard. I strain my ears, looking for a source, and soon I swear it's coming from Harold's little aquarium, from the gray-green creature sitting in that murky water, his skin the texture of charred ham.

He says, Say something to make her happy. The voice is airy as soft feathers.

Martha, I say, barely thinking, that was some breakfast you cooked this morning. Claire looks at me with blank eyes and kicks her shoes off in front of her.

The frog says, Something else, you idiot!

I look at my girlfriend, her hair wet, her feet bare. I say, I think you're it. You're my One Thing. The strange thing is, after I say it, it occurs to me that this might be true.

No, I'm not, she says, but that's real nice of you to say so. She's beaming. She reaches out and squeezes my hands. The frog says nothing, so I guess we're good.

Josie calls the next afternoon for a favor. She says it just like that, as if it is the most natural thing in the world to say, as if I have been performing favors for her all my life. As if her calling out of the blue to say, Hey, Steve, could you do me a favor? was the next, most logical step in our newfound parent-child relationship. It occurs to me as I hold the phone against my ear that I've never heard her voice on the telephone before. It has a crisp, contained quality to it, like those round glass fishing floats on the coast. Dignified, almost. Hard to believe, really, that the woman on the other end of the line was probably spilling out of a halter top in the middle of the Blessed Palms Mobile Home Park. It is this sound, more than anything, that makes me comply.

Half an hour later, I follow the directions she's given me to a run-down little building across town, sandwiched between a Dairy Queen and a dry cleaner. On the small strip of lawn in front of the building there are small pinwheels staked into the ground, plastic birds whose tail feathers twirl in the wind, sprinkler heads in the form of dogs and children. I give the man inside Josie's name and he pulls from behind the counter the most horrid lawn statue I have ever seen. It's a peacock and a toad, snuggled close together as if their very lives depend on the relationship, the peacock's feathers wrapped around the toad's body as if in protection from the evils of the world. The toad looks sorrowful indeed, its mouth turned down, in need of peacock comforting, I suppose. His most salient feature is a bright, paint-sale yellow wart sitting like a parasite above his right temple. I pay the man for the statue. I can't wait to drop the thing off and get home to Claire, now vindicated in my belief that this woman is a complete loon, blood relative or no.

Josie doesn't seem taken aback by the statue, but she doesn't seem too thrilled by it either when I knock on her door and present it to her. Under my feet, the Astroturf is peeling from her makeshift porch, and to the right of the trailer her car sits high on cinder blocks, dark rags and wrenches spread as if in formation underneath it.

Thanks, she says, I'd have picked it up myself, but (she motions to the old Ford next to us) Mike says my car won't be running for weeks.

I smile and nod. I feel like she wants me to ask who Mike is, but I resist, wanting to get home and have this whole business done with. Josie turns around and walks inside, leaving the door wide open. Too embarrassed to just leave, I follow her.

Sit, she says.

Thanks, I'm fine, I say. I really should be going. Josie sits the statue on a counter in her kitchen.

A voice from behind me breaks the silence. What's the hurry? it says. I turn around and see a man probably ten years younger than myself, wearing a white undershirt and blue jeans. It takes just a second, not even a second, for me to realize this man is my blood. He's taller, yes, and more fit than myself, but even to me the resemblance is clear. It's like in the books, when the character says, *All of a sudden, it was like looking into a mirror*, except I swear that's how it really feels. The man's nose, his slightly swollen eyes, the bend of his shoulders. Everything.

Josie says, Mike, Steven; Steven, Mike.

I ask, Is Mike...?

Your cousin, Mike answers. Josie's brother's kid. He reaches out and shakes my hand.

Come, sit, Josie says, and before I know what's happening the three of us are sitting around the table, plates in front of each of us. There are two casseroles (one concealed by bread crumbs, the other tater tots), a bowl filled with green beans and what looks like cream of mushroom soup, and a fourth bowl boasting a cheesy potato dish. My stomach turns at the sight of it, but soon against my better judgment I'm eating, eating as if I've been fasting for days, eating as if my life depends on it. The casseroles are creamy and fresh—I'm unclear what's in them, but every so often I see a carrot spill out onto the plate, a piece of celery, a cube of chicken. I eat and then I eat some more. I eat seconds of everything. I belch after helpings. I scarf it down as if cream-of-everything soups are going out of style, as if Campbell's itself has paid me to, as if in homage to Andy Warhol and his crazy paintings, and damn if it isn't better than anything I've had to this point in my sorry life. And after the dishes are empty, Josie and Mike sit back and smoke, all of us panting as if out of breath. I haven't smoked in years, and I'm not about to start again now, but I scoot closer to Mike and breathe deep, loving the warmth as it enters my lungs. The smell of tobacco fills the room.

As if in a dream, I look at Josie and say, Ma'am, that food could raise the dead.

And she: That's a compliment worth waiting for.

From the counter in the kitchen, the toad still sits under the peacock's feathers. But heaven help us all, the creature is smiling, sure as I am sitting here with Mike's smoke in my lungs.

I'm thinking of that frog, and that meal, just a week later when I call a meeting of the Miracles to tell them I've found my Miracle Reason. Delores is pissed as ever when she walks through the door, refuses to let me take her coat. She sits purposely across the room from Celeste, who looks as anxious as she did last time I saw her. Eben calls the meeting to order and announces the purpose of our gathering.

Delores says, Some nerve you've got.

Scott looks at Claire, his eyes pursed.

Celeste says, Where? Where did it happen?

I say, In my mother's trailer.

It's like this, see, I say. This is my Miracle Reason, my one thing. It's to tell you this: There is no One Thing. There are lots of them.

Nobody says a word.

I think I believe every word of this, really I do. I pause, because I want to find the right words to tell them what I've learned, which is not that they're wrong, but that we're all saved, over and over, all the time, for different reasons. Part of me was saved, miraculously, when I met Claire, and another part in that trailer with Josie. Don't get me wrong, I'm not going to buy lawn ornaments anytime soon, but somehow that hideous place feels like home.

And this one does too—here, with these strange people, I'm starting to feel a tug, a kinship not unlike the one I feel in Josie's trailer, which I suppose is what belief is all about. If that means I have to listen to frogs speak all my life, so be it. To tell the truth, I'd like to hear that voice again, its sound like soft feathers filling my ears the way Mike's smoke filled my lungs. Really I would.

*Me at six, with seaweed, Point Reyes shore, California. After the
sun went down and I was back in the station wagon with my family,
riding on Highway 1 watching the world rush by, it was hard for me
to believe I had not, in fact, just spent the day as a hula girl.*

Christiana Langenberg was born in the Netherlands and immigrated to the U.S.
with her Dutch father and Italian mother. She is the winner of the 2005 Drunken
Boat Panliterary Award for Fiction, 2003 Chelsea Award for Fiction, and her stories
have been published in *Literary Salt, Carve, Chelsea, Green Mountains Review, American
Literary Review, Lullwater Review,* the *Blue Moon Review,* and a variety of literary formats.
She teaches in the English and Women's Studies departments at Iowa State University
and has been instructed to mention that she has four beautiful, amazing children.

HALF OF WHAT I KNOW

Christiana Langenberg (signature)

Christiana Langenberg

The theory is the dog committed suicide. My father tells me this when I get home from school, after he says Luigi is gone, and I ask him what he means. "He killed himself," he begins. So I make my way down the hill from the house, over the long, soft bed of pine needles, and see for myself: Luigi hanging from the leash tethered between two locust trees. One hind leg is barely touching the ground, the other oddly bent, as if he is stepping on something that is not there. The rope is wound around his neck. When I reach him, I walk around to the other side and squat so that my head is at the same level as Luigi's. I turn to look back up at the house. It seems far off and small, as if five people couldn't possibly live in there without spilling out at some point.

My sister and brother appear not to know how Luigi died. Rafaela is practicing her French horn and Hans is doing God knows what in his room. They don't ask me and I don't tell them. I swallow a lot and get myself some ice water. My father buries the dog.

The blare coming from my bedroom is not music. Rafaela claims it is Mozart, but it sounds, instead, like a moose having its toenails removed in short, lyric bursts. I'm not in the room, but I know she keeps tipping the wide bell over to pour her spit on my half of the floor. She says she *must* to do this. From the basement come loud vrooming noises and the squealing of tiny, pretend brakes. I think but do not say, "No wonder Luigi killed himself." It doesn't seem as funny to say when it's actually true. No one is paying attention.

I open Hans's door and he has his entire collection of Matchbox cars lined up like a parking lot on the checkered outdoor carpeting that is his floor. None of my friends' houses have carpet like this. It was *on sale*. It was *practically a steal*. None of my friends have suicidal dogs.

Hans asks me if I want to play Disneyland. This means he needs me to drive the Fisher-Price school bus along the rows of parked cars because it's the tram that takes people to the rides. Never mind that the Fisher-Price people are actually larger than the cars and sometimes I pretend the cars are their skateboards, which makes my brother yell to my mother that I am not playing correctly.

I help him set up a Magic Mountain out of an upside-down wicker wastebasket with a dishtowel draped over it. Then I get started on the Ferris wheel made out of Tinker Toys, but there aren't enough little plastic fins for the ends because my mother has been vacuuming without the lights on again. Hans starts revving his engines, which gets on my nerves. Nobody revs when they're parking. Doesn't he know this?

This make-believe takes hours to play. I don't have hours. In just about three it will be dark and that always changes everything. I am twelve, my dog just killed himself, and I cannot forget what my father said: "That's it then. It's over." He is upstairs, leaning against the kitchen counter, a beer in one hand, the other in a fist in his armpit.

My father is, as my mother is fond of saying, a "quiet water hurries deep" kind of man. She is always running American idioms through her Italian expressions, but I understand what she means. Sort of the same way I understand the basic notion that you shouldn't use a blow dryer near a bathtub. My father carries just under his surface a mysterious potential for danger. Either his own or someone else's. It is a dark space, not to be disturbed. I know both more and less than I need to about what's in there.

I am a clever child, but because I am also quiet, nobody knows this. One of my father's nicknames for me is The Sponge, because, he says, I take everything in. He has a manner of speaking, evenly enunciating all his consonants, which makes everything sound like the truth. Just when I think something is brilliantly clear to me, he makes a tight, clipped pronouncement that throws everything into shade.

At bedtime he tells us elaborate stories of two dark-skinned boys named Hippewa and Chippewa who he says are Indians. They are forever rescuing people and themselves from desperate circumstances. I am riveted by these stories. I know, although I never ask, that this has something to do with his own childhood in the Dutch Indies, and that bad things happened when the Japanese invaded Indonesia in 1942. Families were split up into some kind of camps. I understand words like *malaria, cholera, solitary confinement*, but they don't figure into my sense of camping. Camping is where I can wear my swimsuit all day and toss my polenta scraps under the table for the chipmunks to eat.

Only once, when my father's younger brother Piet visits us from Holland, do I get more information. Uncle Piet drinks shots of gin, squeezes his eyes closed when he laughs, and is willing to talk. "*Het* is just *vater* in *hele kleinen* glasses," he says of the shot glasses on the coffee table. He tells me stories about the camps. In one, my father retrieves his youngest brother Hans from a mass grave because he is not yet dead from cholera, as the guards who dumped him had assumed. Piet describes my father as a lanky and resolute teen, dragging his six-year-old brother out of a ditch in the blazing sun and into the shade inside a hut. My uncle Hans does not die. In another story my father is accused of causing an uprising and endures being beaten until the Japanese guards threaten to involve his mother. Then he is forced to sign a confession, written in a language he does not speak, and thrown into solitary confinement for months. He was fourteen at the time.

My father sits silent in the room while Piet talks. With an itchy clarity, I realize *camp* does not mean camp. I make the mistake of asking him how he felt when all that happened. He says it is past my bedtime and adds, with something like a smirk on his face, "Piet likes to tell stories."

Sometimes my father stalls as he's telling the Hip and Chip stories, when Hans and Rafaela are asleep and he thinks I am, too. In those moments, I watch the moonlight from the window as he turns his face toward it, staring, quiet, staring, until his face disappears into the dark. Time hangs motionless until his eyes come back to where we are. Sometimes the story is simply over at this point and he rises slowly and leaves the room. Other times he stretches his legs on the carpet and launches his standard test to see if we're awake. He whispers, "Then the washing machine said to the refrigerator...," and I say, "Hey!" and he laughs, "I thought you were asleep!" before he picks up the frayed end of the story where he left it.

When I ask my father, "*Waarom?*"—why did Luigi kill himself—he looks at me surprised, and says just one thing. "He knew the consequences." I can tell from the way the muscles in his face make his jaw a rectangle that I am to let this go. I will get in trouble if he knows I slipped out the back door, through the shady tunnel of pines, and saw Luigi hanging—my dog a gray slant between the locust and the oil drum. That detail I keep for myself. He gives me only the ending to this story. Luigi is gone. Period.

That night my father is too tired for Hip and Chip. My mother is busy. I am told to get in bed and go to sleep. But the transition from day to night is hard for me, and it seems I can never just lie down and go unconscious. It is difficult to turn my mind off, to stop thinking the things I'm thinking. My dog is dead. The nightlight might burn out. I could go blind while I sleep. Strangers might come in and steal me. My sister begins her raspy breathing one millisecond after she pulls the covers over her head.

I am taking a chance, getting out of bed after I have been told to stay there. On any given night, this can make my father angry. There is the chance I will say, "Um...," and he will erupt. I am very careful and walk extra softly, and tonight I do not detonate his mood when I appear in the living room to announce, "Rafaela is sleeping creepy." Tonight he is more somewhere else than here.

The outside of him responds to my statement. The book closes, his hands push up on the arms of the chair, and he rises. I follow him down the hallway back to my room. We make no sound. He walks in and shakes Rafaela's shoulder.

She grunts, "Whut?" from under the sheet.

He speaks. "You look like you're sleeping in a body bag. Stop that."

Then he turns and walks out as I stand next to my bed.

My sister pulls the covers up again when he leaves. I know enough to know I cannot push my luck and go out there again. I slide under my blanket and stare at the nightlight. I look around the room until I've pretended all I can that things aren't what they are. The hatchet in the corner is really my broken tennis racket. My sister's brassiere on the closet doorknob is not a vampire bat. Years go by and I am still awake. Rafaela's alarm clock lies to me that it's been five minutes. I'll be awake forever.

I hear reading noises in the living room. A page turns, my father's body settles into the yellow chair, ice shifts in a glass, a throat clears, and another page turns. The distant hum of the sewing machine takes up the basement. The washer chugs into the rinse cycle. The dryer tumbles the buckles on my overalls. I can almost see them going around. My mother and the major appliances are safe.

I tell myself the story of Luigi, but I have to loot my memory in order to do this. It begins a few years back, with our first dog, Gioia. I include all the details. I like details. They remind me of what I know. My family is at the Children's Zoo. My hair is short, too short, and feels prickly on my neck in the humidity. Rafaela, Hans, and I are playing with a puppy in the petting zoo, trying to feed her the pellets we're supposed to be feeding the baby goats. We fall in love with her instantly and work together for once to convince our parents to buy the dog.

Months later, I am looking out the bathroom window at a curious thing in the back yard. My father is shaving and I ask him, casually, "Why is there a poodle stuck to Gioia's butt?" My father curses in Dutch, "*Verdommen!*" and races out the door. Little blobs of shaving cream adhere themselves to the walls as he careens around corners. They look like frosting and smell like lime. Outside, the poodle gets smacked on the rear end with a broom until he unsticks himself from our dog and jumps over the fence.

A brief and utterly confusing lesson in animal sexual behavior follows. The word *sex* is never used. My father talks about *inseam* and *nation* and *fallen opium tubes*. Huh? I expect my mother to measure Gioia for a pair of pants. She just recently fitted the dog for a diaper because she was having her period, so this is entirely possible. The poodle must be on drugs, or at least not from this country, which would account for the opium. Maybe there is something else I'm supposed to understand, here, but Tom and Jerry are on TV in two minutes. "Uh huh," I tell my parents.

When Gioia's six puppies are born, only one has curly hair. The others look a lot like a German shepherd down the street and the runt has distinct basset hound-looking ears. It is then that I understand dog behavior and the link between this mysterious period thing and fertility all at the same time. Gioia is a slut.

I, apparently, am the only one horrified. My father calls Gioia a bitch, but in an un-angry way that makes no sense to me. Everyone else is crazy for the puppies, the children of a dog who has behaved like a *putana*. Gioia is spayed for her own protection. My mother has fallen in love with this dog and Gioia can do no wrong.

I decide people are gross and dogs are grosser. The only redemption for dogs is that they don't know any better.

When Gioia leaps through the screen door to bite the Jewel man in the butt as he is delivering our laundry detergent, my mother scolds me for screaming *butt* out loud when I should have alerted her to the mayhem by hollering that Gioia was masticating the Jewel man's *culetto*. She buys extra cleaning supplies—Jewel Dish Sparkle, Jewel Dust-A-Way—and hisses at me out of the corner of her mouth. She demands an explanation: not for why Gioia spontaneously attached her jaw to the uniformed behind of the poor unsuspecting Jewel man, but rather why I insisted on reverting to crude American words like *butt*. She also buys a product that is actually called Dog-B-Gone, which you're to sprinkle on your garbage can or fence in case a sexual predator like a poodle stops by. Everything remains unused under the sink for years. Butt. Butt, butt, butt.

Gioia bites the Goodwill men when they stop by to collect a large bag of my mother's polyester pantsuits and our seersucker culottes. Somehow this becomes my sister's and my fault, because after my mother frantically sewed zig-zaggy corduroy ribbon around the collars and armpits, which made them itch, we whined and refused to wear them. She called us rotten, ungrateful children. Then she yanked open the rotten drawer and looked for the rotten phone book and called the Goodwill to come pick up the clothing. Rotten children. "*Porca miseria*," she added. We are pig misery.

My mother does not have a driver's license. She was going to take the test once, but then her "legs were getting cold" so she decided not to. I am the only child I know whose mother does not drive and everything comes to our front door. Milk, frozen food, cleaning supplies, the Avon lady, that rotten little neighbor boy with the unkempt hair who likes to play with my rotten brother, and advocates for poor children who will endure itchy armpits gratefully, just so they don't have to go naked. My sister rolls her eyes behind my mother's back. We behave like a couple of *culetto* heads.

Later, as I drag a barking Gioia into the house and the Goodwill men are safely back in the truck, my mother stands with her arms folded across her chest. She can extract guilt from inanimate objects. "You *know* why this happened, don't you?" she asks. "*Capisci?*" This does not require an answer.

The next day, when the needle on her sewing machine breaks I whisper to my sister, "You *know* why this happened, don't you?" Rafaela snorts and whispers, "What turns the corner goes in circles."

Meanwhile, Gioia appears to be going for some sort of record for biting the most philanthropists in one year. The park ranger at Halsey National Forest in western Nebraska is victim number seven. He stops by our campground to see if he can help my father fix the radiator problem on our station wagon. It happens with rocket speed. Gioia's jaw is in his thigh the moment he lays his hand on the car. Like on those science programs my father makes us watch, where the frogs sit quiet and harmless on a lily pad until a violent shot of tongue uncoils itself to maim an innocent fly a few feet away, I have no time to think. The leash burn on my palm remains for days, like a stigmata.

Even more amazing, the ranger laughs it off and rubs his pant leg where there are neat little holes in the shape of Gioia's mouth. He and my father shake their heads and agree, "That's some watchdog!"

The next day Gioia stays in the tent until the car is fixed and my father drives into town to get the ranger a bottle of whiskey. The ranger is downright jovial, Rafaela asks him to sign her autograph book, and Hans sits in his jeep making pretend driving noises. My mother, bent over the camp stove stirring the *pasta con melanzane*, invites him to dinner. "It's nothing fancy." I think they have all gone insane and wonder if I am adopted. None of them seem capable of seeing any of the contradictions here.

I never thought of Gioia as adopted, but I do think of Luigi that way. I wonder how that started. Gioia was as much a part of our family as a brother or a sister; Luigi was always just a dog, visiting.

I think of the day Gioia died, my mother's relentless sobbing, the smell of wool mittens drying on the woodstove, and the silence, except for the crying, everywhere. The details are so ready in my mind, it could be now: January 7 and twenty-four degrees, the temperature dropping three degrees an hour, a blizzard on the way. My father picks us up early from school so we can make it home before *real* snow hits. The snow is falling thick and fast as we get out of town. It looks pretty real to me. Flakes the size of doilies billow around the car as we move through them.

Seven long miles later, when we finally get to the edge of the driveway, there is a mound in the middle of it and I tell my father I think I see a foot sticking out. "*Dio mio santo*," says my mother. "Don't be ridiculous," adds my father, but he stops the car to check it out. It is Gioia, her skull crushed and her body already frozen stiff. My mother gasps and begins what will be days of weeping.

My father figures Gioia must have been chasing a car on the road and the driver swerved to either miss or hit her, and then she was dead; and the driver knew this, stopped the car long enough to carry her body up to the driveway. I want to know why, if the driver took this trouble, he didn't leave a note, and my father says, "What is he going to say—'Sorry I killed your dog'?"

We keep her in a box in the garage until the blizzard is over and my father can think of a way to get a grave dug in this cold. I go out to the garage to see her, but Rafaela and Hans don't. She looks like she's sleeping. I know it's because my father has turned the smashed part of her head toward the bottom of the box and draped most of her with an old towel.

The next week Gioia is buried in the walnut grove and we get Domenico, a two-year-old mutt from the Humane Society. They tell us his name is Jeff, but my mother renames him Domenico because it is a Sunday when we get him. No doubt because of this, he runs away after six days.

My father decides it might be better to get a younger dog, one we can train, so we go back to the Humane Society and get Bruno, a fat, brown puppy who looks like a Saint Bernard. I imagine when he grows up I will train him to find people lost in blizzards. He will have a little barrel tied just under his neck for medicine, or notes—I haven't decided which—and he will look just like the dog in a book I have. My other favorite book is the Dutch one where three horses—my favorite is the black one, Swaartje—walk around on their hind legs in dresses and pearls, but I realize that will never happen.

Rafaela and Hans think of Bruno as more of a foster dog than a real dog, because he is so different from Gioia. He is cute, but they quickly convince me he is stupid. Where Gioia watched cartoons with us, Bruno is only interested in following my mother around and eating. She does things like warm milk for him and pours it over his dry dog food because she feels bad he has to eat in the garage. He eats all of his food and the cat's, too, and then emits the world's worst scorched-tuna-and-onion farts. It is too disgusting to bear, and the clincher is the way my father puts it. "Imagine, out of a dog's anus, drifting through the air into our noses and down into our lungs." I feel like I've just been force-fed dog poop. When Bruno gets an infection in his foot from a locust thorn, and my father says, "I'm thinking of taking Bruno back," we look at each other and shrug.

Besides, after paying to have Moretto neutered the month before, there is no way in hell my father is taking another animal to the hospital. No way in hell, *verdommen*. We only got to keep the stray kitten because he felt sorry for it when my mother, annoyed by its incessant mewing outside the front door, yanked the door open and flung cold water on the cat. In January, in Nebraska, where we measure temperature in terms of wind chill.

It was not the embarrassment of the kennel that my father fashioned out of chicken wire to take the scrawny, pitch-black cat to the vet. It was the shock of the $58.50 that led him to believe he could heal things himself. After all, he is a plant pathologist, and the beauty of science, according to my father, is that it is so logical. A couple of weeks after Moretto's neutering, when the cat got an eye infection, my father brought home boric acid from his lab, added a dab of Neosporin, and, ta da!—the cat, by then referred to by my father only as Fiftyeightfifty, was cured.

But Fiftyeightfifty is a cat, not a watchdog, and it is determined we need a watchdog. To protect us from burglars or robbers or mean people looking to kidnap children of Dutch-Italian descent living in rural Nebraska and sell them into white slavery in South America. So we are told, and so we believe. My parents both lived through World War II as adolescents, and were intimately acquainted with the potential for random violence. Their parenting is laden with doom-related manifestos. "Familiarity breeds contempt." "Most people, given the opportunity, will stab you in the back."

The odd thing about these phrases is that they are delivered as calmly as, "Please pass the salt."

It goes something like this. My mother reminds me to clean my room. I say I am going to the pool with my friend Lori, and I hear a breezy, "Familiarity breeds contempt," as she floats through the room with the vacuum cleaner.

The phrase I hear most is, "Remember, you are not immune to tragedy." My brother thinks it is funny to say, and tosses it into conversations during board games. "That's Boardwalk. Gimme $40 or your Get Out of Jail Free card…Remember…you are not immune to tragedy." His eyebrows arch and his voice takes on the same lilt as my parents', and we hold our stomachs and laugh until we fall over.

"You sound like idiots," my mother says. She has just sewed a sleeve on a dress backwards.

But sometimes at night, as I am listening to my older sister, asleep and senseless, breathing into her pillow on the other side of the room, I am filled with a cryptic expectation that at any moment something bad will happen. Happiness is fragile. We are ducks sitting down. It is just a question of time.

Not surprisingly, I become afraid of the dark and refuse to sleep without a nightlight. If I am going to wake up suddenly blind at three a.m., I want to see that I can't see. I tell my mother this one night as she is basting the hem of a chartreuse skirt—which looks alarmingly close to my size—in the living room and my father is reading *Time* magazine. I have already gotten my sister in trouble for when she slinked out of her bed and turned off the nightlight, which made me scream so hysterically my father rushed into our room and slammed on the overhead light because, apparently, he thought I'd been shot. My sister was spanked for turning off my light and for laughing when my father said *shot*.

I am now out of bed for the third time. I tiptoe to the edge of the hallway and hear my mother say, "*Dio mio santo!* This again." I know I need to present a dire reality. When I get to the part about how I'm afraid I won't know I've just gone blind, she interrupts me.

"Ach! *Ma dai!* Don't be ridiculous!"

It annoys me that she thinks I can occupy the condition of being ridiculous when I am brimming with fear. I continue around the coffee table to tap my father's compassion, and he tells me the story of some kids who were messing around one day when they should have been in bed, and one kid tipped over another kid's chair and he landed flat on his back, and, kablammo, blind forever. My stomach tightens.

"Get to bed," says my father, and turns the page.

My mother, her mouth full of stickpins, mutters, "Perfect. That's just perfect."

Bruno is returned to the Humane Society because we can't have a watchdog who is prone to injury. And besides, there is a colleague of my father's who has a friend who has some puppies, German shepherd mix. My mother is again in charge of naming it. I want a girl dog. We get a boy dog. Luigi. A big puppy with enormous, clumsy feet. I can tell by the way my mother pinches her neck skin that she is ready to be disappointed in the dog, and I resolve to be his best friend. When his huge tail sweeps my mother's ceramic crucifix off the coffee table one too many times, I suggest we create a nice play space for him outside.

My mother is oblivious to what happens on the six acres outside the house, but order is very important to her inside. She reminds me that Gioia was light on her feet whereas, "Luigi gallops like a bool." "A bool?" I ask. "A *bool*," she answers tightly. "Oh, a bull. Like a bull in a candy store."

The pen my father fashions for Luigi is three hundred feet down the hill from the house. It is flanked by the pigeon coop on one side and a huge garden on the other, upwind from the septic lagoon. Rafaela, Hans, and I help by putting a chicken-wire fence around some metal posts until Rafaela gets bored and accuses Luigi of being hyperactive. She is taking Advanced Placement Psychology in the tenth grade so now she knows everything. She suggests we adjust his diet. No red food coloring, especially. Hans tells her to go on a diet because her brain is fat.

I make a sort of swinging gate for the pen out of pieces from the scrap wood pile and a couple of rusty hinges I find in the bucket labeled *Nails Still Good*. But Luigi regularly leaps the fence in his re-lentless need for human contact. That's when my father tethers a long rope between the two trees in the pen and clips his leash to that. He spends the first week winding himself around the trees and yelping for assistance.

My brother and I feel sorry for Luigi, and build a ramp up to an old oil drum from which he can survey the property and see the house better. This works so well we begin work on an entire jungle gym for him, until Hans drifts off-task and gets in trouble for nailing a long slanted board across the entrance of the septic lagoon and painting *Big Shitter's Ranch* on it in drippy, blue letters.

It takes my mother a few days to notice. When my father deposits two five-gallon buckets full of zucchini and beans at the kitchen door and hollers at her, "We must eat more zucchini!" she rockets into a nasty mood.

"*Vai al diavolo!*" she responds, but she's in the middle of kneading bread, so she can't chase after him.

My brother stands over the bucket, which, he mutters, is a buttload of zucchini, and shakes his head. "Jesus, Dad," he says. "The war. Is over."

I am certain he'll get slapped for this, but my father is already back outside, and my mother just says, "*Ma dai!* Don't be such a stupid boy."

Later she stomps down to the lagoon where we are playing with Luigi who is chasing the geese around the perimeter. Hans wants to see if Luigi can actually catch Fernando, a riot of irritation and flapping wings. We see our mother locate our father. He is grafting fruit trees, and her voice carries across the water as she makes a rapid slicing motion with one hand across the top of her head, shrieking, "I've had it up to *here* with your rotten zucchini."

It is at this moment that my father notices for the first time Luigi's excited barking. "Make that dog stop tormenting the geese!" he yells. Then my mother, just as quickly over her mood as into it, points to the sign on the lagoon gate and asks, "What does this mean, Big Sheeter's Ranch?"

My father wants to know what Luigi's and our problem is that we *insist* on *torturing* the geese. I point out that the geese are actually mean to us, they lower their heads and charge us when we're near the lagoon. Luigi is our bodyguard. But my father is mad at my mother now and insulted by her inadequate zucchini consumption. I try to lighten the mood and suggest maybe Mom can knit us all sweaters out of those yard-long Chinese green beans that are taking over the trellises. He reminds me there are starving children in Bangladesh and I am lucky to have food on my plate. Then he tells us, "Luigi will leave the geese *alone.*"

He's been touchy all week, since that mink raided the pigeon coop and bit the heads off all the pigeons without eating them. He drove immediately into town to look under the freeway viaduct for more pigeons that had fallen out of their nests. There were always some that needed rescuing. He buried the dismembered pigeons under his fruit trees while the new ones fluttered and flapped in a cardboard box nearby. I wondered if they could sense the mayhem that preceded them and if they were scared of more than being in a new place.

My father is strange about birds. We had pigeons in town, too, when we lived there, before the animal-control people suggested it wasn't exactly legal to build a coop in your backyard. We'd just gotten to where we'd named them and could tell them all apart. The beige one with the white flecks was my favorite. But the coop had to go. My father was going to have to take them back to where he found them.

I had gone to the pool for the whole day with Lori. We were walking our bikes back to her house at 5:00, even though we were supposed to be back by 4:30. Lori's mom didn't worry as insanely as mine did, and I could just call home when we got there to say I was on my way. As we were waiting to cross the busy street two blocks from Lori's house, we saw Pam, her older sister, standing perfectly still on the other side. Uh oh. They'd sent someone after us. We were in big trouble. But Pam just stood there, looking more past us than at us, her face as white as paste. I turned around to look, too. Nothing or nobody I knew was there. When we were right up next to her, I could see that her face looked more gray, like papier-mâché. Her eyes looked blank on the sides. She said very little. Lori was to come home immediately and I had to go straight to my house. Their older sister Debby had been in a motorcycle accident with her boyfriend and had been taken by helicopter to the university hospital in Omaha.

I knew enough to know that meant she was going to die. I rode my bike home so fast I thought I was going to throw up. Everything I passed that looked familiar wasn't.

When I walked in the door my mother hugged me hard for a long time. She already knew about Debby. She called me *tesoro mio*, followed by the Dutch word for sweet, but her pronunciation of it is a little off. Where there should be a gargly sound after the *s*, she can only produce a hard *c*, which makes it sound like she is calling me Scott. Tesoro Mio Scott.

That night even dinner smelled strange. There was a rich tomato sauce, and I could detect the garlic and red wine in it, but I didn't know what the smooth dark lumps were. They looked like mounds of mud, or the cases that Silly Putty comes in. We had liver often enough, but this wasn't that. My mother also frequently served other organs, like kidney ragout and sautéed heart, which I actually liked, but this wasn't that. I sliced into the small half-dome sitting on my plate, and the texture was something like rubber turkey. The flesh was dark as night. My mother kept wiping her eyes with her napkin and taking sips of her wine. When anybody asked her something she'd look up sort of spacey and say, "What, Scott?" She re-piled her peas into what looked like a replica of the displays of green apples at the grocery store.

I put a piece of the meat in my mouth, and it squeaked between my teeth, and resisted chewing. "What is this?" I asked.

My mother looked at my father.

"Squab," he said. "Eat it. It's good."

Rafaela looked at me funny. I looked at Hans. Uh oh. He was using both hands to shimmy his glass of milk back and forth. This would make the bubbles on top go away if you did it right. Hans liked his milk even on the top. He was being extra careful because if he sloshed there'd be trouble.

"*Basta,*" said my mother, "I can't eat this," and Rafaela's face flooded with relief. Dinner was over. The dishes were scraped into the sink. Food was *wasted*.

It wasn't until later, when I was waiting to fall asleep, that I asked my sister, "Is squab the same as pigeon?"

"Yes," she said.

"Then why do they call it squab?"

"Because it sounds better than sautéed mourning dove."

I twisted the satiny edge of my blanket around my finger. "I thought he said he was going to bring them back to where they belonged."

Rafaela was quiet for a while. "Well. I guess he thinks he did that."

My turn to be quiet. Blanket twisted. Sheet pulled up to just under my neck. "He always said a half-truth is worse than a lie."

Silence from the other side of the room.

"I can't believe he thought we could eat our own pets without knowing it."

Nothing. Maybe she was asleep. I could think of nothing else to say. I was stuck on the image of me with a piece of Enrico in my mouth. I felt like a cannibal.

We move out to the country and life slows down. It takes me longer to become a teenager than it did my sister. Even at almost thirteen, I am still playing with my Skipper and Twiggy dolls in my closet. Sometimes I put them in my beach bag and Luigi and I walk the mile down the gravel road to Kildeer Lake, which sounds like Kill Deer to me. I expect to find the beach littered with deer carcasses and coyotes smacking their lips, yanking back arteries that snap like elastics, but this never happens. Usually, I am the only one there. Luigi bounds around in the tall prairie grasses, and I shove my dolls' long skinny legs into the sandy lake bottom, which makes the same slurpy sucking noise I imagine quicksand does. Then I become the giant who saves all their lives. Sometimes I dig torture pits for the dolls and booby trap the bottoms with slivers of twigs, like the bamboo pieces Hip and Chip use. The unsuspecting dolls fall in, but they are never fatally wounded. Other times I fill the holes with silt from the lake's edge and pretend they are pockets of quicksand, but this never really works, because when I take part in the dialogue I can't be completely innocent. I already know the surface will betray them. This makes their escape neither difficult nor impossible.

Once Luigi comes up behind me with a baby rabbit in his mouth. "Drop it!" I scream, and he does. The rabbit lies either stunned or dead at my feet. Oh my god. I smooth its fur over its ribs, expecting to feel guts and blood, but suddenly it rights itself and hops in a wobbly line toward the grasses. "That was sick!" I tell Luigi. "You're sick! We're going home."

When I tell my father about it later he says, "What do you expect? He's a dog."

Hans has witnessed the exchange and follows me outside to watch me fill up Luigi's water pan. I can tell from his face that he has decided to see this situation more clearly than I can ever dream of. "Remember—," he begins.

I roll my eyes. "Not the tragedy thing."

He shakes his head. "Don't tell people your problems...ninety percent of them don't care, and ten percent are glad you have them."

I'd forgotten that one.

So now it's the end of the day, Luigi is dead and there is no conversation. None of this makes sense to me. It seems Luigi would have told me somehow if he was depressed. I feel desperate enough to consider any answer, so I ask Miss Psychology. "I just want to know, if a dog was really unhappy wouldn't he let somebody know?"

Rafaela sighs heavily. "Well, I just want to know if you're an imbecile. *Deficente!* That's Zoology, not Psychology. Dogs communicate nonverbally, since, you know, they're animals?"

I stare at her. She can't be my sister; she doesn't even look like me. "I didn't mean I think they can actually talk," I tell her. "You'd better watch it or I'll give you The Treatment." This is my ultimate weapon against her. It is my best-kept secret. I volunteer to set the table, and when no one is looking I lick her silverware, and it dries clear so she never knows she ate my spit. It makes her crazy not knowing what I've done. Right away she shrieks, "Mo-o-m!" but I go outside so she doesn't pursue it.

Everything looks the same but nothing feels that way. It's like I have to look at everything to make sure it is still there. I sit down on the deck and look under the bushes where the hose attaches to the house. It is always dripping. A daddy longlegs moves delicately up the hose, stretches over the leak, and reaches the brick foundation. Next to me is the space where Luigi would be if he wasn't dead. He used to let me lay my head on his back like a pillow.

I am starting to feel sleepy, and give myself the task of noticing the very moment when I switch from awake to asleep. I realize there is much that I don't know and little to be certain of. Luigi was alive this morning and now he is dead. The one thing I know is that dogs will put up with a lot of crap because they want you to love them. And then I am asleep.

There are no more dogs after Luigi. Moretto lives long after I graduate from college and move to Minneapolis for work. He goes deaf at seventeen, but is such a good mouser, nobody really notices. One morning my father steps into the garage, over the gift-carcasses of two field mice on the welcome mat, and raises the garage door, which has stopped working electronically. He taps the horn, a signal to my mother that he will soon be out in the driveway and she should lower the door against the cold. He turns the radio to the classical station and backs out.

It is the sound of Moretto's head popping under the car's back tire that makes him stop. My mother, still in her nightgown, wrings her hands together, and says, "*Dio Mio!*" over and over. "Oh my God!"

My father says, "This has nothing to do with God. He just didn't hear me." When my mother tells me that, I wonder about the pronoun reference. She goes on to say my father walked around in circles in the orchard muttering to himself until he decided to bury Moretto under the cherry tree. It is January again and the ground is frozen. It took him hours to smolder a small fire under the base of the tree, she tells me, and then hack through the snow and dirt until he could scoop out a small grave.

I am four hundred miles away, working in a treatment center for emotionally disturbed children. I am hearing all this on the employee lounge telephone. People are staring at me because I am not saying much into the receiver except "Jesus."

"He didn't suffer," my mother says, and I know she is talking about the cat. Still, I imagine how awful it must feel to be my father, even if it's an accident, to be responsible for the end of a life.

I tell my mother this and she says, "The apple, *quando casca*, rolls near the tree."

"Jesus," I tell her. "Look, I have to go. I have to work."

• • •

On my last day at the treatment center, before I move on to begin graduate school and the rest of my life, I help an eight-year-old girl prepare to go to court. She has to testify against a former foster parent who physically abused her sister. She is thin and pale, her hair dull from years of malnutrition, but she is fierce as she looks in the mirror. "Don't I have nice eyes?" she asks me and herself in the mirror.

I step in front of the light to peer over her shoulder and her smile broadens. There are both our faces in the mirror, but I look only at hers, those deliberate blue eyes.

"I like how those dark spots—" and she taps on the mirror to point to her pupils "—get bigger or smaller. Depends on the light."

"You're very smart," I tell her, and help smooth her hair back with a purple headband.

"It doesn't match," she shrugs. "But it doesn't matter." She cups her hands over the headband and steers her head side to side to see how she looks without it.

"Y'know, Michelle," I tell her, because I've been trained to do this. "It's all right to be afraid."

She looks surprised, her eyes unblinking. "Of what?" she says. "I don't have to save the whole world. Just me and my sister."

One month into my Reader Response Theory class, Beth, a classmate, asks me to watch her golden retriever overnight while she goes to retrieve an antique rocking chair from her grandmother's house in Madison. She will be gone only one night, she promises. There's not enough room in the truck for both the rocker and the dog. Sally is a good dog, extraordinarily mellow, like a piece of furniture, except that it yawns and needs to be let out to pee.

Sally is on the tail end—which is exactly what Beth says—of some medication for a tucked vulva. "I am not touching your dog's vulva," I tell Beth.

"Oh for god's sake, they're pills," answers Beth.

"Oh." I look at Sally, who is carefully licking her vulva. "Well, then I can smash them up in some ice cream, right? We used to do that with my dog Luigi's pills when I was a kid."

"You had a dog?" she asks, incredulous.

"Yes." I'm puzzled that she's surprised. "Didn't everybody? He committed suicide when I was twelve."

Beth stares. "You're shitting me. Suicide?"

"Yes. He hung himself. Jumped off the roof of his doghouse with the leash around his neck."

"Jesus…"

"I know. He didn't really seem depressed."

"Didn't leave a note?" she smirks.

"Funny." Now I'm annoyed. I've never understood why this is so difficult to believe. "Look, I am not lying. The dog offed himself."

Beth nods. "Okay. I've just never heard of that before." After class she decides there's room in the truck for Sally after all.

Two weeks later, Beth has to return the rocking chair to Madison because her grandmother has become depressed and Beth's mother, whose other grandmother killed herself, thinks the chair better come back lickety-split. "The chair," she says. "We need it back. Now."

Sally is over her vulva situation and I am allowed to watch her overnight. She accompanies me to my meeting with a nervous accountant who is paying me too much to edit a proposal he's written for a small business grant. He is thin and sinewy and I watch the muscles in his jaw flex and unflex like a rubber band over the corner of a box. Sally lies on the floor with her head on her paws and snores. His name is Kurt, but when I tell him, "You write in curt sentences," he doesn't laugh.

He says, "Can you fix that?" His eyes are cheerless.

"It's not all bad," I answer quickly.

After two hours of what turns into an autopsy of his prose, he gives me a check for $150 and says, "I couldn't have done this without you." He shakes my hand. Sally sniffs his ankles and we leave to walk the ten blocks home, my head still busy with the mistakes I didn't even touch.

Beth calls when she reaches Madison, just after I have had two glasses of wine and fallen asleep. The next morning she repeats for me the conversation I don't recall having. She says she asked how the dog was doing and I said, *What dog.* She said, very funny. I said, *Heh heh.* Where is the dog? she asked. *Stretched out along the foot of my bed, like letterhead in a large font.* You're letting her sleep on your bed? *Not on my bed, at the end of it by the footboard, and I didn't start out sleeping this way, there were thunderstorms.* Oh, said Beth, I forgot to tell you about the thunderstorm thing. *Uh huh,* I said. What is the dog doing now? she asked. *Sleeping.* How does she look? I whispered, *Her front legs are slightly curved backward and her hind legs are the same. It looks like the end of my bed is in quotation marks.*

I take to calling her Stationery Sally. I tell Beth to be sure and spell Sally's new name correctly. Stationery. With an *e.* Beth says I'm in danger of becoming freakishly obsessed with meaning.

A few weeks later, Beth's grandmother dies of natural causes, and the rocking chair gets to come back again. Sally and I look at each other. Sleepover?

This time the neighbors are having a loud party involving more cans of Miller Lite than I can count from my bedroom window, which faces their backyard deck. I'm tapping my foot on my footboard, along to Reba McIntyre, and it's midnight. Sally is equally bored. She keeps sighing and repositioning herself. Not very stationary.

For a while I try copying the dog. Head on left front paw, tongue sticking out to the right. Hind legs straight back, Ow, my pelvis doesn't do that, head under the bed. Reba gets switched for Wynona. Sally lifts her head up and bonks it on the rail. "Ow," I tell her. "Want an ice pack?" She puts her chin on my right paw. Wynona is loud. Someone turns her down a notch. Relief.

Beth calls to check up on us. "What're you guys doing?"

"Enduring," I say. "Here, listen to this." I put the phone up to the screen so she can hear the racket.

"We natives call that a hootenanny," she says. "They're not bothering anybody. Just shut the window, tune it out, and go to sleep."

I make her wait while I shut the window and get back in bed. Their voices, off key next to Wynona's, wrap around the west side of the house and come in that window instead. "Do you hear that?" I ask. "I couldn't sleep if you paid me!"

"What's the dog doing?" Beth asks.

I look over the side of the bed. Sally is lying on her side and has pulled a small blanket across her middle so that all I can see is her head and then her tail. "Sleeping parenthetically."

We are having a beer at the sidewalk café across from campus. Beth is reading the student paper, which, I tell her again, is an exercise in futility; there are always so many mistakes in it. "Did that accountant's check ever clear?" she asks me out of the blue.

"Yeah, I got that Sylvia Plath book with it. *Johnny Panic and the Bible of Dreams.* Why?"

She lowers the paper and watches my face before she begins reading.

"What?"

" 'Kurt Johnson, twenty-five, was found dead Tuesday morning of a self-inflicted gunshot wound to the head. His brother Kevin'—God I hate when people start all their kids' names with the same letter— 'told investigators he'd been depressed for some time.' "

I can think of nothing to say. Stationery Sally's tail is brushing the instep of my right foot. Beth's hair is glossy and blond. Kurt was not immune to tragedy. And now neither is Kevin. The sun is warm on my arm. At the edge of the table a sparrow is eating the blue corn chip we laid out for him. We are wearing the sunglasses we think make us look like Audrey Hepburn and Grace Kelly.

"Period, the end," says Beth.

A year later, Beth moves on to a PhD program and I rent a house with a large, fenced yard. I acquire a grad student, Jane, for the summer, who will live in the basement. Jane was my officemate Mary's roommate, but their apartment had been overrun by mice. "They're practically kicking back in the recliner and learning how to use the remote," said Mary. "Next they'll be squeaking in Italian. *Topi miseria,*" she added. She was heading to Italy on sabbatical in a week and she needed the whole crisis to be resolved in forty-eight hours so that she could practice her Italian in peace and have a good trip.

162

I offered to come over and set six traps under the sink where most of the poop, which looks like caraway seeds, had collected. "Jesus," I told her.

"Tell me about it," Mary said. "It's like a plague."

Two days later, two traps had either gone missing or walked off under their own power. "Okay, that's it for me. They can have the place," said Jane. "When do I move?"

I helped her haul her things over to my place. Jane has a schnauzer named Vif, which means *lively* in French, as opposed to *mouse killer.*

Everyone loves the dog. Jane loves the dog. My neighbor's children love the dog, although they think his name is Beef. They share all their food with the dog, including lollipops.

"Are you sure this'll be okay?" asks Jane. "You really don't seem like a dog person." She regards me suspiciously.

"You're probably right," I tell her. "But we'll see how it goes."

So this is how it goes. The dog is not mine and I do not love the dog. I feel obliged to love the dog, but I simply can't do it. He licks my legs after I put on lotion, eats my shoes, and does not come in when he's called. I have to be told to pat him on the head in the morning when he flings himself against my leg like a pogo stick, as I move in the direction of the coffee.

Jane says, "He just wants to say hi."

One day Jane is sick and taking codeine cough syrup. She stumbles out of bed to let the dog out at 6:30 a.m., falls immediately back to sleep, and forgets there is anything other than a dark world with no coughing. It is raining. Hard. I realize I'm going to have to be the one to let the dog back in and towel him off. Then I'll have to give him a treat to coax him into the kitchen while I put up the baby gate to block his entrance to the living room. I loathe this part. I loathe cajoling the dog. It irritates me beyond reason that the dog won't just do what he's supposed to do. I stomp my feet and hiss his name. He smiles at me and lies down under a lilac bush.

I go drink another espresso and hope the dog comes to the back door on his own. I listen for the percussion of his nails on my storm door. Nothing but the drumming of rain on the roof. This morning

Vif has decided to loll around in the yard and bark at nothing, like a hunk of beef with vocal chords. The rain lets up a little. I stand at the back door in the drizzle. "Vif!" He stares at me. "Vee-eef!" It appears he does not understand English. He cocks his head and looks at me as if he has never in his life heard his name. Never before heard me say, "Vif get off the couch, Vif, get off the table, Vif—*no*! Vif, are you insane, get off my bed."

So I leave the dog outside, figuring Jane will wake up soon enough and let him back in. I'm not five miles down the road and the sky opens up to release vats of rain, drops the size of hula-hoops on the asphalt.

Later that evening, Jane tells me she woke up at nine o'clock and frantically searched the house for Vif until she found him, drenched and shivering, under the maple tree. "He looked so sad," she says. "He could have caught his death of cold." Vif is sleeping in the chair in the living room next to the giant Style Me Barbie head I got as a gag gift on my last birthday. A decapitated doll as a pillow for a mindless dog. "Take a picture," says Jane. "Preserve the moment."

It is Jane and Vif's last night in the house before they move out. Outside it is humid and stormy. "We're going to die," she says, mesmerized by the incessant tornado coverage on the local TV channel. "Look, there's a red blob and two more behind it, heading right for us." I glance at the Doppler screen where the meteorologist is gesticulating, with large rotations of her arm, at the *affected area*. If it were a target, we'd be the bull's eye.

"Oh relax," I say. "We are not going to die. Just grab a beer and come look at the sky. It's really amazing." The clouds look like lava boiling, heading north at forty miles an hour. The lightning is horizontal and frequent. I have never been afraid of things I can see coming.

Jane's line rings and she goes to the basement to answer it. Vif follows her.

Thirty minutes later, the storms have passed, and she comes upstairs, her eyes red from weeping.

"What's the matter?" I ask, and my stomach tightens.

"My lover just broke up with me!" she begins. She yanks open the fridge door—"I need a beer. Or six."—and one of the racks inside the door breaks off. Condiments spill into each other. The floor is a lake of mayonnaise, pickle juice, and soy sauce. "Perfect, why don't I just shoot myself," Jane says. She stands at the edge of it, drinking the beer as if it's a long, liquid aspirin. Vif leaps up, grabs a plastic bottle of ketchup, and heads for the cream-colored carpet in the living room. "Vif, get back here," she says, halfheartedly, and reaches for another beer.

I want to be compassionate, but I'm also suddenly so full I feel like I need to be wrung out, not to mention I want to grab the dog by the neck. As a result, something like a two-lane highway comes out of my mouth. "*Vif!* Jane, I'm so sorry. *Give me that ketchup!* Did you have any warning? What was the reason? *Drop it!* You must feel so—stunned. *Are you insane?* Betrayed. *For god's sake, Vif!* How did you leave the *Get down!* conversation? *No!* Let me get you some kleenex. Do you want to talk about it? *No, off the couch.*"

I finally capture the dog before he punctures the ketchup, and plunk his writhing body outside so I can clean up the kitchen. Jane anesthetizes her breakup. I tell her two things I believe. One. You won't always feel this bad. Two. Feelings never killed anybody. As I say them, they sound so hollow they practically echo, and she nods in a glazed sort of way.

Beth is in town for a concert and staying at her sister's when she calls to tell me she has an extra ticket. I haven't seen her since Sally was put down after an unexpected and difficult litter of puppies. I remember Beth kept one and named her Smoochie. Smoochie is in the back bedroom taking a nap. Smoochie is only six, but in the last stages of liver failure, and Beth doesn't know what to do. When she wakes up, Smoochie comes loping down the hallway, dragging one paralyzed leg behind her, but wagging her tail. She is Sally reincarnated, and I take a step back without meaning to. Her tail thumps the carpet and she nods her head at us and smiles. The eighty-five pounds she used to be is at least half gone, says Beth. She looks like a radiator with a hairy rug thrown over it. I make myself pat her back and all I feel is bone.

We help her down the stairs so she can go outside. She shuffles onto the grass and pees on herself. "She can still go outside to pee," says Beth, and we help her back into the house. She lays a towel on the floor and Smoochie settles onto it.

During the concert I cannot focus on the music. I wonder if we will find Smoochie dead when we get back. I lean over Beth's sister and ask if we should have left the dog alone. Beth nods. "It's okay. She'll be fine." But as I lean back into my seat I see her look at her sister out of the corner of her eye. They both bite their lips. I chew mine until I've eaten off all my chapstick. Maybe we're not immune to tragedy, but another day or so of Smoochie's zest for life could make us feel invincible.

When we get back, Smoochie is at the door, tail wagging. We look at each other like bandits, as if we've just stolen one more day from the future.

In an unusual turn of events—unusual because neither of us ever really spur the other to loiter in Nebraska—my brother convinces me to meet him for the weekend at my parents' acreage. Amazingly enough, it is neither humid nor buggy. If we didn't know Nebraska, we'd think we could live here all the time. We sit out on the deck to have a glass of wine and relax.

I look down the hill and point to where the tire swing still hangs. Hans reminds me that rubber lasts forever. He says the tap water in the house still smells like *caca di galina* as it did when we were kids, and he shakes his head when my mother offers him ice for his water. "No chickenshit cubes for me," he says.

"Ach," she frowns. "Why do you insist on being so crude?" She claps his face in both hands and kisses him loudly on the cheek.

I wince. Hans winces. "Why do you always have to kiss me right *in* my ear? Now I can't hear a thing." He pulls on his earlobe and stretches his jaw.

My mother goes in to peel potatoes. "My, how you exaggerate!"

Hans looks at my father and wags his index finger at him. "I've told you a million times not to exaggerate."

Since when did they become such good friends? Did I miss something?

I can hear water running inside. The smell of rosemary and sautéed onion makes its way out the kitchen window.

My father suggests we walk down to the walnut grove so he can show us the no-till, organic garden he's just put in. "Cabbages the size of your head," he brags. Past the fruit trees, past the grape arbor, past Luigi's pen still there between the locusts. I ask under which tree Luigi is buried and my father says he doesn't remember. "Don't rub your eyes after picking those," he says when I touch the tip of a habañero to my mouth.

"Remember when Luigi killed himself?" I ask Hans. He is holding his wine glass in one hand and the herbs I've picked in the other. My father is guarding his eyes against the sun. He sets a five-gallon bucket near my feet.

"Luigi never killed himself," Hans responds calmly.

I look up. "Yes he did."

"No he didn't."

"Yes he did."

My father says nothing. There is not even a look on his face that indicates he heard us.

"I saw it for myself," I insist, and point behind me. "Up there." I can still see it. Luigi hanging. The rope rigid with weight, the color of sunlight not unlike today.

Hans is looking at me funny. "You saw Dad shoot the dog?"

"Dad shot the dog?" I echo. I am not looking at my father.

"Yeah."

Now I am. "You shot the dog?"

He waits for only one second. Then he nods. Just like that. And he looks the same as he always has.

"You shot Luigi?"

He nods again. "Not with a gun. With potassium chloride."

"You shot the dog?"

He nods and looks annoyed, as if he is pointing directly at something and I am unable to see it.

"But why?" This can't be right.

"He was killing the baby goats."

"I don't remember any baby goats."

"At the neighbors'. He was jumping the fence. He had to be stopped."

Hans shrugs, takes a sip of his wine. This makes sense to them. All of it does. "You don't remember the baby goats?" he asks, as if I've simply forgotten.

"How long have you known this?" I ask him. My stomach tightens.

He shrugs again. "Since it happened?"

"You knew *then*? And you never told me? We played Disneyland? Are you insane?"

"I thought you knew."

"How could I know? What I *thought* I *knew* was that Luigi killed himself. I *saw* him hanging at the end of his leash."

"No you didn't," says my father. "I had already buried him when you got home."

"No. I saw him dead, hanging from the rope."

"No you didn't."

"Yes I did."

"Well, he didn't die by hanging," says Hans. "The rope was just a restraint before the injection." He adds this like he knows.

"You knew this?" I ask. "You saw it?"

"Well, I didn't *see* it, but I know it happened."

They are both so calm, so nonchalant, that I feel like I am making this whole scene up in my head. Maybe if I ask them more questions and their lips move, I'll know I'm not standing here alone. "So why didn't you tell me the truth instead of letting me believe he committed suicide?"

My father's eyebrows go up and down. "I don't know. I didn't want you to get upset. Besides, the dog was responsible. You can't have that kind of disregard for life and stay alive."

"I'll show you where I moved the asparagus bed," he tells Hans, and they disappear around the mulberry tree, leaving the bucket for me to fill with whatever I want to take home.

There is no place for this in my head. That he murdered the dog, that I thought all along the dog committed suicide, that somehow these two parts of the truth are not supposed to collide, but rather make up the whole story, and *that's it then, it's over.*

I am unable to move. It is all so tidy and green. There are plants everywhere, as far as I can see, teeming with perishable food. I feel clammy and sweaty and like I'm going to throw up. But the biggest betrayal of all is not all this loud, rampant life nurtured by the carcasses of hapless animals. It's the quagmire of perception and memory; it's my own stunning inability to dismiss their points of view. Maybe it's time to stop absorbing everything, stop accommodating everyone's version of the truth, and simply assign meaning to my view of it.

"Careful with those peppers!" my father calls back, but it's just a disembodied voice. I can no longer see him from where I'm standing. It could be the wind through the walnuts for all I know. "All of them, even the bells, are hot!" it says.

During the four-hour drive back to Iowa I am listening to the public radio station at low volume, paying attention when I feel like it, digesting tiny pieces of information like snacks for my mind. When I hear that new research has revealed the average life expectancy for women in this country is eighty-three, I feel alarmingly old. I remember when eighty-three seemed ancient. Now it doesn't seem like enough, and forty can't possibly be considered middle-aged, can it? I wonder if I can remember everything from the first part of my life that I'll need for the next, and if I've paid attention to all the right things.

The announcers move on to the life expectancy of the sun. They are talking about the solar eclipse that will occur in about twenty minutes. Their voices orbit my head. I am driving with my sunglasses on even though it is partly cloudy, because if I take them off I squint; but if I leave them on it seems too dark. Either way, it may not matter. I'm not likely to notice any eclipse, unless I pull over and do that thing with the two pieces of cardboard.

I remember doing this for the first time when I was a child. I must have been about six, because we were still living in town at the time, and everyone on the block was going to meet in the middle of the street at exactly the right time to view the sun passing in front of the moon, or the moon passing in front of the sun. I can never remember which way it goes. I had my two index cards. One with the hole punched in it and the other just plain. My father must have told us fifty times to be sure we didn't look directly at the sun or we'd go blind like Galileo. I was so afraid of going blind I refused to go outside when everyone else was filing out into the street, and I missed the whole thing.

There is a rest area coming up and I pull over into the parking lot. I have fifteen minutes before the eclipse. This time I really want to see it; I want a sense of what it looks like, without blinding myself, if possible.

I look around the front seat for some white paper that is thicker than notebook paper. There is only the extra cardboard coffee cup the girl put around my hot chocolate this morning. I snap out the scissors on my Swiss army knife and cut the bottom off the cup, then cut the whole thing in half. In a few minutes I have two rectangles that look like small canoes with no ends. I sit on them carefully to flatten them.

During the shows of family vacations, while the slide carousels were reloaded, my brother and sister and I would make shadow puppets. We didn't always know what we were doing, but it was fun to see our fingers become animals' heads on the wall. Using my left hand as a model now, I draw a tiny profile of a dog's head on one rectangle. It is half the size of the nail on my pinky. I cut out the dog and check my watch.

The sun is behind me and I drop my glasses down my nose to see if I can notice any difference. Not yet. Trees, picnic tables, other people's cars, everything looks the same. I hold the card with the hole in it over the one that is solid, and I wait. It is a long two minutes. I consider turning my car radio on to get a countdown or something, but then I might miss it all, so I just wait. I realize time doesn't matter. I may still not be ready for whatever it is I might see.

Finally something about the air just *feels* shaded. I stare at the cards in my hand. There is the dog's whole head, bright white on the card.

And there, right in front of me, right as I'm watching, it goes half-dark. Or maybe half-light. Depends on how you look at it.

INTERVIEW WITH MARY GAITSKILL

Mary Gaitskill

by Sarah Anne Johnson

Mary Gaitskill's most recent book is the 2005 novel Veronica, *which was nominated for a National Book Award. She's also the author of* Because They Wanted To, *which was nominated for the PEN/Faulkner Award in 1998, the story collection* Bad Behavior, *and the novel* Two Girls, Fat and Thin. *Her stories and essays have appeared in the* New Yorker, Harper's, Esquire, Best American Short Stories *(1993), and* The O. Henry Prize Stories *(1998). Her story "Secretary" was the basis for the film of the same name. The recipient of a Guggenheim Fellowship, she teaches creative writing at Syracuse University and lives in New York.*

Photo credit: Joe Gaffney

Mary Gaitskill

Many of the writers I've interviewed were inspired to write by their early interest in reading. What drew you to writing fiction, and what did you do to develop your craft?

It's really hard to say what draws you to writing. Early reading had a lot to do with it. Even before I read or was able to read much, my mother read to us, so I had a very strong concept of stories. When I was six, when I first learned how to write, one of the first things I did was try to write a story.

Did you go to a writing program?

No. When I was in school, there were very few writing programs. I remember hearing about Iowa, but I had no interest in it. Now it's become something that people feel they have to do, which I think is very unfortunate. I taught myself to write by reading and writing a lot and by not showing it to people constantly. That's the thing about the writing program that bothers me, this idea that you need to show it immediately to a group of twelve people. They're not going to have a deep understanding of your work even if they spend the entire two years with you. It's very difficult to have a deep understanding of another person's work. It's a very intimate thing, how a story is working on the inside. It's very difficult to comment on that. All you can comment on is the outside.

I've worked very alone and very privately. In the past I occasionally showed things to people and they almost never liked them. When I was younger I was aware of writing groups, but I never wanted to do that, and I think it was good that I didn't. You really are alone when you write, and these groups give you the illusion that you're doing it with other people, and you really can't be.

Do you think the group detracts from finding your own way?

Not for everybody. Some people feed off the energy of a group—these people are typically the people who dominate the group. Ultimately, I think even they need to get out of the group at some point, but for a time it can be inspiring for that type of personality.

You've said that some of your favorite books are classics such as Ulysses *by James Joyce,* Lolita *and* Pale Fire *by Vladimir Nabokov, and the stories of Anton Chekhov. How does the work of other writers influence you, and how do you use your reading life to inform your writing life?*

I don't know the answer to that. I don't think that anyone does. Influence is completely indiscriminant. It's an unconscious process. I'm sure that I have been influenced in various ways by writers that I've loved, but I also think I've been influenced by writers I've read very casually. I've been influenced by trashy writers as well as by really great writers. I've been influenced by music, by things I hear on the news, by newspapers, movies, cartoons. You're influenced by almost anything you absorb. You learn from very high-quality writers but the learning doesn't take place on a rational level. Someone can point out how a writer is doing something and you can copy it, but it doesn't work. If you're a really good copier, all you're going to wind up with is a weak version of the superior writer's idea.

What reading great writers can give you, especially if you reread them, is a better apprehension of depth, which, again, is not a rational process.

Myla Goldberg also cited Pale Fire *as an influential book in that it experimented with form and was about the unreliability of memory. What draws you to the book?*

Its beauty mostly, its ridiculousness, its comedy, its poignancy in the sense that it's a story of misdirected love. It's about the sense of a beautiful dream world that shimmers under a prosaic and dull reality, and trying to find a bridge to that world through love or an ideal or a poem. There's a section that I always read to students, which is about a minor character. She's the girl that the narrator was forced to marry. She's not important at all. She shows up in one or two sections. He must marry her for social reasons even though he's not interested in women, generally. He won't have sex with her and she doesn't understand why not, and she becomes more and more despairing. There's this gorgeous section where he remembers the first time he told her that he didn't love her. She sinks down on the grass, and he immediately changes the subject. He says that in spite of his lack of love and interest in her in life, his dream life made "extraordinary amends." In his dream life his love for her exceeded in passion and tenor anything he ever experienced with anyone else. It's that strange misconnection with an imaginary connection underneath that's poignant and very true to human experience.

You've written short stories, novels, nonfiction articles, and essays. Do you feel more comfortable in one form or another? Rick Moody said that when he writes nonfiction he can then go back to writing fiction and feel refreshed.

There was a period of time when I really enjoyed writing essays. I haven't been interested in them lately. Something that really annoys me is when people try to interpret my fiction through what I've said in my essays, because they come from totally different places. Someone with the very strange name of "Wide-Even" very laboriously tried to unravel my fiction using things I'd said in disparate essays on a variety of subjects. At one point he said that I insist, through my fiction, on a fully sexualized society. I certainly don't need to insist on any such thing. We're already there, regardless of what I say about it.

An essay is a much more rational medium. I can say much more directly what I mean and hope that there's a minimum of misinterpretation. Usually people can understand essays better than they can fiction because it's a more direct expression of rational opinion. The relative simplicity of that is sometimes a relief. Also, I think it develops your skills even though it's a different form. Any kind of writing that you do is in some way developing your skills. You have to express yourself clearly in an essay just as you do in fiction, though the clarity takes a different form.

Novels and stories occur for every writer in different ways. Edwidge Danticat told me, "The stories come sometimes in one line or one scene. I've had many, many stories where I had ten pages and nothing was happening, and I put those away, sometimes for many years." How do your novels or stories come to you?

Similarly to what she was saying. I sometimes get an idea for a book or story with an image, or a single event, or a personality. *Veronica* was more about a personality through which I connected to the subjects of illness and mortality and beauty. It was a crude juxtaposition that had a lot of power for me—and I'm not using the word *crude* in a negative sense here. The novel I'm working on now started with an image of the weather being embodied in human form. I have no idea what it has to do with the book in rational terms. Before that, I was thinking of the book in terms of characters and how these characters would come into play with each other. But I didn't sit down to write until I got this image of the weather as people.

Danticat went on to say, "When you have nine stories together that are going to be a book, over the years you move away from them and they become different. There's a deepening that comes with time." When you gather stories together for a book, how do you see them differently? How do you make changes to accommodate the book?

I do see them differently. When they get into relationship with one another they take on a different meaning. Thus far I haven't made that many changes to accommodate a book—only one, really, which was in the last collection of stories. I took out one story because it repeated the circumstances of another story too closely and it was the weaker one.

When you're working on stories are you thinking about the collection?

What happens is that I start out just writing stories, but at some point when I have five or six of them, I do start thinking in terms of a collection. Then it can change because I start thinking about how these ideas work together or how they might be varied.

How do you arrive at an order for stories in a collection?

To me, the story that follows the previous story ideally is a story that further develops a theme or emotional tone in the previous story or turns a corner somehow.

Your collection Because They Wanted To *opens with the "Tiny, Smiling Daddy," a story about a man thinking back on his ambivalent relationship with his lesbian daughter. What drew you to exploring this father's point of view?*

That was a story that took a long time. I wrote it originally when I was writing the stories that went into *Bad Behavior*. The original version wasn't as developed. In that draft, the daughter hadn't written anything—there was a phone call that triggered him thinking about her, which was much less dramatic. I don't remember why I chose to write it from his point of view. In general, I think it can give a story a very interesting energy if you write from a point of view that you're not naturally sympathetic with or that's somewhat foreign to you. I

176

tell my students, if you're going to write a story from your real life, what can make it interesting is to write it from the point of view of someone besides yourself, ideally a person you didn't like.

The story ends when he remembers how Kitty told him she was a lesbian, and he screamed, "You mean nothing to me. You walk out that door, it doesn't matter. And if you come back in, I'm going to spit in your face." His wife was consoling him, but she slides away from him on the couch and he is left with the violent words in his head. What makes for a strong ending to a short story?

That one works because you get a feeling of remorse, but because of all the other thoughts he's had, his feelings are more complicated than that. He's someone who would have difficulty expressing them even to himself. He's had these feelings and thoughts, but they've created a lot of confusion for him. At the end it's allowed for him to see the contradiction between what he's said and what he actually feels.

In general, I'm not sure I can tell you what I think constitutes a good ending. I think often it's an ending in which the story is cracked open. I just assigned Flannery O'Connor's "Everything That Rises Must Converge," where you're seeing these very nasty, rigidly de-fined characters act out their personalities again and again. At the end a woman is knocked down and has a stroke, and the son falls apart. They are cracked open; they can't hold onto their characters anymore. There's a huge outpouring of emotion and dark mystery that's an in-tense contrast to the repetition and rigidity that went before. Another good ending is a scene that contrasts what the characters are saying and doing with what they really feel, or an ending where you finally get all the information about what's been going on with the characters and it opens up at the end. Or one in which the scope of the story is dramatically changed and you suddenly have an apprehension of another world totally outside that of the story, which may supersede the story—the end of "Signs and Symbols" by Nabokov might be described that way, or Chekhov's "Gusev."

Some writers write the entire first draft of a novel and then go back and revise, while others work through each page until it's perfect, taking their time reaching the end. Ann Patchett was the only writer I've interviewed who thinks a book out in her head and then sits down to write it out in a couple of drafts. What is your process like for writing and revising a novel?

I definitely don't think it all out in advance. I wish I could. Usually I get a basic idea. Sometimes the idea is more or less fully formed, like with *Veronica*. With *Two Girls* or the one I'm working on now, I have an idea for the ending. Typically, I have a basic situation and a thought for an ending, but I don't have any idea how to get there. I'll make notes in the margin about things I want to happen somewhere in the novel. Occasionally I'll write a scene without knowing where it belongs, but I know I want it there somewhere. That happened repeatedly with *Veronica*.

Veronica contains references to artists, music, the modeling business, and Paris, to name a few topics of interest. How much research did you have to do, and how did you go about it?

Most of the research I did involved the modeling world, about which I knew nothing. I was amazed at how different it was from what I pictured. In my original draft, before I did the research, Alison became a model when she was twenty-eight. That would never happen; that's when she would be quitting. A model starts her career between the ages of thirteen and eighteen, and realizing that changed things quite a bit. I talked to models. I read books written by models, some of which weren't bad. I read about the modeling industry. I talked to a photographer and a hairdresser who'd worked on modeling shoots. I went to a couple of shoots and a go-see.

How did you find all these things?

A friend knew a couple of the models I spoke to, and they introduced me to others. Once I knew them, I asked them if I could go with them to a photo shoot or a go-see.

Veronica opens with the main character's mother telling her children a fable about a little girl who gets carried away with her good looks and her good fortune. "Because I sat against my mother when she told this story, I did not hear it in words, only I felt it in her body. I felt a girl who wanted to be too beautiful. I felt a mother who wanted to love her. I felt a demon who wanted to torture her. I felt them mixed together so you couldn't tell them apart." The story that follows could be viewed as the narrator's attempt to sort out these aspects of her own life.

A friend of mine was disturbed by my use of that story. The story is a very old-fashioned fairy tale and, as such, it's very punitive. It takes a certain delight in torturing this girl. My friend was bothered by this, because she felt that most girls would want to be beautiful models, that this was only human. She felt that I wanted to punish the character in a puritanical way, and I can see how she felt that way. But I wanted to use the power of that old story and that old point of view, which I find to be very deep. It's true that it doesn't really allow the complexity of human beings as we've come to see it—a very forgiving and indulgent sort of complexity—but it is deep nonetheless. My friend was also troubled that I referred to Alison and Veronica as demons. But I hope it's clear that I don't mean them to be literal demons—all human beings could be said to be these demons thrashing around in their confusion and self-destructiveness. Sometimes it seems we're lost in ourselves and become lost in the world.

BookForum *said, "Veronica is a story that is dismantled into existence, as if the reader were examining a skeleton, bone by bone, without knowing what it was, how it connected, with only the vaguest sense of how it related to the human body." How did you arrive at the elusive, associative structure for the narrative?*

It was very hard. It was intuitive. I knew I wanted to blend the different time frames. I didn't want to divide the story into different sections with the past, the far past, and then the present where she's older. I wanted to blend them together. When people think deeply about anything, their minds dismantle time and see things together and I wanted to capture that feeling where things are happening all at once.

It's layer upon layer.

Yes, and the layers are shifting and changing places.

Did you have to pay specific attention to the transitions so that readers would know where they were?

Sometimes that happened naturally, and the line breaks were helpful. But sometimes I used words or images as cues; I'd repeat a certain word, but use it in a different context. Say, in the present I'd have Alison opening a metaphorical door with an image or thought, and then in the line break she'd be in the past literally opening a door. I could create a subliminal connection that way.

This is not a book that I thought would do well. I thought people would lose patience with the language and the moving back and forth in time.

What about the language did you think would bother people?

I thought people would think it was overly associative, that there was too much emphasis on the language. I thought it would be seen as too dense or metaphorical.

You've said that you wrote the first draft in 1992, and then didn't write for a while. What happened during that time, and how did you get reenergized to work on the manuscript?

I was writing during that time. I wrote the stories for *Because They Wanted To*; I wrote most of them after I put *Veronica* aside. I wrote a screenplay that didn't go anywhere, and I wrote other short stories, and I started this other novel, so I was doing quite a bit of writing between 1992 and 2001. Though I did go through a period of time when I wasn't writing very much. The years right after *Because They Wanted To* came out, between late 1996 and 2000, I wrote very little. I wrote journalism, but there was a year when I didn't write any fiction at all. I felt a kind of revulsion against fiction.

Did it freak you out?

Yes it did. I thought, God, I have to write, otherwise what else am I going to do, yet I hated it. I didn't want anything to do with it. There was a period of two years where I wrote only one story, and I didn't enthusiastically get into it again until four years later. I didn't want to write, not even journalism. Part of it was that I was changing and the way that I had written and the place I was coming from was changing. I was also going through physical changes, what they euphemistically call the "change of life." It was like the ground was shifting under my feet, so it was hard for me to write from a solid place. It's like I was used to looking out a certain window for inspiration, and I was trying to look out that same window and it was closed. It took me a while to find a different window to look out of.

When you started working on Veronica, *did you feel a new kind of energy? The writing feels heightened, as if you've experienced a breakthrough of some kind.*

It felt different even in 1992. I rewrote the original, but the actual images and the things I was trying to describe were the same. Even at that time it felt different, but it was very crude. What was different about it was that the emotions were much more raw and so was the writing. That's part of why I found it hard to go back into. At that time in my life, when I did a draft I worked meticulously and slowly so that when I went back to revise it, it was all there. With this book, I wanted to get the emotions on the page in a more powerful way. I didn't want meticulousness. I forced myself to write it really fast. I wrote about 125 pages in a year, which for me is very quick. The problem was that it was so crude that I didn't know what to do with it. I didn't have the tools to deal with the material yet. When I tried to revise it in 1994, I was using the voice and the style of *Because They Wanted To*, which is very different from that of *Veronica*, and it just didn't work. At least I had the sense to know that in the first thirty pages. The original draft was the seed of something that wasn't ready to flower until later, but I'm glad I wrote it down. I wound up using almost all of the material. I even used a lot of the material I did for the revision in 1994, because the ideas were there, I just hadn't found the right language.

The main character in Veronica *is Alison, a model, but readers don't get the glamorous story of a model they might expect. What drew you to writing about the ugliness and falseness inherent in the beauty industry?*

I've been in situations that people would consider glamorous, and it usually is mixed with ugliness and crudeness and competitiveness, so that seemed realistic to me. In the modeling industry, that contrast is heightened because it's very young girls thrown into a world that they know nothing about. I'm not saying that all girls who are models have the kind of experience that I describe Alison as having. That's a particularly bad experience. Some people do very well. A lot of it has to do with a woman's personality. Some women thrive in that atmosphere and have a kind of shrewdness that enables them to exploit the business more than it's able to exploit them. It depends on what kind of person you are.

But innately there's a lot of potential nastiness when it's very young girls being encouraged to focus on their looks as the most important thing about them. Nobody's saying it's the most important thing, but it's why they're there. It's all anyone cares about. There's talk about the model's personality being important, that you need to see their personality on their face, but the fact is that in the magazine pictures you don't see much personality in their faces. It's really not the point.

If you have vulnerable young girls encouraged to focus on something that is very temporary, when they lose it they're going to experience it as much more painful than most pretty girls in a different situation. It's also a very sexually charged atmosphere, particularly in Europe in the seventies and eighties. My sense in talking to people is that it's changed, but back then it was an environment that was a field day for predators. So the ugliness is there alongside the glamour.

This novel is infused with music. Alison's father plays music for his friends so that they might understand his feelings. "Time parts its shabby curtain. There is my father, listening to his music hard enough to break his own heart. Trying to borrow shapes for his emotions so that he may hold them out to the world and the world might say, Yes, we see. We feel. We understand."

It's the way I feel about music. I love music and it fascinates me as an art form because it can do things words can't do. You can have the illusion when you listen to music with someone or even with a whole crowd of people, that everyone is experiencing the music the same way you are, even though they're probably not. There's an incredible sense of unity, the feeling, real or not, that you're all in this current of energy in the same way that you don't get even if you read a book as part of a group and discuss it. Music is so much more direct and visceral. It's really physical. I'm envious of that and fascinated by it, and mostly I really enjoy it. I love the way it can describe so many things so quickly and with such nuance in a phrase of sound.

In describing Veronica, Alison says, "From a distance, her whole face looked askew, puckered like flesh around a badly healed wound." How do you arrive at these evocative details, and is it difficult to find the details that nail the most essential aspects of character?

An image will spring into my mind, then I have to search for the right words to describe it. Translating the visual picture into words is the real task.

At one point, Veronica says, "How do you think Stalin and Hitler wound up killing so many people? They were trying to fix them. To make them ideal. There's violence in that, hon." You do not idealize your characters, choosing instead to show their faults as well as their virtues. Do you agree with Veronica that there's violence in trying to idealize people, or characters or anything, for that matter?

I do. It's not murderous violence necessarily, but both Hitler and Stalin were after ideals that were impossible to achieve—ideals that at first blush were quite admirable. I hear something like it in the way that people talk about their health, mental or bodily. People think that if they eat everything right and exercise and take the right herbs and supplements that they're going to have perfect control over their health, mentally and physically. I try to take care of myself, too, but sometimes there's an obsessive, rigid quality that has a total lack of gentleness or respect, that wants to force the body and mind into this perfect instrument, which it can't be.

It makes me think of TV shows where stories are tied up in a nice neat little bow or end happily. It seems an idealization that becomes reductive.

Yes. I'm teaching a literature class and I'm having them read short stories from different eras. A lot of the stories have been quite unhappy. The characters die at the end or lose everything. One of the stories was from pre-revolutionary China, "The True Story of Ah Q." The man who wrote it was one of the first people to write in regular language rather than the Confucian style. Ah Q is a bum, a drunkard, and the other characters are shopkeepers or petit bourgeois. This drunk guy constantly gets in preposterous, ludicrous situations; he's an utterly ridiculous person. Then at the end he's arrested for something he didn't do and he's executed randomly. He's being wheeled through town in a cart. People are following, and he feels like he's being followed by a wolf pack. He tries to sing an operatic song because that's what criminals are supposed to do. He wants to gesture with his hands but they're tied. For the townspeople, it is a very disappointing execution because he doesn't sing anything. The students didn't want to read about this guy. They seemed to feel that reading about a bum was a waste of their time.

Veronica ends: "I will get something to eat at the Easy Street Café and talk to my friend who works there. I will take the bus home and talk to Rita, standing in the hall. I will call my father and tell him I finally heard him. I will be full of gratitude and joy." This reads like a prayer. How did you arrive at this ending for the story?

It seemed like what Alison would think and feel. The sadness is that it will be hard for her to live up to that attitude. In the previous paragraph, she thinks she's going to be like the little bird in the fairy tale, which spends its life giving to others—but there's a limit to how much she can give to other people because she's ill and she's poor and she's tired. At the same time, she's realizing that she can still give to the world in terms of small things. For that, it's not too late. Given where she's been and what she's seen, it's very possible that she would feel that way and want to change her life and give to people in the way that she's been given to by Veronica in particular. I've found that sometimes the people who have had the hardest lives have the most ardent, ideal dreams.

What advice do you have for new writers working on their first stories or novels?

Don't ask for advice.

Sarah Anne Johnson is the author of *Conversations with American Women Writers* and *The Art of the Author Interview*, both published by the University Press of New England. Her fiction has appeared in *Other Voices*. She is the recipient of a Jentel Artist Residency in Fiction, and she teaches The Art of the Author Interview in the MFA programs at Bennington College and Lesley University. www.sarahannejohnson.com.

VERY SHORT FICTION AWARD WINNERS

1ST PLACE

Janice D. Soderling receives $1200 for "Rented Rooms."

Soderling's bio is on page 186, preceding her story.

2ND PLACE

Natasha Singh receives $500 for "Seeing the World Whole."

Before my father lost his eye, he saw the world whole. His dreams lived along the lines of railway tracks; they were dressed in silver and traversed the arched back of Rajastan to Tamil Nadu.

Natasha Singh received her MFA from Sarah Lawrence College, and her writing has been published in numerous anthologies and select journals. She is a recipient of grants from the Canada Council, Ontario Arts Council, and the Toronto Arts Council. Natasha currently resides in New York where she is completing a memoir in essays.

3RD PLACE

Sali Dalton receives $300 for
"Uncle Willie, My Green American Eagle."

People say monkeys and parrots are similar in intelligence. Well, monkeys are dirty and destructive, and don't show affection like a dog, but manage to force you to love them like your own child. Parrots are different.

Sali Dalton tells us she was deceived into marrying her white African boyfriend upon his graduation from Stanford in 1951, and moving from the freedom of Steinbeck's California to a land ruled by the Old Testament, where women were chattel and slavery a way of life. She says Joan of Arc's spirit enabled her to fight against Apartheid, spousal abuse, freedom fighters, the police, and jail. After she was forced to leave in1979, her farm people haunted her dreams, demanding she write about their lives of witch doctors, extraordinary animals, and a haunting love that broke the rules. The author now lives in Tampa Bay, Florida.

---

*We invite you to visit **www.glimmertrain.org** to see a list of the top twenty-five winners and finalists. We thank all entrants for sending in their work.*

*The United States was nearing the end of the
Great Depression of the thirties. Hard times.*

Janice D. Soderling was born in the United States, but lives in Sweden. Her work
has appeared in significant literary magazines in seven countries, and her poems were
twice selected for the *Anthology of Magazine Verse & Yearbook of American Poetry*. Janice
keeps a roof over her head as a self-employed writer/translator for academic, scientific,
and high-tech business spheres.

RENTED ROOMS

Janice D. Soderling

There is a succession of rooms, all of them temporary, as life is temporary. Some of them, many of them, are filled with laughter, with friendship, with affection, with hope. People gather around a table sharing the moment's contentment, the latest gossip, the last slices of cake, picking the crumbs from the platter, delaying the fading of a day that no one wishes to relinquish. Pink and crimson stripes melt across immense clouds, pour into the hollows of evening.

A woman in a worn apron lifts its bib over her head, begonias bloom in terracotta pots on the window sill: a fluttering white curtain, the dishes stacked in the sink, waiting. Hands touch as chairs are moved closer, scraping against the floor, a sound that makes the room seem a permanent place even when the sun is declining, even when good-byes must soon be said.

Sounds accumulate in the pockets of a new day; someone beating a carpet with rhythmic, desperate strokes; small particles of dust fly like frantic gnats. Someone is hammering nails to build a staircase. There is the dull slam of a car door, the sound of angry wheels grinding in the gravel as a car pulls away. Dogs bark in the distance, warning strangers. Birds chirp and ruffle their feathers, waiting for rain.

In the bedrooms, the many bedrooms, the best and the worst is enacted.

A room like a gray-walled cell, the bars are built into the mind, as is the gloomy damp, the concrete floor. Sleep brings fitful, cold dreams, a death-like touch. A woman and a man wake on opposite edges of the bed and avoid each other's eyes; grim-browed, they pull on their clothes without speaking. All their words have been used up.

Other rooms, other nights, where the darkness is pried open by a flickering candle and illuminated by the meeting of bodies. A woman sits astride the man she loves; they move easily as fish swimming, hair brushes across skin; mouths, tongues, fingers, sweet-flowering genitalia find the spaces waiting in the soft half-shadows. Love, the magician, love, the great illusionist, the healer of all wounds, strokes the heart, creating and re-creating the reasons to go on.

A fire is lit in the fireplace, silent flames flicker and shift; there is the thud of a log plunging into gray-toned ashes. The fire dies down, darkness slips in under the door.

A slatted crib, a folding cot. A child whimpers in fever. The mother carries it in her arms, rocking it as a lifeboat rocks its passengers. She sings a lullaby, low-voiced, unceasingly. She sings to ease the child's pain, an incantation to absorb its suffering into herself and free the small, scorched body. Later, turning the pages of a calendar, she weaves tales of distant kingdoms and armored knights on horseback, wizards and queens and the pot of gold at the end of the rainbow. The tooth fairy, she says, will come in the night; it does come, leaving a coin in exchange. Other presents, other surprises, equally wondrous, fall from her hands cupped like a miniature cornucopia: brightly painted Easter eggs are stacked in a woven basket; there in the toe of a Christmas stocking is a rough-skinned orange, walnuts, and peppermint candy. Gifts from the overflowing heart, from the thin purse. Gifts of love. The child, the children, grow tall and go away to inhabit other rented rooms.

We crowd our rooms with objects, planning to stay there forever. Promises, pledges, empty boxes waiting to be filled. Oh, the items we collect to make it all seem less destitute, to fetter ourselves, and someone else. Ropes, chains, invisible knots. Shiny knives gleam and glitter, the blade of an axe cleaves the firewood, splits the head of the sacrificial animal. Steel guns are loaded. Words eject like bullets, hard and heavy; the damage they do can never be completely repaired.

Doors open to other doors and to the worlds outside. City sounds. The steady hum of traffic on the street below, a siren wailing like a banshee, like a woman abandoned. Water gushes from a faucet into a dingy hotel sink; there is the whir of an overhead fan, or of myriad-eyed flies looking for open sores. A knock on the door. The rent falls due. Again.

A circus comes to town, a brass band, a gaudy parade. The arena is populated with clowns rolling their sad, painted eyes; with collared dancing bears lumbering to the sound of a barrel organ, bald, mangy patches scarring their fur. The flippers of trained seals continue to applaud the little poodles walking upright as long as they are able.

"I was there," people say, awed, like travelers returning from a holy pilgrimage, like refugees from a theater of war. "I saw it all. I stayed until the very end. You can never know what it was like."

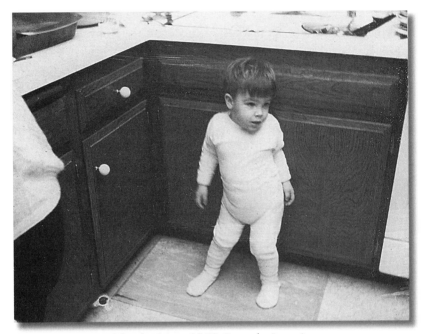

Thanksgiving, 1968. Love the jammies.

Andrew Roe's fiction has appeared in *Tin House, One Story*, and *Opium*, as well as the *Glimmer Train* anthology *Where Love Is Found: 24 Tales of Connection*. His book reviews and articles have appeared in the *New York Times*, the *San Francisco Chronicle*, Salon.com, and other publications. A Pushcart Prize nominee, he lives in Oceanside, California, with his wife and son.

PLEASE DON'T TELL ME THAT

Andrew Roe [signature]

Andrew Roe

The dream was about horses. I was riding one. At least I think I was riding one. Because really, what I remembered most later, right after waking up, during that fuzzy but somehow also kind of clear spell of time when dreams are still picture-fresh and haven't started to run away from you yet—what I remembered most about the dream was this: the feeling of movement. There was the wind pressing against my face, the soft coolness of that. And my body rising up and down. And closing my eyes. And then with the wind again as I seemed to go faster and feel lighter, all without having to hold on to anything. It was perfect. And then, finally, forgetting my name and who I was and all the things that were piling up and not going away. But it all stopped suddenly, a rope pulled me back, back, because my brother, Ryan, has apparently hit me. Hard. Twice.

"Get the fuck up," he says, pounding my shoulder a third time just because.

Ryan is older, fourteen as of last month, when he announced that he would be spending his birthday with his new high-school friends and not his family. Recently, too, he decided that cursing makes him cool. And who knows. Maybe it does. I wouldn't be the person to ask.

Still cloudy headed, still pasty mouthed, I mutter something back to my brother. Not words really, more like caveman moans. The idea behind the sounds, though, is pretty much *Hey, what gives, what's going on.* Ryan understands. More and more we don't even have to speak

Glimmer Train Stories, Issue 64, Fall 2007
©2007 Andrew Roe

to communicate. It's mostly our faces and our eyes and the way we nod or point. And that's usually enough. He's my brother, and I know him better than I know myself. We share a room, a bathroom. And, of course, our parents. We know things that no one else in the world knows.

"Dad," he tells me. And that's all he has to say.

But there's one last thought before Ryan rips off the blankets and calls me a dork-wad and I have to admit defeat: can you close your eyes in a dream, can you fall asleep in a dream, can you know that you're both sleeping in your bed and also sleeping in your head?

It's strange being awake this early. Everything seeming different because on any other day you'd be asleep and unaware right now. The alarm won't go off for another hour at least, and the world outside is dark and quiet and unknown. People still sleeping or maybe rolling over, taking showers, spraying on deodorant, zipping zippers, doing whatever it is they do in the morning. Except, I guess, people who live in different time zones. To them it's later in the morning or afternoon or even at night, their day might even be over, those people across the oceans in places you see on maps and globes but which still somehow don't seem real.

I start getting dressed, my clothes cold from the night before, which I hate, which means I'll never be warm all day. It's Tuesday. Tomorrow is Wednesday. I listen, but there's nothing. Which is weird. The silence. No TVs, no dishes, no doors. And no Ryan complaining about this or that, or me being told that I pay attention too much. It's rare, the quiet now, like finding a quarter in your pocket that you forgot about, and if it wasn't for my brother digging like a dog for a pair of clean socks I'd be able to almost enjoy it.

Secrets are hard to keep in our house. That's because you can hear everything from everywhere. And that's because it's mostly empty and there's not much furniture, and so sounds echo through the rooms and down the halls and up the stairs. We're renters, is the thing. We don't own the house, it's not actually ours, and everyone in the neighborhood seems to know this. Because our lawn is brown. Because we don't have a barbecue in the backyard. Because the leaves never get raked. People walk by with their dogs on leashes and their babies in strollers and instead of saying hello they smile without showing their teeth.

But I remember the first day we moved in, six months ago, and how it was this big deal, moving from an apartment where not all the windows opened to a house—a house!—where you had to walk outside to get the mail. Even though we couldn't afford to buy what the house needed, what would make it more of a home, we'd go from room to room, excited by all the space, the possibilities there. My parents talked more, watched movies together. Ryan and I tried harder, too.

It didn't take long, though, before our new life felt like our old life, with just a different place where we slept. Once we were sort of settled in, the neighbor ladies with the hair and nails brought us casseroles and cold-cut platters. They looked around: Where was the fluffy sofa? The dining-room table and matching chairs like so? The glass cabinet with snow globes and sports trophies? The framed pictures of kids who get straight A's and make their beds without being told to? We had none of that stuff, just the basics, what you could pack in a rented U-Haul trailer, our dad's truck, and our mom's Nissan Sentra. They looked and looked and looked but didn't find what they were looking for. They asked what kind of mortgage we had. My parents were melting, their bright future slipping through their fingers like sand. Ryan burped. The ladies didn't come back.

Just as I finish tying my shoes (they're tight, I'll need another pair soon but I haven't said anything yet), Ryan buzzes past me and says, "Move it, ass-dick, let's go."

And so we barrel down the stairs like firemen who just got a call. I ask Ryan for details about what's happening, and he says shut up and mind your own beeswax, jizz-head, and I say come on, and he says all right: "Dad shows up and I'm like dead asleep and he wakes me up, he keeps shaking me until my eyes open, and I'm like what? He's got the breath, okay, and but he tells me to wake you up, too, and to then meet him in the truck in the garage, pronto, in five minutes, which was like five minutes ago already. There. Satisfied, Sherlock Holmes?"

From the kitchen comes the tired rumble of the truck's engine. And then there's nothing to do except go into the garage, and there's our father in the front seat, waiting. We squeeze in, squeeze together, the three of us, and try not to look at him, but we do anyway. His eyes are red and puffy, and his mouth is open like he's just heard something he can't bring himself to believe. He hasn't shaved. His whiskers seem sharp, sharpened, like they could cut your fingers if you touched them for too long. Basically he looks like he's been up all night. Which he has, I guess.

I notice the car doesn't have much gas, maybe an eighth of a tank. I don't say anything, but I'm worried. I don't know where he's taking us. Or why.

For just a moment, a blink-and-you-forget-it-before-you-even-know-it one, as we're backing out of the driveway and onto the street that's our street, technically, but has never really felt like our street, I think that maybe he's kidnapping us. But since nowadays he usually didn't want much to do with us, why, I wonder, would he go to all the trouble and risk of going to jail and winding up on *America's Most Wanted*? It doesn't make sense.

He stops the truck. We're not moving. Ryan and I look at each other, then at the house, out there in the dark and cold, no lights on, and with our mother sleeping inside.

He says, "You guys have never seen where I work, have you?"

We both shake our heads: no.

The walls are thin. I walk in on conversations. My mom calls her sister practically every night. I don't sleep well. Plus how sound travels, the echo effect. This all means, then, that I know more than I probably should. Ryan, he doesn't listen as much as I do. Especially now that he's older, wants a guitar, has touched girls behind the Circle K on Lincoln Boulevard.

"What's the point?" he likes to say. "What's gonna happen is gonna happen either way, the folks are the folks, and I'll be outta here when I'm outta here, so what the fuck?"

And I guess he's right.

First side streets. Then the freeway, where there are only a few other cars, all with their headlights on, two white beams pulling them forward against their will. I watch them as they pass or we pass. The people inside hold their giant lidded cups of coffee and take long slow sips like they're drinking a secret potion that makes them live forever, or at least longer. Their hair is still wet from the shower and they check themselves in the rearview mirror. They sip and stare. I imagine they all have their radios going. The news. Traffic. Weather. Sports. The voices of men and women who tell you about the world.

As he drives, my father has a toothpick in his mouth. This is normal. More often than not there's a toothpick between his lips. Now he scrapes his teeth with it while his other hand rests on the bottom part of the steering wheel, the way he always drives, like he's barely controlling the car. When he's done working his teeth, he sucks on the wood, switches it from one side of his mouth to another, as if he can't decide which is the better place. Then, sticking with the right side, he lets it dangle there. It's so familiar that without a toothpick his face seems wrong. When I picture him it's always with the toothpick, a small pointy weapon that's part of his mouth, a warning.

My mom hates the toothpicks. She tells him use some floss, it's gross. He tells her he likes the old-fashioned things, if it was good enough for his father, then it's good enough for him. And every time she finds a soggy toothpick on a table or counter or even the floor, she holds it up, like evidence, as if saying, "See?" and then throws it in the trash.

He changes lanes, then changes back when the car in front of us is going too slow.

"Aren't you guys excited?" he says. "You should be excited. But you don't look excited. Don't you want to know what your father does for work, where he goes every day?"

We did. We definitely did. We only knew that our father worked in an office and wore a shirt and a tie and slacks and his blue windbreaker, and pretty much everybody there was stupid except for him and this one other guy, Donald, who came over to the house once and broke a lamp. But we were silent. We were stone. We were TV sets without the sound on.

"Come on," he keeps going. "This'll be fun. I know it's early, but Christ. Perk up already. Show some enthusiasm for your old man. We're the men here. Just the men. This is what I do every day. Make this drive. Look out at this road, these streets. Count down the minutes until I get there. Ten. Nine. Eight. How many miles are left. Getting closer and closer. And I'm not doing this for my health, you know. If it was up to me…God, you guys are thick. What am I going to do with you?"

He looks over his shoulder and changes lanes again.

Ryan is a better name than Steven. I've given it plenty of thought over the years, and I'd take Ryan over Steven any day. But that's not the way it worked out. I'm Steven. Ryan is Ryan. That is something that isn't going to change. Even if, when I get older, and I do all the legal stuff you have to do to officially change your name, I'd still know, deep down, underneath the new car shine of Keith, of Kyle, of Tyler: I'm Steven.

And Ryan would always be older, too.

Now there's Tony Pennisi. Now there's Rory Hines. And Charlene Moorehouse, with her tight shirts that show off her navel ring. They call. They come by. They leave and go places. Ryan is home less and less, and I want to be gone, away, too. Instead I stay in our room, reading the books I check out from the library, finishing one and then picking up another, thinking of what I'd be doing if Ryan were there.

Ryan says there's things I don't understand, that I'm still just a kid. His world is getting bigger. And mine, it seems, is getting smaller.

We reach the right freeway exit and now there's some light in the sky, cracks of color here and there. Every now and then I look at the gas gauge and worry. We go on one of those streets that seems to repeat itself every few blocks: gas stations, Home Depots, Taco Bells, Burger Kings. After that some apartments or a storage place or a used-car lot, and then the same scene all over again.

"I'm hungry," I announce. It's one of those things where I hadn't planned on saying anything, it just came out on its own.

"It's not even light yet," my dad says, and then makes a fist with his right hand and blows into it several times; the heater in the truck only half works. When he's done, he goes on: "Who gets hungry this early? Usually you'd be asleep right now. How can you possibly be hungry?"

"Well I am is all," is what I say.

Right then we happen to be passing a McDonald's, big surprise. I can tell he's in one of those moods where he's too tired or too distracted to argue. So he turns into the drive-thru. The voice from the speaker where you order is all *wah-wah-wah* like the teachers in Charlie Brown.

Me, I get Chicken McNuggets. Because that's what I always get at McDonald's. With barbecue sauce. Ryan orders two sausage McMuffins and a large fries. My dad: coffee plus a hash brown.

"Don't eat yet," he instructs us. "It's not much farther. Just wait."

So we wait, the bags of food on our laps. The bags are warm. We can smell what's inside. Suddenly, though, I'm not so hungry anymore. It's another one of those things: You think you want something, then you get it, then you don't want it anymore. It loses something between the wanting and the having.

"I feel like I'm always failing you somehow," he said one time.

They have these conversations that are really the same conversation over and over, with different words but the same meaning.

I'll be in my room reading, listening.

"Please don't tell me that," she said back. "Please. I don't want to hear it. I don't want to know."

The parking lot is empty. In front of us is the place where my dad works. It's one of those buildings where the windows are black on the outside so you can't see in. Next to it are two other buildings exactly the same. There's grass and plants and trees and flowers. Everything wet from the night before. The asphalt, too.

Andrew Roe

Like I said before, we know our father works in an office, and that also he complains about having to be there all the time. Other than that it's pretty much up to our imagination. Work is just a place he goes, like we go to school, you don't have a choice about it. When he comes home and plops down on the couch or drags himself upstairs, we all know to let him be, to let him settle in before we say anything. Sometimes it's five minutes. Sometimes it's longer.

Still, I'm curious. About what he does all day, what he says to other people and what they say to him. In movies and TV shows I keep an eye out for anyone who acts like him and dresses like him so I might get some clues. "They forgot the fucking catsup," Ryan announces. And Dad just shoots him this look like: That's my territory, don't even think about it, bub. Ryan gets quiet, eats, licks his fingers like he's in a commercial.

It's silent then as we sit and eat in the truck. The smell of the food is heavy: the chicken, the barbecue sauce, the McMuffins, the fries. It's hard to think of anything else but the smell. My dad isn't drinking the coffee because it's too hot. He takes off the lid and the steam rises up and mixes in with his breath, which I can see. It's that cold.

And then my dad says, "I wanted you guys to see this. It seemed important a few hours ago, earlier, back at the house. For some reason. For some reason it seemed important. I had something I wanted to tell you, too. But now. Now I don't know. It's just a building. It doesn't mean anything…"

And his voice trails off, drifts away. The thought dies. He stares down at his lap like he's maybe searching for it, the thought. I try to think of the times when we have actually looked each other straight in the eye, longer than just a glance, the smallest recognition before moving on.

We eat some more. Ryan scarfs. But I'm going slow. Like I said, I'm not even hungry. So it's eating just for show. Because I wanted it and now I have to follow through. Not eating would be admitting I couldn't finish what I said I'd wanted. And there is always the possibility that this would not go unnoticed.

He starts again with: "This is it, though. This is where I come, every day, day in, day out, rain or shine. Right here. Where we are right now.

I drive, I park, I walk. I take the elevator or sometimes the stairs if I'm feeling a certain way. The same people, the same faces…"

Only he's not talking to us. He's talking to someone else, maybe my mom, maybe just himself, maybe Jim Morrison, who he's always listening to and who my mom says my dad kind of looked like when they were younger and he had long hair down to his shoulders. But he's definitely not talking to Ryan and me.

He's still going: "But when you stop and think about it, what I do, what I'm doing, not just work but more than that, the bigger picture, the facts of it, the grand scheme of things…"

Ryan farts, something he can do, magically, whenever he wants. We wait for a response. But it doesn't come. Our farts, our fighting, our fears—he's a long way from all that now, it seems.

"This…"

My father shakes his head. This what?

He's digging for the words, the right words. I'm thinking that he might get there if he keeps going. It's like he's about to break through. But then, no. He stops, pulls back. The words are gone, lost in his throat.

"Your grandfather, my father," he backs up, starting over, "he worked with his hands. With his hands. He helped build homes, buildings, things that mattered." I watch him stare ahead, at the office where he worked. "Me, what do I do? What do I do? I process claims forms. I get paper cuts."

He looks at his own hands, like they have let him down, one of many disappointments he's had to live with.

"This is stupid," he finishes, firing up the engine. "This is fucking stupid. This isn't working. I don't know what I was thinking."

Then a pause. He picks his teeth again with the toothpick. Then a little later, after the toothpick has been tossed on the dashboard: "Look. I don't expect you guys to understand this. This is all way over your head. It's complicated. I remember when I was your age, or ages, where I was at then. There's only so much you're capable of absorbing. You're kids still. But things happen. Things change. People have their reasons, okay? People do things. It's just the way it is. And sometimes, most of the time, you don't even know why they did what they did, not until a long time after. Way down the road. And even then, when it's way later, when years have gone by, sometimes you don't know even then, not ever. You just don't know."

And that's it. He stops. He doesn't say anything else, though for a while I think he might. So we finish eating, crumple up the bags, and drive back home. Above us, the sky continues to come to life.

The gas, I want to tell him. We should get gas. He won't make it back to work, no way. But I keep quiet because I know sometimes that's best.

When we get home my mom is up, freaked, saying she was worried like crazy, she just woke up and everyone's gone, what was she supposed to think. Her hair is all tangled and wild and sad, and there are places where it's no longer blond, patches that are not cooperating. Cigarette smoke sits in the air. She was just about to call the police. Good thing we got back when we did.

"Where were you?" she asks him, not us. But he's walking, in motion, not stopping to make this a full-blown conversation.

"Out," he says. "Out in the world. I wanted to show them something."

"I was worried. First you don't come home till I don't know when. Then I wake up and the boys are gone. I know you've been home at some point because of the empties on the kitchen table and the toilet not flushed. So what—what was I supposed to think?"

But that's it; he doesn't say anything back, just continues his march through the kitchen and heads upstairs, and then we hear a door closing. The sound echoes and the three of us stand there and listen to it until it fades and is gone.

School hasn't started yet but it will soon. I get the sense that this could be one of those days where we don't have to go and my mom writes us a note. She's good at writing notes. They're very detailed. Sometimes she even looks stuff up in medical books to come up with new illnesses and viruses. The people at school seem impressed by this. Is your mother a doctor or nurse? they asked once. No, we said. What does she do? Silence. Should we or shouldn't we? Ryan took care of it. She works at Photo Barn, he said. Then they were like: Oh, I see.

"What about school?" I ask.

She's pacing in the kitchen in her ratty old-lady robe (she's got a brand-new one, leftover from Christmas, but she's never worn it), the pack of cigarettes showing through the front pocket like always. But she's not smoking. But thinking about the next cigarette, you can tell. And you can tell this, too: She'd also been up for most of the night. On her face is the blurry mask of someone who hasn't slept. That, plus the idea—stretching across the forehead, curling around the mouth—that there's some kind of decision being made. Right now. At this very moment. Her eyes are narrowed, focused, like a pitcher eyeing the outside corner of the plate. Her face says, is saying, whatever—it says she's moving from one thing to the next. Today, tomorrow—they will be different. Maybe. Because, you know, I've seen the look before. It doesn't necessarily last.

"What?" she says.

"School," I repeat. "It's starting soon. Are we going?"

"Go upstairs," she tells us. "Both of you. Now. I'm thinking. I'll let you know. I'm thinking."

Upstairs in our room, and right away Ryan dive bombs onto his unmade bed.

"This is fuckin' bull-twat," he says into his pillow.

I'm not sure what he means: our parents, getting up early, driving to my dad's work, not going to school. Or maybe none of the above.

I want to tell Ryan the dream about the horses but I'm pretty sure he'll say dreams about horses are for wusses—fuckin' wusses. So I don't.

But I think about the dream again. In fact I try to relive it as I lie down on my bed and close my eyes. I try to get back to that place in my mind when I'm moving and the wind is in my face and things haven't already happened yet and the world spins and shines just for you. It's a long, long time before I open my eyes. And when I do I look out the window. I see that the sun is up and it's completely light outside and I'm only a little bit afraid. 🏇

Here I am with my grandfather, looking. At what, I don't know. Maybe a car wreck or maybe a vast body of water. Something that makes my mouth hang open. I chose this picture because of the way we're aligned, the old man and the young man, like some reflection off a magical mirror that tells us where we're going, where we've been. Though my grandfather appears serene, he was in fact a fiercely intelligent, wildly cantankerous man. In all of my memories he is talking. He had so many stories to tell. And when he told them he would shake his finger and smack his lips and rock in his rocking chair with such force that I sometimes worried he might topple over backwards. I still hear his voice, raspy and excited, bouncing around in my head, working its way into my fingers and then my keyboard.

Benjamin Percy is the author of two books of short stories, *Refresh, Refresh* (Graywolf, 2007) and *The Language of Elk* (Carnegie Mellon University Press, 2006). His fiction appears in *Esquire*, the *Paris Review*, *Best American Short Stories*, *Chicago Tribune*, and many other publications. His work has been read on "Selected Shorts" on National Public Radio and his honors include the Plimpton Prize and the Pushcart Prize. "The Caves in Oregon" will appear in his most recent collection.

THE CAVES IN OREGON

Benjamin Percy

This afternoon, a hot August afternoon, the refrigerator bleeds. Two red lines run down the length of it—and then a third, a fourth—oozing from the bottom lip of the freezer. This is what Kevin finds when he returns home from his job at the foundry and flips the light switch repeatedly without success, when he stands in the half-light of the kitchen and says, "Shit."

Already he can smell it, the blood. And when he draws a steadying breath he imagines he can taste it, too—the mineral sourness of it. He is a big man—a man who spends most of his days with his hands taped, swinging a fifty-pound sledgehammer—and he must bend his body in half to observe the freezer closely. The seal of its underside has gone as red as a tendon. Little droplets are gathering there, swelling fatly, and then, too heavy, they fall and race for the floor.

Right then he hears Becca, her car grumbling up the driveway, as she returns home from the community college where she teaches. He hears her keys jangle, her footsteps on the porch, in the hallway. She calls out his name and he says, "In here," and she begins to say something, something about the garage door failing to open, her voice cut short by a sharp intake of air when she sees the bleeding fridge.

"Power's out," he says, and she gives him a tight-faced look as her teeth take tiny bites from her cheeks.

"I just got home," he says. "Like, five seconds ago. I was just about to start cleaning."

She drops her keys on the counter. Against the Formica they make a noise like bottles breaking. Her voice is a coarse whisper when she says, "Wonderful." She leaves him in the kitchen, her high heels clattering down the hallway. He can hear her burrow roughly through the closet, and a moment later she returns with an armful of beach towels. She throws them down at the base of the fridge and tells him to get the cooler.

"The cooler?"

"Yes, the cooler," she says, with more than a little impatience in her voice. "You know, the *cooler.*"

He retrieves it from the garage and with some hesitation sets it on top of the towels, watching his wife as he does so, hoping this is where she wants it. Then he retreats from her and crosses his arms, his hands tucked into his armpits. For a moment his wife stares at the freezer, her head cocked, as if listening to something in the far distance. He watches her back, the rigidity of it. A long brown ponytail curls down her spine like an upside-down question mark.

And then she suddenly brings her hand to the freezer door and pulls. At first it resists her, and so she brings her other hand to the handle and leans backward. Then, with a sort of sucking, sort of gasping noise, it opens.

The sight of it reminds Kevin of the time he had his wisdom teeth removed. His dentist had given him an irrigator, a plastic syringe. Twice a day he filled it with salt water and placed its needle into the craters at the back of his mouth—and from them, in a pink rush, came scabs, bits of food. That is what the freezer looks like when its door opens and the blood surges from it—all down the front of the fridge, dampening their photos, glossing over their magnets, until the front of the fridge has more red on it than white.

Becca makes a noise like a wounded bird. She turns her head away from the mess and squints shut her eyes. Her pants, her shoes, are splattered with red designs. A tremble races through her body and then she goes perfectly still.

Kevin goes to her and places a hand on her shoulder, and her shoulder drops a little from the weight of it. He feels as if he is touching a banister, a rifle stock, something hard and unbending. "Let me do it," he says. "Please."

The kitchen is loud with the noise of dripping.

"I hate this house," she says. "I hate, hate, *hate* this house."

"You go sit down and I'll take care of it. You rest. You need your rest."

She raises her arm, long and thin, her hand gloved with blood, like a stop sign.

"Okay," he says, and his hand falls away from her when she bends over to reposition the cooler. And then, with her arms out as if to hug, she reaches into the freezer. There is a surprising amount of meat in there, and she hooks her arms around it, the pile of it, and slides it out all at once. The T-bones, pork chops, bratwursts, chicken breasts, all splat into the cooler, one on top the other, a mass of meat along with two ice trays and a sodden box of baking soda. A hamburger patty misses its mark and plops on the linoleum, making a red flower pattern.

By this time Kevin has removed from beneath the sink a sponge, a roll of Bounty, and a Clorox spray bottle. He tears off five lengths of paper towels and lays them in the freezer to soak up the blood pooled there, while Becca plucks the photos and magnets from the fridge and tosses them in the cooler. Then she kneels with a bouquet of paper towels in one hand and the bottle of Clorox in the other. At first, when she sprays, when she wipes, she only smears the blood, making it pinker, making swirls like you see in hair and woodgrain. Then the blood begins to come away and the fridge begins to look like a fridge again.

Thirty minutes later, when she at last finishes, she says, "There." She is damp with sweat, with gore. She runs a forearm across her forehead and takes a deep, shuddering breath. Her blouse, once beige, now clings to her redly, pinkly, in tie-dye designs. She strips it off and tosses it in the cooler, along with her skirt, her bra and panties. Her shoes she sets aside. Naked, she goes to the sink and runs the water and soaps up her arms and feet and splashes her face, and when she turns toward Kevin her face is calmer, paler, drained of its previous flush.

"Sorry I snapped at you," she says.

"It's okay," he says, raising his voice so it follows her down the hallway, to their bedroom, their bathroom, where she will climb into the shower and leave behind a pink ring at the bottom of the tub, as she did several months ago when she began to hemorrhage, when she lost the baby.

The power went out because of the cave.

The cave—a lava tube—runs beneath their house, their neighborhood, and beyond, a vast tunnel that once carried in it molten rock the color of an angry sun.

People say Central Oregon looks like another planet. Mars, maybe. The reddish black landscape is busy with calderas, cinder cones, lava blisters, pressure ridges, pressure plateaus—much of it the hardened remains of basalt, a lava that spreads quickly, like thin porridge, flowing sometimes seventy miles, its front fed by lava tubes, like their lava tube, one of so many that network the ground beneath Bend, Redmond, La Pine.

Sometimes the caves collapse. A tractor-trailer will be growling along Route 97 when the asphalt opens up—just like that, like a mouth—and the rig will vanish, crashing down into an unknown darkness. Or someone will go to their driveway and find it gone, along with their car, their johnboat, replaced by a gaping hole. Or a hard rain will come, dampening and loosening those unseen joints beneath the surface that send the ground buckling. Imagine five acres dropping several inches, maybe even a foot, in an instant. Imagine fissures opening in your lawn. Imagine septic tanks splintering, sewage bubbling up from the ground like oil. Imagine power lines pinched off and neighborhoods darkened for days.

It's upsetting, not trusting the ground beneath your feet.

Their house is part of a new development called Elk Mound. It is located on a spur of basalt overlooking a coulee crowded with juniper trees that deepens and widens on its way south to accommodate the spring-fed Newberry River, which winds through the Aubrey Glen Golf Course on its way toward Bend, just five miles south of them.

Theirs was the last house in the development to sell, a year ago. It had been built over the mouth of the cave. To pass inspection and ensure no vertical settlement, the contractor widened the foundation, bolting it to the bedrock with twenty Perma-Jack brackets. The realtor advertised the cave as a "natural basement with cooling properties."

In the living room there is an insulated steel door. Somehow, through the cracks around it, the breath of the cave finds its way in, smelling faintly of mushrooms, sulfur, and cellar-floor puddles. Beyond the door a steel staircase, nearly forty feet tall, descends into darkness.

Becca teaches in the Geology Department at COCC. She often wears her hair pulled back in a ponytail and khaki pants with many zippered compartments. She keeps a special toothbrush by the sink to scrub away the crescents of dirt that seem always to gather beneath her fingernails. In everyday conversation she uses words like igneous, tetrahedron, radar mapping. The cave, to her, was the equivalent of a trampoline or fire pole to a child. It was cool.

And so they bought the place for a song.

Three years ago Kevin met Becca when skiing at Mt. Bachelor. She was standing at the summit of the mountain, at the top of a mogul field, when he slid off the chairlift. It was her honey-colored hair that first caught his attention. The wind blew it every which way, so that with the blue sky all around her she looked as if she were underwater. She wore this white outfit that stole the breath black from his chest. He unwrapped a Power Bar and hungrily ate it. When, five minutes later, she still hadn't moved, he approached her.

He asked if she was okay, thinking she might be afraid of the long drop before her, but she only looked at him curiously, completely unafraid, and said, "I'm fine," with the breath trailing from her mouth.

To their north the spine of the Cascade Range continued with the Three Sisters rising through a thin layer of clouds, like gnarled vertebrae. Becca pointed her pole at the saddle-shaped place between the South and Middle Sister and said, "I'm just studying that moraine over there."

He had never heard that word before—moraine—and it made him picture a great flood of water, frozen in its tracks.

Then she adjusted her goggles and gave him a smile, and took off down the mountain, her skis arranged in a careful pie-wedge that curled the powder over, exposing in her wake a broad, zigzagging track of blue.

And he followed. And one thing led to another.

There was a time, not even five months ago, when she would sneak up behind him and pinch his butt and yell, "You're it!" and run from him, squealing, as he chased her through their new house, over the couch, under the dining-room table, finally catching her in bed with his hands made into crab claws that touched her roughly all over.

Afterward they would drink beer and watch the Late Show, and she would laugh with her head thrown back, smiling so widely he could see her back teeth, her fillings giving off a silvery light.

They were pretty happy.

Then she was late. A few days passed, then a week, then two weeks, before she sent Kevin to the pharmacy. At this time she knew, because she had always been like clockwork, had never been this late. But she wanted to be certain. She wanted some bit of proof she could point to and say, "There."

In Aisle 5 the shelves were crowded with dozens of pink boxes. Not understanding the differences between them he randomly selected one—an expensive one with a picture of a rose garden on it—and on his way to the register grabbed a pack of gum, a Butterfinger, an *Us Weekly*, trying to clutter the register with other things. The checkout girl wore blue eye shadow. He thought it made her look very sad.

At home, when he handed his wife the box, she turned it over and scrunched her eyebrows and read its back as if for nutritional information. "Is this even a good one?" she asked, and he said, "Yes. It's very reliable." He leaned toward her and tapped the place on the box where it read *98% Accurate!*

This seemed to satisfy her and she went into the bathroom with the kit and closed the door, and he could hear the cardboard tearing, could hear her swearing when she peed a little on her hand, could hear the muffled roar of the toilet when she finished.

There was a lengthy silence and then she emerged from the bathroom. She had a plastic stick in her hand and she was shaking it and looking at it between shakes like an undeveloped Polaroid.

"Well?" he said.

She looked at him with a blank expression and held on to the stick a second longer before handing it to him. He took it with two hands and brought it close to his face. At the end of the stick, in a tiny window frame, there was a plus sign. It was an absurd shade of pink—the kind of pink that pink would wear. "Plus means what?"

"Plus means pregnant," she said.

His eyes grew larger and he felt at once lightheaded and ebullient and fearful. "You're kidding me?"

She pressed her hands hard against her face. "I am not kidding you."

"You're shitting me?"

"I am not shitting you," she said, and looked at him through her fingers. "I'm serious."

Kevin, open mouthed, considered her. "You're serious."

"I'm being seriously serious. We're having a goddamn baby."

Kevin works at the foundry, the Redmond Foundry, which produces over two hundred alloys. It is a high-ceilinged cinderblock building whose inside is black with dust and red with fire. All around him men wear heavy leather aprons and canvas gloves and tinted goggles. One of his main tasks is shaking out—which means breaking up sand castings to get at the metal castings cooling and hardening within them. His sledgehammer is like an extension of his body. When he leaves work his hands are still curled in the shape of it. All through the day he swings it again and again until the weight is nearly impossible to bear, until his face goes as red as the liquid metal glowing all around him, and his veins rise jaggedly from his arms. When he swings, his breath goes rip-rip-*rip*, and the hammer blasts open the sand casting with a *crack*.

A cloud of particles rises from it and sticks to his sweat. And there is the alloy, like a fossil fallen out of mud, to toss in a nearby bin.

His wife thinks he should go back to school—he is capable of so much more, she says—but the pay is good and nobody bothers him and he likes the rhythm of the work, the mindless repetition.

Sometimes, if someone calls in sick, he'll work the induction furnace or the electric-arc furnace, getting clamps in the right places, arranging molds, making sure they're free of dirt, and then pouring into them the hot metal that looks so much like lava.

Weekends, they used to explore the cave. They would throw on their jeans and fleece and tie their hiking boots tight, and descend into the darkness with their Magnum flashlights throwing cones of light before them. Down there no birds chirped, no dogs barked, no planes growled overhead. Occasionally they could hear the traffic humming above them, but otherwise, their noise was the only thing. And so their footsteps, shooshing through black sand or clunking off rocks, seemed so loud. And so they spoke in whispers. And when they spoke—saying, "What was that?" or, "Watch your step," or, "I love how old everything smells down here. It smells like it's a hundred million years old."—their breath fogged from their mouths.

When a vein of quartz would catch the light, Becca would put her hands to it. Its rock would be slick, and jaggedly streaked pink and white, like bacon. She'd remove from her backpack a pick and hand it to Kevin, and he'd swing it in a short arc and chip some of the quartz from the wall. And she would collect it to take home and stack neatly across her bureau, across bookshelves and windowsills, so that after a while their house seemed to glitter from every corner.

The cave would branch off into narrow corridors, scarcely wider than the Korean hatchback Kevin drove, but the main tube reached thirty, forty yards across, like the hollowed passage of an enormous worm. It seemed to go on forever. They wondered if it had an end.

Sometimes the blackness would go gray, and they'd click off their flashlights and pick their way through the gloom until they came upon a sort of skylight, where the roof of the cave had collapsed and now let in the sun. One time they found a dog—a German shepherd—hanging from such a hole. It had been lynched by its leash, its leash tethered to something aboveground and out of sight, perhaps a tree. And the dog dangled there, spotlighted, turning around and around.

There were things—a far-off moaning, a bundle of bones, a dark shape scuttling just past the reach of their flashlight—that scared them. Rocks scared them. Rocks cluttered the cave floor, some of them the size of melons, others the size of elk. For this reason they bought REI spelunking helmets. Sometimes the ceiling would come loose with a click of stone, a hiss of dirt, nearly noiseless in its descent, but when it impacted, when it slammed to the cave floor, it roared and displaced a big block of air that made them cry out and clutch each other in a happy sort of terror.

But that was before.

Becca doesn't like to go down in the cave anymore. Not since that day in July when the bats came. It was early evening, and they were sprawled out on the couch watching *Wheel of Fortune*. She was four months pregnant and her belly was beginning to poke out enough that women would stop her in the grocery store and ask. A safety pin held her jeans together in the front. Kevin was drinking a Bud Light and she was drinking water. She let in enough liquid to visibly fill her cheeks, and then swallowed in tiny portions, her cheeks growing smaller and smaller until sunken. He liked watching her drink. She drank water as if it were wine, not as a necessity but as a pleasure, trying to make it last longer. She looked at him looking at her and said, "Do you hear that?"

"Hear what?"

"That."

He picked up the remote and hit the mute button, and the applause of the audience fell away, and a hush descended upon the room. He heard nothing and said as much.

Becca had her head cocked and her hand raised. "Just wait," she said, and then, "*There.*"

And there it was, a scritch-scritch-scritching at the steel door.

For a long time they simply looked at each other, and then she pushed him and said, "Go see what it is," and he said, "All right already," and got up from the couch, and slowly approached the door, putting his ear to it. The metal was cold against his cheek. From here the scratching sound sounded more like the sound of eating, of teeth mashing something into a paste.

Becca said something he couldn't hear and he pulled his head away from the door to say, "What?" and she said, "You think it could be a wild animal?"

"Don't know." Right then he opened the door, and the bats came rushing in, a dense black stream of them. They emitted a terrible screeching, the noise a thousand nails would make when teased across a chalkboard. They fluttered violently through the living room, the kitchen, the hallway, battering the walls and windows, seeking escape. Kevin screamed and so did Becca, and the noise of flapping, of air beaten in many different directions, was all around them.

Somehow Kevin ducked down and pushed his way through their black, swirling color, and ran for the front door and threw it open, and not thirty seconds later most of the bats had departed through it, disappearing into the twilight gloom.

Becca was on the couch with an injured bat fluttering limply in her hair. "Holy shit." She had a hand between her breasts, over her heart. "Holy fucking shit. What the fucking shit was that?"

The next morning she woke up complaining of cramps.

Even before she was pregnant she would talk about her pain incessantly, saying her back hurt, her neck hurt, her feet hurt, her head, her stomach. If it were touchable—like, the space between her eyebrows—she would touch it. "I think it's a tumor," she would say, not joking, completely serious. "Feel this. This does not feel normal."

And Kevin would say, "I'm sure it's nothing."

"I'm sure it's nothing," was what he said when she complained of cramps, when she limped to the shower with a hand pressed below her belly.

"My lower back," she said. "On the right side. I really, really hope I'm okay. I'm pretty worried about the way this feels."

212   *Glimmer Train Stories*

And then she began bleeding. A rope of red trailed down her leg much as it would trail down the freezer. And Kevin, now in a panic, wrapped her in a bathrobe, and with shampoo still in her hair drove her to St. John's where she delivered, with a rush of blood, the baby that looked like a baby, a little girl, only too small and too red, smaller than his hand.

Becca was convinced it had something to do with the bats. Perhaps she had been bitten or scratched, and perhaps some parasite with leathery wings and claws traveled through her bloodstream and did ruin to her. When she told the doctor this, vines of sadness trembled through the skin around her eyes. They ran blood tests and found nothing. No, the doctor said. Not the bats. It was just one of those things.

She didn't like this. She didn't like to think that her own body could turn on her, collapse upon itself. So she said, "What does he know? Doctors don't know anything. One day they say eggs are good for you. The next they're bad. How can they have the answers when the answers are always changing."

Right then Kevin could see the pain between her legs in her face. Still can to this day. Sometimes he imagines a rotten spot inside her, like a bruised bit of peach he wants to carve away with a knife.

Tonight they find a bat in their living room. It is tucked into a corner, where the wall meets the ceiling. Kevin can see its heartbeat pulsing through its thin, leathery skin. Maybe it is one of the old bats that never escaped, or maybe it is a new bat that somehow found its way inside, its tiny brown body crawling through the heating ducts, the walls.

Kevin wants to surround it with something—maybe a glass or a Tupperware container—and carry it outside and release it. When he says this, Becca looks at him as if she wants to spit. "I hate this house," she says. "I hate this stupid, stupid house." Then she grabs the poker from the fireplace and holds it like a spear, and jerks it forward, impaling the bat.

When the metal moves through it, it makes the smallest scream in the world.

• • •

They haven't had sex in a month and a half, not since the miscarriage.

In the back of the closet, on the top shelf, beneath his sweaters, Kevin keeps an old copy of *Penthouse*. He bought it at a gas station several years ago and sometimes sneaks it down to read when his wife isn't home. He likes having something hidden from her, something that belongs to him alone, a small betrayal.

Becca has a rule: If you don't wear a piece of clothing for a year, you get rid of it, and right now she is going through their closet with a garbage bag, filling it with clothes for Goodwill, when she finds the *Penthouse*.

Kevin comes out of the bathroom to find her standing there, with her legs spread apart, the magazine crumpled up in her fist. "What?" she says. "I'm not good enough for you?"

"It's not that."

"Then what is it?"

This is a question with a lot of barbed wire around it, and when he doesn't answer she rips the magazine in half, and then in half again, and throws its pages to the floor and stares at him, panting. The way her anger grows reminds him of an umbrella, a big red umbrella, suddenly sprung.

"Look," he says, exasperated. "You want to punch me? Would that make you feel better?"

Her eyes narrow with anger, and he motions her forward with his hands and says, "Come on. Hit me, why don't you. You know you want to. Do it." He can see her little hand balling into a fist. And then she draws it back and gives him a glancing blow to the shoulder. "Is that all you've got?" he says. "Come on. You can do better than that. You hit like a girl. Hit me like you mean it."

This triggers some switch inside her. She makes a furious little noise and charges forward, and hits him again, and this time his shoulder seizes up with hurt.

"That's better," he says.

She has a look of complete rage or religious exaltation on her face—he isn't sure. She is breathing hard. He can hear the air coming in and out of her nose. "What else do you want me to do to you?" she says.

"You tell me."

She points her finger at him and tells him to take off his shirt. And he does. Bare-chested he stands before her, swaying slightly. She reaches forward and twists his nipples—hard—and when he screams she smiles, and pinches between her fingers a clump of chest hair, and rips it out, leaving behind a pink place where the blood rises in tiny dots. And he screams again. And their eyes hold together like the pieces of a puzzle.

She throws him against the wall and kisses him, roughly kisses him through all their laughing. And they tear the clothes off each other, and he picks her up and pushes her against the wall and enters her. And she is bucking her hips against his and he can feel himself losing control, can feel the heat rising in him, moving through the tunnels of him and nearing eruption, when all of a sudden she pushes him away and says, "That's enough."

When he asks what's wrong she absently scratches her bare breast and stares down at her feet as if the answer lies somewhere underground.

It is easier for Kevin. He can lose himself in the rhythms of his hammer, can smash the frustration from his body. Every day at work he drinks a milk jug full of water and sweats out every last drop of it, and it is more than a little like crying.

Right after the miscarriage he thought a lot about the baby, the little girl they never named. How she might have smiled ridiculously at him making funny faces. Or used the coffee table to pull herself up and take her first teetering steps. Then he drank himself to the very pitch of drunkenness, and that was enough. The baby has almost disappeared from his memory, almost.

Sometimes he will say something—maybe he will be watching CNN, and maybe they will broadcast a dead Iraqi child lying in the middle of the street, and maybe he will make some offhand remark about how lucky they are, how very lucky—and only when he sees the crumpled-up look on Becca's face does he remember and say, "Oh."

She cannot not remember. A playground busy with children. A dirty pacifier abandoned in the aisle at Wal-Mart. The purple teddy bear she bought and set among her rocks on the bureau. On a daily basis all of these things fly into her eyes and thump around inside of her skull, like bats, leaving the poisonous dust of their wings. She keeps her lips pursed around the edge of a pain he can only imagine and she cannot seem to forget.

Midnight. He wakes up to find his wife gone, the shape of her head still imprinted on her pillow. He calls out her name, and when she doesn't answer he gets out of bed and walks down the hall and into the living room, where moonlight comes in through the windows and makes the decorative rocks set here and there sparkle.

He observes the steel door hanging open—and there, surrounded by blackness, a palpable blackness, strange and horrible, which seems to ooze into the house, stands his wife.

He goes to her. If she hears his footsteps, if she feels the weight of his hand on her shoulder, she gives no indication. She wears one of his T-shirts and nothing else, her feet tight together, her arms at her side.

From the door a cool wind blows, bringing cave smells, of guano and mold and sand and stone. He closes the door and hoists up his wife, and cradles her in his arms, carrying her to the bedroom, to bed, where she finally comes alive and says, "No," and jumps up and goes to her dresser and opens its drawers. She steps into her panties and zips up her jeans and pulls a fleece over her head, and asks, when she begins lacing her boots, whether he is coming or not.

Their flashlights are the only lights. There is no moon down here. Beyond the cones of yellow light there is nothing, everything utterly black. Dark as only a cave can be dark. The longer they walk, the closer the walls seem to get, the narrower the passage.

Becca leads the way—her body tense, her shoulders bunched up nearly to her ears—down a series of unfamiliar corridors, taking a right at each junction so they will know to always take a left when returning. Around a bend, among a pile of rocks, a pair of eyes brighten redly, then vanish, and Kevin spends the next dozen yards sweeping his flashlight back and forth, waiting for something to materialize and come rushing toward them.

Becca moves her pale hand along the basalt, steadying her passage and crumbling away the green-and-gold patterns of lichen growing there. Occasionally she pauses, close lipped, as if contemplating something visible only to her, before continuing forward. Her flashlight makes giant shadows that seem to knock against each other.

Then the channel opens up into a space as big as a banquet hall. Its floor is strangely clean, absent of rocks. From the ceiling hang roots, like capillaries, groping for purchase. Kevin gives one a tentative tug, and when it doesn't give he tries swinging from it, and it carries his weight, and he flies from one side of the cave to the other, like something out of a Tarzan episode.

Becca has a small smile on her face when she walks the room, touching the walls and looking all around her, as if committing the space to memory. And then she locks eyes with Kevin and brings the flashlight to her face, throwing shadows across it. They seem blacker than the darkness of the cave.

Her light clicks off and she becomes a gray shape in the near distance.

He waits a moment, surrounded by his own ball of light, before clicking off his own light. And the next thing he knows a cloud of darkness settles around them. He can hear her feet whispering across the cave floor, and then her voice playfully calling out to him, "Marco."

He can hear the saliva popping in his mouth when it rises into a smile. "Polo," he says, and moves toward her voice with his hands out before him, his fingers like the snouts of moles, routing through the dark. When he touches stone he hears her voice again, saying, "Marco," behind him now.

This continues for a few minutes, with her always eluding him. He can hear her voice and her footsteps, and by the time he races to where she was, he knows she is already gone, but not where, not exactly.

All this time the roots startle him, coming out of the dark to lick his face. More than once he screams. And this is how she finds him. He can feel her hand at his elbow. It squeezes him and rises to his chest and pauses there. "Hey," he says, and she says, "Got you."

Both of them click on their flashlights at once. And they blink painfully, seeing a yellow light with a few filaments of red running through it. The black liquid of the cave oozes at the edges of their vision as the world takes form and they stare hard at each other for a long time. Then, as if something has been decided between them, she grabs a fistful of his shirt and pulls him down to the sandy floor where she brings her mouth roughly against his. And this time she doesn't stop him when he peels off her pants, and explores the slickness between her legs with his hands before climbing on top of her.

Together they move slowly, with the deep rhythms of a sleeping chest, until they are finished—and this takes a long time—so long that their flashlights begin to dim and eventually black out. And they are alone in the dark, huddling together with the cold creeping into their bare skin.

When they finally untangle themselves and rise from the cave floor, he takes off his belt and runs it through his back belt loop only, so that it serves as a sort of leash. She grabs hold of it and follows him as they continue back the way they came. They can hear dripping sounds of water, and the hushing sound of wind, and the booming sounds of rocks falling somewhere deep in the cave. But they aren't afraid so much as they are resigned to making it home. Kevin reaches his hands before him and moves them in a slow, scissoring motion, as if clearing the cobwebs from the air. And he lifts his feet high and brings them down carefully, and when necessary warns Becca: "There's a big rock here, about knee-high, so don't bang into it."

Every time the cave walls fall away he follows the left passage, groping through the dark, and eventually they find the staircase. They climb it and close the steel door behind them. The air is warmer up here. It feels soft. A patch of dawn sky is visible through the living-room window.

Becca goes to the kitchen and pulls out a gallon of milk and, before pouring it into a glass, stands there, backlit by the fridge, her face in shadow, looking at Kevin as if wondering how they found their way back.

The Last Pages

Dorothy Ann with Mom, Dorothy Grace, 1945.

Here I am again at the beach, and while it would be lovely to pretend that I often strike a pose that captures a tendency toward seriousness and introspection, the more likely truth is that I am camera shy, it was hot, I was sweaty, in the company of friends, and someone said, "Hey Christiana!" so I turned in that direction to see what was the matter.

My children look at this photo and say, "Tie-dye, again? You are such a hippie." I look at it and say, "I like how dark those glasses are. I wonder where I put them."

I know from my own children, who are at varying developmental levels, that sometimes very peculiar things matter a great deal to them. Turns out imagined children can be even more tenacious. I wrote "Half of What I Know," because the narrator wouldn't let me not write it.

As I sat down to think about what to write for this page, I looked at the photographs I thought I'd randomly selected. In the first I am a child on the Pacific Coast, dressed (by myself) as something else. In the other I am an adult on the Atlantic Coast, dressed (once again by myself—some things remain constant) entirely as myself. Most of my fiction

takes place in psychological landscapes, though it seems clear that certain moments in any *place* can be something we fully inhabit. The landscape of childhood in particular strikes me as rife with story potential: the setting changes, the point of view shifts, and the conflicts reveal themselves the more we pay attention. Then again, as my grandmother was always fond of saying, "You take yourself with you wherever you go."

—*Christiana Langenberg*

Rules I Regularly Break

Show don't tell
Get the lead runner
TV in moderation
Write what you know
Swim with a buddy
Only cross at the light
Feet are for the floor
Stretch adequately
No U-turn
No horseplay
No jokes
Pringles—not for breakfast

—*Susan Perabo*

Perabo's senior fiction workshop. Me, appropriately, in shadow.

This is a "To Do" list I found in a notebook recently. There are notebooks all over our house; we're all note takers (writers, typists). This one is in my husband's handwriting. These two words, crossed off, say as much about our writerly, familial life as one could expect two crossed-off words to do. It's practically a Zen koan.

—*Antonya Nelson*

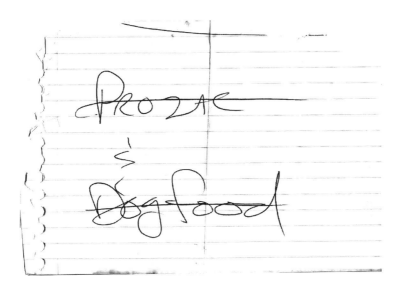

My kids have recently become obsessed with chihuahuas. I'm not sure where this came from, but for the past year they've begged obsessively for a little yappy puppy each. We have enough cats and dogs in our house as it is, so, needless to say, two chihuahua puppies is not something I'm willing to give in on. But who wants to be the bad guy every day, saying no to something their child wants so desperately? On an impulse, I came up with this stroke of genius: "When I win the Pulitzer Prize, you'll each get a chihuahua." My husband rolled his eyes. Since then, they've told everyone they know (or happen to pass on the street) that, *When Mommy gets the Pull-it Surprise, we're gonna get chihuahua puppies.* It's been a nice little ego boost for me, because they each fully expect that someday this blessed event will occur. My husband, on the other hand, thinks I'm being cruel. Really, where's the faith? Hey, I intend to keep this promise. Someday, even if my kids are grown and wrinkling like I am now, I'll show up on their doorsteps with a basket full of yapping puppies. And they'll know why.

—*Elissa Minor Rust*

Glimmer Train Stories

My sister Julie and I have for years loved to host theme parties. The theme of this one, which we held in September 2005, was "Dress Like a Tramp: Julie's Turning Thirty!" Here Julie and I (I'm wearing the cowboy hat) are making a costume change with help from our friends Aaron, T. J., and Drew.

—*Cheri Johnson*

My son was born on March 17, 2006. A St. Paddy's Day baby. So we gave him a good Irish name—with a dash of literary allusion—Connor. As the cliché goes, since he came into the world, everything's changed. There's the expected stuff, like the exhaustion, the sappiness, the protectiveness, the love like no love you knew before. And then there's the unexpected stuff. I'm now part of some secret society I never knew existed. Before, I never noticed babies unless they were sitting next to me on a plane or in a restaurant, and then it was with great annoyance. Now I see them everywhere, along with their paraphernalia. You pass some guy with a stroller in the mall, no matter how crowded it is, you notice each other and you give each other the nod. You're constantly sizing up other parents and their babies, thinking, "My kid is cuter," or, "My kid is smarter," or, "My kid sleeps through the night, sucker." It's weird and disturbing and not something I ever thought would happen to a hairy bastard like me. And here's the other thing, the thing that helped me write this story. If I see something happen to a baby in a movie, or if I read about something happening to a baby in a story, I nearly crack. And let me be honest with you: I've got a stone-cold stomach. It's hard as hell to make me cringe or tear up. But that shit is like kryptonite to me. I remember reading an

interview with Elie Wiesel. He was talking about watching Nazis toss infants over a fence. Some of them got tangled up in the barbed-wire and just hung there. I wept. Which is significant. I'm one of those people who never cries, and here I am roughing away the tears from my cheeks. I channeled this new-found empathy when writing "The Caves in Oregon," and I think—I hope—I managed to do it with sentiment, not sentimentality.

—*Benjamin Percy*

This picture of me was taken aboard a ferry crossing the Saguenay Fjord in Northern Quebec on the way to Tadoussac.

—*Deborah Tarnoff*

Growing up, there was always something otherworldly about the trips to my father's office in downtown Los Angeles—only thirty or so miles from the suburb where I was born and raised, but it felt very far, far away. Here is my father—who died in 2004—behind his desk, looking very businessman-like, circa 1970. I should probably point out that the father and family situation in "Please Don't Tell Me That" couldn't be further from my own, but I suppose the raw beginnings of the story stem from the excitement of those visits. Initially the idea was to have a vaguely desperate/thwarted father reaching out to his son in an attempt to bring them together, to show his son, by taking him to his workplace, something about himself that he couldn't articulate verbally. Later, after a few unsuccessful attempts, the point of view switched to the young son and the story finally could be written.

—Andrew Roe

No one had to ask this sixteen year old what she wanted to be; she told anyone who would listen. *I am going to be a writer.*

She wrote the school song and commentary for the Future Homemakers of America fashion show (local, very local). She worked on the school paper and the high-school annual. Then she got busted.

She traveled a crooked and bumpy path with lotsa water under the bridge before she learned not to mix her metaphors, but the ambition never changed. And her favorite book is still the dictionary.

—*Janice D. Soderling*

I tend to write fiction that has either a heavy dose of autobiography or a heavy dose of magical realism or the fantastic. I don't really mix the two, and I'm not sure why. I certainly don't feel compelled to be truthful when writing anything autobiographical (I'm much too lazy to be that detailed, which probably is why I never considered journalism). Honestly, I'd prefer life to have more magic in it. I don't mind the inexplicable. It gives me something to think about besides whether I have to vacuum the living room again.

My husband took this picture the day after I completed a week-long charity bicycle ride across Montana. It was one of those rare moments when you know you are strong enough and capable enough to conquer the world, should it require conquering.

—*Susan Petrone*

M y little author. My little artist. Daddy wants to thank you—and your mommy—for being everything in the world.

—*James Sepsey*

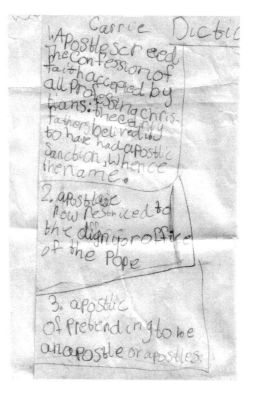

Hermann (right), youngest of ten, trying to survive WWI.

COMING SOON

As I watched the cousins it occurred to me that baseball was the one sport that wasn't a metaphor for war. There was no struggle for turf, no real contact. The point, if there was one, was to get home safe.

from "Jubilee" by Garth Risk Hallberg

The air was hot, but he could not tell if the heat emanated down from the sky or up from the earth. He stepped over a dead man who was wearing a fine wool jacket, holding onto its lapels as if it might do him some good. Where had he gotten a jacket like that?

from "The Shelter" by Kim Brooks

A bleached blond woman in a sequined sweatshirt appeared at the door. "That statue is for the feast," she said, "and my husband's chair of that feast, and the feast's next week. The saint stays right here." She pointed to the floor with both hands.

from "Saints Alive" by Scott Anderson

All the respectable people, the parents with kids to raise, moved out.

from "Child of God" by Jennifer Moses